CVC
5

T0163306

CVC

Carter V. Cooper

SHORT FICTION ANTHOLOGY SERIES

BOOK FIVE

SELECTED BY AND WITH A PREFACE BY

Gloria Vanderbilt

Library and Archives Canada Cataloguing in Publication

CVC / selected by and with a preface by Gloria Vanderbilt.

(Carter V. Cooper short fiction anthology series ; book 5)
Issued in print and electronic formats.

ISBN 978-1-55096-490-5 (paperback).--ISBN 978-1-55096-491-2 (epub).
--ISBN 978-1-55096-492-9 (mobi).--ISBN 978-1-55096-493-6 (pdf)

1. Short stories, Canadian (English). 2. Canadian fiction (English)
--21st century. I. Vanderbilt, Gloria, 1924-, editor II. Title. III. Series: Carter V.
Cooper short fiction anthology series ; bk. 5

PS8329.1.C835 2015   C813'.010806   C2015-903604-6
                                                    C2015-903605-4

Copyright © with the Authors, and Exile Editions, 2015
Text Design and Composition by Mishi Uroboros
Typeset in Garamond, Mona Lisa and Trajan fonts at Moons of Jupiter Studios

Published by Exile Editions Ltd ~ www.ExileEditions.com
144483 Southgate Road 14-GD, Holstein, Ontario, N0G 2A0
Printed and Bound in Canada in 2015, by Marquis Books

We gratefully acknowledge, for their support toward our publishing activities,
the Canada Council for the Arts, the Government of Canada through
the Canada Book Fund, the Ontario Arts Council,
and the Ontario Media Development Corporation.

The use of any part of this publication, reproduced, transmitted in any form
or by any means, electronic, mechanical, photocopying, recording, or otherwise
stored in a retrieval system, without the expressed written consent of the
publisher (info@exileeditions.com) is an infringement of the copyright law.
For photocopy and/or other reproductive copying, a license from
Access Copyright (800 893 5777) must be obtained.

Canadian sales: The Canadian Manda Group, 664 Annette Street,
Toronto ON M6S 2C8 www.mandagroup.com 416 516 0911

North American and international distribution, and U.S. sales:
Independent Publishers Group, 814 North Franklin Street,
Chicago IL 60610 www.ipgbook.com toll free: 1 800 888 4741

In memory of

Carter V. Cooper

The Winners for Year Five

Best Story by an Emerging Writer
≈ $10,000 ≈
Lisa Foad

Best Story by a Writer at Any Point of Career
≈ $5,000 ≈
Nicholas Ruddock

CVC

BOOK FIVE

PREFACE

I am proud and thrilled that all these wonderful writers are presented in this edition of the *CVC Anthology*. Though I, and those who loved Carter, still hear his voice in our heads and in our hearts, my son's voice was silenced long ago. I hope this prize helps other writers find their voice, and helps them touch others' lives with the mystery and magic of the written word. And so, as we conclude our fourth year of this annual short fiction competition – open to all Canadian writers – I have awarded two prizes: $10,000 for the best story by an emerging writer, and $5,000 for the best story by a writer at any point of her/his career. Hundreds of stories were received in 2014-15, and from the 14 that eventually were shortlisted, I selected the winners, being those that most appealed to me, as a writer, as a reader, and as a lover of the written word on paper. About the winners, I have this to say: I love everything about the construction of Lisa Foad's story, "How to Feel Good." Not a word too much. Not a word too little. Perfectly put together, a story that will not tell you how to feel good about yourself but will grab your obsessive attention from the first sentence and in one way or another, will tell you a lot about yourself. Nicholas Ruddock's "Mario Vargas Llosa" has narrative daring. To openly and successfully adapt the narrative framing of a great writer's vision to one's own narrative line – and in doing so, to discover, in an often lyrical prose, a magical new continent that are the lives of Latin American immigrants in

Toronto, one of North America's largest swarming cities – is daring, and took great imaginative gumption.

And I want to give a big thank you to the readers who adjudicated this year's competition: Norman Snider, screenwriter, essayist and fiction writer; Frances Mary Morrison, senior television producer of documentaries; Jerry Tutunjian, executive magazine editor; Matt Shaw, short story writer and copy editor... all of whom have played their own special roles in the development and support of emerging writers.

Gloria Vanderbilt
May 2015

Veronica Gaylie

TOM, DICK AND HARRY

Tom lies in St. Paul's Emergency, pacemaker jumping like a sockeye salmon while he teaches two nurses four verses of "Danny Boy." They release him and by the time the taxi pulls away eight nurses stand outside waving to him. He says, Cordova Street's the best home he ever had. Three square meals, a radio and people who listen to him sing Hank Williams: lawyers, hockey players, priests and shrinks. My mother says, Ach. He doesnae see the neighbourhood, he jist looks at the flowers.

He spends his days at the courthouse, gets free coffee from the court coffee lady who never in her life gave away anything for free. But Tom has a way about him. He was in fact up to three free coffees a day, overdid it a bit, and the coffee lady had to say, Eh, Tom, I didnae mean it quite like that. Said, I mean, I didnae mean three free coffees noo, and Tom looks up at her and says: You're right, Mother. From now oan, it's only wan.

By the time McSorley's hockey trial hit he was back up to three and that day, court packed, standing room only, the guard said to Tom, Okay, big guy. Go on in. And Tom looked aroond, Big guy? Who's eh talking tae? The way Canadians say things, Tom jist loved it. People in line looked at Tom, who wasnae tall, and said, Hey, why does he get in? And the guard stared back and said, Because he's one of the family.

And Tom went right in.

Later Tom was interviewed on CBC about the trial from an old-timer's point of view, except they got Tom who looked straight into the lens with his blue eyes and snowy white hair. Standing there with his free coffee, he said, It was tae hard te see oan TV. Ye really couldnae get a good angle oan things.

The reporter told Tom to walk into the sunset, an old-timer shot to close the show, Folks, there goes the old-timer, walking into the distance, walking slow, but Tom, camera rolling, live TV, walked slower than they wanted him to. Behind him the camera rolled, the reporter's voice slowed and slowed, tried to keep pace with Tom walking slow: Folkss…there goes the old-timer…walking…walllkingg…

But Tom walked slower than slow. Tried to drag it out, you know. By the time he pressed the button to cross the street, they liked Tom old, but not so slow.

Now Tom has a way of walking slow. Not like he was before. The night he staggered in circles around the backyard drunk, shouting,

I'm a fucking Scot!
I'm a fucking Scot!

Before that, he made everyone laugh. Found cigarettes in his ears, made coins disappear. When Granda died Tom handed in his gloves at the bus mechanic depot and walked and walked and did not stop. All the way to New Westminster.

They gave him electric shock. (I did not care what the neighbours thought.)

Back in Glasgow, he might have been the one with a football kick called The International, but in Canada, he did magic tricks, alone, on the living room loveseat.

⁂

Tom, Dick and Harry wanted to leave Scotland forever.

Everyone nodded. It was understood. Fish and chips only went so far; life was dull. Souvenirs of Rome over the mantelpiece, a papal plate, a little ceramic dog that changed colour when it rained; knick knacks only went a certain way 'til notions of New York called you away.

On the morning the boat left, waving goodbye to the three raw loddies, Tommy still in boy scout shorts, the mither saw

> the little blue light on the back of her hand
> that she always saw before bad news.

Over there, the way people leave. You tried and tried but could not get away. You'd stare at a dripping sink for years, thinking you had lots of time then, one day, you'd turn around, see dust falling slowly in the living room sun and suddenly you'd know a whole life could pass while that dust fell slow, settling on the shoulders of a bottle of HP. Then you'd know. (Time to go.)

In the living room after the others left, their cousin Tom wondered if he'd ever see North America, the Fraser River, the Pacific Ocean. He wondered if he'd ever see film star Nelson Eddy as an RCMP walking out of the Canadian evergreens.

Thoughts trickled like this in a world of fish and chips and arguments over where a picture of a soldier should go, over the mantel or under the bed because a generation before in Ireland they knew what a picture of a soldier meant. And up and down from the wall the old picture went: the father up, the mother down, no time for it to even leave a mark of where it might have been. It was a smoky world.

My mother worked for a chimney sweep in a shack in a lane because alone, in the coal dust, she could read.

To dream of tap dance shoes, ruby red, in a black and white reel. To leave a place of chest pains called carbuncles of the heart. A place of meat-pies, neeps, sprouts, cabbage, and the potato. Later that day the mither peeled potatoes for chips, golden,

how the sun streamed in.

How anyone understood a word the faither whistled through his toothless gums: Where's meh wallies?

He lost the real ones picking up chairs with his teeth to impress the ladies.

Generations stood on the mantelpiece in photos, in bright hats on vacation: big smiles, crooked teeth.

Other times it was just the clock in the living room, ticking. And dust falling. You waited for a sign. Sure enough someone said,

> The day Tom, Dick and Harry left,
> the blue light on the mither's hand was lit.

※

Tom went. Dick went. Harry went.

It was easier for Dick who was tall, suited his clothes, a Dapper Dan, presented himself well. He worked as the corner man in a vaudeville show. Americans liked personality. *Put it there* went over big and with his suit and that height, Dick landed Maître D' in a fancy restaurant.

> Dick fell in.

Everyone said they couldn't do enough for him. Good tips. They said,

> Ach, the lad did well fer ehsel over in America.
> Aye, Dick wi ehs fancy new teeth.

At home, the mither beamed in her new red woollen coat while they three raw loddies flew over the ocean. Imagine. America. All that smart chat, just like you see in the pictures. Ach, the variety. The selection on the shelves.

The get up an go.

One day after work Dick went out the back way and was never seen again (murdered – for his tips). No one really knows how he got lost but he was found in a river no one had heard of:

the Hudson.

Back home Sam the head of the family put the phone down, then picked it back up again and called Harry in New York.

Yer comin haime right noo.
An bringing Tammy wi yeh.

But Harry, in his new fly chat, said:

No can do.

Sam put the phone down. Dust fell slowly back home in the living room sun, first time in months. The room filled with it. Sam closed his eyes.

Small world it is.
An tha silly sun oan all days as this.

Back in New York, Harry felt bad. He was just a kid. He knew you didn't move to America to dwell on things and if back home you're killed going out the front door, in America you're killed going out the back way,

this was no matinee.

No Nelson Eddy. No RCMP walking out of the Canadian evergreens. No Fraser River you learned about in school, but a brother, gone.

Harry in New York put down the phone. Got on with things. Sam got down and prayed, and Mary, their sister, left.

✕

You think, Mary's there. Mary with her good heart and head. Mary in her brick Bronx bedroom. Visiting Mary went like this. You'd knock, then hear her walking down the hall saying,

Just a minute!

Unlocking bolts and turns,

Just a minute!

Unhinging chains and locks and ties,

Just a minute!

Finally she'd shove the big dresser out the way, the door opened, and Mary stood, smiling, saying,

Come away! Come away!

With that black hair. The whole place smelt like chips. To the kitchen, the red, shiny tablecloth, the kettles, ironing boards, armchairs covered in clothes,

red, white and blue

the look of rooms where people leave for work every day.

Outside she was just the same. Mary in those black heels, serge suit, lapel brooch, walking down the street, back straight. She had a way of striding, that Toibin walk, handbag tight under her arm. She said,

It's after three, the trade schools are oot!

And right on cue, you'd see faces peek around corners but with Mary striding that way with her purse, blue eyes meaning business, they left her glittering brooch alone.

And then, even with Mary there, even with Mary all put-together, it happened to Harry.

For a long time the story went:

Ach. Flamin black soot came doon tha tunnel
an choked ehm dead.

(Ah was jist waitin oan it).

Harry was a driver for the old New York subway system, night shift. Back home, Harry had been the one in uniform, the one with a good job,

> no like Dick wi ehs head a way up in the clouds,
> flyin roond wi aw tha money.
> Bad fellas waitin fer ehm oot back.
> Ach. Wi ehs beeg reed open face an aw.

Someone said,

> It's no good over there in America.
> Tommy, Ahm tellin yehs.
> Jist look at Harry.
> Dead of emphysema.
> Doon tha hole night an day wi oot a bit ay air.
> (Jist like the coal mine).

As if he never left.

Dick went. Harry went. Now one left in New York not counting Mary. Tom. Tommy, the eldest, was different. Tall, lean, a scout leader, he wore short pants and laughed at everything everyone said

> when eh wasnae oan ehs knees, praying.

America. He loved it over there. But for Tommy, last one left, it didnae look good.

One day he asked Mary,

> What are the odds that oot of three brothers…
> what are the odds, Mary? Aw three?

Mary stood, handbag under arm, blue brooch glittering in the afternoon sun, and told him.

✕

The other Tom's father, Willie, was in the first war, on watch, Vimy Ridge. Stood in the middle of no man's land beside his friend Archie Geddes, who he looked out for, who looked out for him. Archie's father had his head blown in two in the same war months before.

Willie on the battlefield, moonlight on the back of his hand, smoked cigarettes to make time fly, and when he lit a match he'd say:

> Make sure yer hands donnae shake
> so yeh donnae upset the other man.
> Always keep yer hands steady fer ehm.

The faither wouldnae have said donnae. Though that night, all the wouldnae, couldnae, shouldnae, didnae, hadnae, wullnae, cannae, disnae and wisnae in the world didnae matter because just then, at the base of their post, a shadow appeared.

> It wisnae tall
> an it didnae hae a head.

Jesus, said Archie Geddes under his breath, while Willie turned white. Was it man or woman? It reappeared, seemed to float just above the ground and then it floated across no man's land where it disappeared,

like the toot.

If it had been raining, it could have been a soldier running from the rain, but it wasn't raining. If there had been fire, it could have been someone ducking bullets, but there was no fire. Just the two men in no man's land saying,

Tha wiz a big yin.

Willie's face went aw peelly wally. He stood poker straight and said,

Tha wasnae a yin.

No, said Archie.

Yeh couldnae hae a square go
wi an apparition such as this.

A sight like that could make the mind wander and hours later, Archie was still talking about it, lighting matches, hands shaking.

Hey, Wullie, why don't yeh fling yer wallies, aye yer teeth, doon there.
Kinda provoke the thing.

Willie went for a look through the mud. Nothing there. Not even a footprint. He went back to the post and told Archie, who stood and held his rifle in such a way so his hands would not shake,

No point callin tha in, eh?

No, no point, said Archie.

How yeh gonnae explain te yer CO
yeh saw a figure runnin headless
through no man's land
an it didnae leave a footprint?

It could have been an apparition. They'd seen a lot of death. It could have been a dream. But that night, at post in the middle of no man's land, Archie asked Willie,

Ehm,
What are the chances
ay a faither an son dyin in the same war
the same way?

The night was clear and Willie said,

Ehm,
let me see.
Two men... wan war.
Same family.

He counted on his fingers, like there was a method to it.

Ah'll tell yehs tomorrow, Archie.

The next day the battle was over.
Later someone told Willie about Archie:

> Ehs two legs
> jist ran oan ahead.

> Wan, two,
> wan, two.

✖

Mary says,

> Jist donnae ask, Tom.
> Yeh know how it is.

> Oh ach, the old blue light, says Tommy.
> The mither's superstition.
> Cannae a fella escape?
> In America they'd call it a coincidence, Mary.

He stormed out the back door, jacket flying over his shoulder,
American fly chat gone,

> Wull yewz aw no go away noo! The lot ay yehs!

He left Mary in the kitchen with the dripping sink and the
falling dust, and Tommy and Granda Dick back home was still
talking about the all-new Tommy, over there in America.

Sam told her over the phone,

Ach. Mary. Why did yehs let ehm go?

That could have been it. But the story goes. Tom went out as the handsome one – the dancer, the talker, the crooner, the kind that made people say,

Too bad. Eh could sing.

As a waiter at a private club up the Hudson River he did well

well fer Dick wi ehs tips
well fer Harry
wi ehs burnin eyes
an burnin lips

and at the end of the night there was drink with the other waiters, all the champagne that was left.

Ach. Tommy.
Eh wasnae tall but eh had lotsa pals.

And the night they were all driving home, singing away, that black hair in the wind (inherited from the Gallachers, McNamaras and McNamees) the driver hit a tree and everyone died

but Tom.

Forehead sliced on metal, brains burst open like a soup tin, and when they found the wreck Tom was gone. He just walked away. They found him in a field, sitting up (still in his good suit). When Mary heard the news, her voice just went. Back home, Tommy and Dick said,

> Ach. New life in America.
> Two dead – wan wi no voice.
> Wan wi no head.

In Tommy's last letter home, he said he had a toothache. Back home that was it. Show over.

> No more ay this family's goan te America.
> Over the bodies ay Tom, Dick an Harry.

When it was all over, someone said,

> Wan thing Ah'll say aboot America:
> it may be violent
> but they know how tae look after their dead.

✕

And the other Tom, cousin Tammy, Gallacher's brother. Not as dramatic (but nonetheless). Tom's brother Willie, who was tall, left for the front at Union Station in Glasgow; the whole family went to see him away. Willie had that black hair like the highlanders, and in a uniform,

> ach.

Aw the women were looking over.

He had his cousin Tommy's teeth. Granda Dick's cheekbones. He played violin.

The mither said,
Willie. You'll play the violin on yer maw's deathbed.

At the station Willie took Tom aside and told him man to man,

Tom.
Between you an me brother.
Ah know Ahm never coming back.

For a second they stood smoking, eye to eye, Tommy holding it in. Like Jimmy Cagney in *Angels with Dirty Faces*. He already knew the rest. So he said,

Don't tell meh, Wullie.
Let's jist leave it like this.

Poor Tom. One minute smoking a cigarette with your best friend, and the next.

The one who left.
The next one who left.

The mither dabbed her eyes and God knows Willie waved his arm outside the train and she waved back with that white hanky right to the end of the railway bend.

And that could have been it. Later when two soldiers showed up at the door

    clock ticking
    dust falling

everyone in the neighbourhood heard. The mither fell to her knees. Gallacher screamed. Someone said in the last months of the war, they sent all the Scots in. The Glasgow Highlanders.

That night the faither's hair turned pure white in his sleep. Gallacher lost her sense of smell. Couldn't eat.

Willie. Who suited his clothes. He always knew what to say.

    Played the violin.
    Brave.

    The way he left that day.
    Tall.

Christine Miscione

SPRING

The day Joan Rivers died, I received an email from Hybrid-Co Canada offering me free Internet for four months if I removed my irate blog post examining the current degree to which they are fucking idiots. I made the post seven months prior, in the dead of winter, when I was broken-hearted and holed up in a new apartment for six days. "We would like to apologize for any inconveniences we may have caused you between January 30th and February 5th of this year. We understand you were not satisfied with our services at that time."

Later that day, Eric and I had sex on the floor. The TV was still on in the background. From underneath him, I couldn't see, could only hear it. A drum circle emerges at Times Square in Joan Rivers' honour. Joan Rivers is remembered for her anti-feminist humour. Joan Rivers loved aging elephants. Joan Rivers' acid cackle as he came inside of me.

Afterwards, washing myself in the bathroom, I noticed scraped skin on my back, right along my spine. The blood was beginning to seep and it reminded me of what it might be like to bleed through cheesecloth. He was apologetic. He took my hand. He said he just got carried away, and next time we'll use pillows, and he's just so "madly" turned on by me. How could I blame him?

Things that make me wish I could live forever: Summers in Montreal. Wine and careé pistache in Parc La Fontaine. The sun setting behind the factories in Mile End. Gypsies dancing around the fountain in Square Saint-Louis. "Scarborough Fair" with all the windows open, the leaves beginning to change.

The Plateau sparkled the night of Joan Rivers' death. It was hot. I was walking back to my apartment from Eric's thinking, Does this go on forever? Then my mother called.

"I'm going to break up with him," I told her. "It doesn't sing the way past love has."

"You're just not ready yet, hunny."

"What if I never am?"

The morning after Joan Rivers died, I woke up feeling like I'd contracted some kind of disease. I walked rue Saint-Denis. I watched the street cleaners. I sat on a bench outside Mont Royal station and tried not to throw up. At noon, still feeling sick, I ate a ham and mayonnaise sandwich on baguette and drank two screwdrivers. Self-censor my blog? I get paid good money for being honest, or at least appearing that way. No, I will not self-censor. I will not be quelled by some formidable Internet company who pays people to scour the web trying to sanitize its image instead of putting money towards rectifying idiocy in the moment idiocy occurs – especially idiocy occurring in the middle of a brutal winter, when one's heart has just recently been ripped out and spat on, and one lacks the self-composure necessary to avoid being hyperbolic.

"Hi there, ma'am, I'm Joseph. I'm sorry for the inconvenience of that long wait and I thank you for your continued patience."

"I want to talk to Audrey."

"I'm sorry, ma'am, I cannot give you Audrey at this time."

"But, I just talked to her two seconds ago before the phone got disconnected."

"I'm sorry, ma'am, but I cannot give you Audrey at this time."

"That's bullshit. I don't want to have to repeat everything to you for the gazillionth time – transfer me to Audrey now."

"I cannot transfer you to Audrey, ma'am, but I can help you with any of your concerns."

"You're not helping me unless you transfer me to Audrey *immediately*."

"Ma'am, I don't know who Audrey is."

Sunflowers in buckets at Jean-Talon. "'Across the Universe'"as the nights grow longer. The smell of cloves stuck in oranges. Chickadees.

Hybrid-Co Canada emailed me again a few days later and upped the ante: free Internet service for six months if I delete my blog post immediately. "We have reassessed your situation and feel that because of the gross inconveniences you experienced between January 30th and February 5th of this year, you deserve a greater promotional offer."

I ignored it. Instead I googled: "how to tell if he's a re-bound" and "how to break up with the rebound you've assured isn't a rebound."

I cleaned the bathroom and the baseboards and thought only about how, according to *Gigi Style*, you can tell he's a rebound if running your fingers through his chest hair makes you gag. *Chatelaine* says it's most obvious if his choice to sleep buck-naked on a nightly basis makes you gag. *Woman,*

Naturally says he's likely a rebound if you don't give a rat's ass that all he wants for his birthday is you prancing around in the faux-satin polyester nightie he gave you "just because." Here's my take on it: he's definitely a rebound if you've woken up next to him on more than one occasion expecting to see your ex.

I decided I better do some real work. My weekly deadline loomed: five blog posts by Sunday night. Celebrity gossip, product name-dropping, la vie domestic. I'm just an "everyday gal" according to my website, not according to my paycheque. What I am is a well-paid sell-out. So I hammered out a blog post, trying to forget real life. This time my observations on expiration dates – how the BB: NOVEMBER 16 on my "delicious" jug of "Simply Orange'" OJ contracts time. "I'm constantly living two months in the future," I wrote. Then, parenthetically: "'How funny, the idea of buying OJ and then dying before it does."

Mont-Royal Avenue with wreaths and tinsel. The strings of twinkle lights on balconies bounding Parc Baldwin. How the city feels endless covered in snow. Our Christmas tradition of goblets filled with Turkish Delights; ordinary socks hung on the mantel with care; me singing Christmas carols in broken French, him on the keyboard.

"Ok, ma'am, what I'm hearing is that you'd like to install a second Internet line at your apartment?"

"No. I'd like *my* dryloop disconnected from *his* apartment on rue Marie-Anne, where I *used* to live, and I want it reinstalled in my *new* apartment on rue Rachel, where I *currently* live, so I can keep the same account."

"So you no longer live in your same residence, ma'am?"

"I no longer live at my *previous* address. Like I already said, I just moved two days ago."

"And what was the reason for the move?"

"Why does that matter?"

"Ma'am, I'm just trying to see if you qualify for a free reinstall."

"Fine. I moved because my boyfr—*ex*-boyfriend and I couldn't agree on whose house to go to for Christmas, and then I wrote this blog post, and yeah, that's why."

"Oh, I see."

"Yeah. Turns out stuffing your face with sugar pie may actually save a three-year relationship."

"Oh… Well, I'm sorry to hear about that, ma'am. Unfortunately, though, there will have to be a charge of $50 for the reinstall."

"What, my reason isn't good enough?"

"It isn't on my list for complimentary services. Sorry about that, ma'am. So, it says the name, uh, Mr. Jean-Paul Badeaux, as the account holder at the previous address?"

"Yeah, that's my ex-boyfriend. As I said, he paid for the *landline*, I paid for the *dryloop*. My dryloop phone number is 514-330-9982. It's only an *Internet* line. It's a separate account."

"Ok. With the snow and everything, we can only guarantee a technician sometime between February 1st and 3rd, 9 a.m. to 9 p.m."

"Really? A three-day cushion? And I have to be home all the time?"

"Yes, ma'am. Sorry about that, and thank you for your continued understanding."

"That's bullshit."

"Oh, and to confirm again: you want your name as secondary account holder taken off Mr. Badeaux's account and put on the new dryloop account?"

It's the hardest thing – trying to forget someone during a Montreal winter.

For two weeks after Joan Rivers died, I was getting heavier. I didn't know it. I thought only about my fans: the 345,000 hits my blog received this fiscal year. I googled "rebound advice" and listened to "Fifty Ways to Leave Your Lover" on repeat – to lighten the mood. I thought about the other him, the one I shouldn't. The man who loved me into this loss. When Hybrid-Co Canada's third email arrived, their tail way up between their legs, all I thought was, Nope. That is not enough to buy me, assholes.

Staring at the moon over the city. The radiator humming. Our scarves drying. His homemade valentines written in rhyming couplets.

"It's 8 p.m. on the third day – when the *hell* are they coming?"

"Ma'am, it says here that a technician went two days ago, but was unable to complete the job because you didn't specify the nametag for the new dryloop."

"First of all, it's not a *new* dryloop. And second, I can *guarantee* you that no one showed up."

"Ma'am, it says here the customer doesn't need to be home to install a dryloop. It's done remotely."

"I was told I needed to be home the whole time."

"Sorry, ma'am. I'm unsure why someone would tell you that."

"So what you're telling me is I didn't need to be home all day for the last three days, in the dead of winter – couldn't even go out to buy a new kettle or a hot water bottle or a duvet, and all I have is a shitty fleece blanket in this new apartment because he took the duvet, and the kettle too, because they were his, and *fine* I get why he'd take them. But I sat on my ass for the last three days, reading and rereading that fucking blog post I should've never made on Christmas morning right before I left him sleeping, all because I refused his French-Canadian Christmas – I refused the sleigh ride too – and now, after three days of that regret, realizing how much my life is in fucking shambles, I *still* don't have the Internet because apparently I didn't give you an arbitrary nametag for the 'new' dry-loop, which isn't even new, and you're telling me I didn't need to be home the whole time? Why didn't anyone call me?"

"I'm so sorry about that, ma'am, someone should've called you."

"I want a technician in immediately. I want someone in right now!"

"Ok, ma'am, let me check my database for the next available technician. One moment… Ok, it says February 5th, 9 a.m. to 5 p.m., the next available."

"That's bullshit. You get a technician in tonight."

"I'm sorry, ma'am, but it's a computerized system."

"So what?"

"I can't override it."

Peonies in glass dishes. Mornings spent reading on the terrace. Daydreaming of having his baby. The way spring doesn't feel ephemeral and secretive if you stop to watch it unfold.

"Have you considered our offer?"

Screwdrivers – another name for woman's best friend? I was listening to the neighbours fucking through the wall, wondering how making love would sound different. Three shots per eight-ouncer of orange juice. Five ice cubes for good measure. But let's not kid ourselves. The ice cubes have the same dimensions as my baby toenail; the eight-ounce cup has shrunk with age.

"Have you considered our offer?"

Fine, maybe. If this is what it takes to save some money and have my experience last winter legitimatized and honoured for the degree of bullshit that it was, then maybe I'll do it. Maybe I'll take down the fucking blog post. Not like I haven't done it before. The Christmas Day Abomination. I took it down in one fell swoop, and all of its ninety-eight blistering comments too. I'm not above going back on my word, apparently.

On the last day of summer, I googled "fertile synonyms" and called my mother.

"What do you mean *free,* hunny?" she said.

"For nine months. Unlimited use."

"Well, that'll sure save you a lot of money."

"Yeah, I guess. But part of me thinks Hybrid-Co Canada should rot in Internet hell for what they put me through. Why should I play along with their little sanitizing game? It was the worst winter of my life."

"Hunny, it's *free* Internet. See it as compensation for what you went through. "

"I guess."

"I think you should take it."

"We'll see. And, Mom?"

"Yes, hunny."

"I'm pregnant."

Silence.

"What do you *mean* pregnant?"

"I must've been really fecund, Mom, what can I say."

"Oh, hunny. Why do you always make things harder for yourself?"

The next day was autumn. I peed on a stick in Eric's bathroom to prove my findings. As I was peeing, I thought of how when the seasons change, I talk about it like I'm surprised it still happens.

"You done yet? I really have to know."

I ignored him.

"Are you sure you know what you're doing in there?"

"Hold on, I'm almost done," I said, letting the tap run. I was sitting on the toilet staring at the stupid addition sign like I'm now officially plus-one. I could hear the TV in the background. Eighteen days after her death, Joan Rivers' dog undergoes plastic surgery to appear perpetually in mourning. Twenty-five people attend the grand opening of The Joan Rivers' Skate Park in Oklahoma City. Joan Rivers' former co-stars fulfill her last request by handing out creamed salmon in Dixie cups at her favourite nail salon in Manhattan. I wanted to write an email to the other him. I wanted to say, "Look what you made me do. You got lost and I found him. Now what?"

Kisses on rue Saint-Denis. Kisses on the corner of Parc and Mont-Royal. Falling asleep on his chest on a bench near Sherbrooke Metro.

Spring, the doctor said. That's when my free Internet would expire. "Spring," I told Eric a few days later over the phone. "What should we do?"

"Well, I've been thinking, and I honestly just want you to do whatever you feel comfortable with. I want you to decide."

"So, you don't care if this baby is dead or alive?"

"Oh, no, that's not what I meant. I mean, I respect you, and it's your body, and I just want you to do what you think is best. Whatever you decide, I'll be good with."

"The fact that you are unwilling to fight for your own flesh and blood makes me think why bother, and not want to go through with it."

I hung up on him thinking of how a person is a manifestation of a moment they were never part of. Their mother "gets" pregnant, like she's contracted a disease, but doesn't know it. And the moment could unfold to include Joan Rivers' cackle christening a one-sided climax on a hardwood floor near a garbage can, and afterwards: scraped spine, a faulty embrace, and the temptation of free Internet dangling in the mix. How does that origin affect destiny? Then baby starts making its face at a time when up above no one knows it exists. I doused myself in screwdrivers. I radiated my abdomen with my laptop blogging in bed.

I hung up and also thought of how we're making a *human being* together, and how I'm certain I don't want it to have his spinelessness or his hair. Then I put on my jacket and I walked to rue Marie-Anne, to my old apartment. A light was on in the front room. The dream catcher I made him was still hanging in the window. I stood there, and it was chilly, and I decided, Fuck it. I'm going to delete my blog post. I'm going to take the free Internet. I'm not selling out any more than any other day, right. Then I thought of how there were certain things in life that made me wish I could live forever. Coming home to this apartment was one of them. The smell of garlic and basil because he's cooking. Making love to him in our clawfoot bathtub. The yellow kitchen with the purple cupboards. Maria Callas singing "O Mio Babbino Caro" on vinyl, a breeze through our front window. His boyhood in the way he sleeps.

"Hunny, sometimes our greatest loves aren't the ones we marry."

Josip Novakovich

DUNAVSKI PIRAT

Not having seen my old friend Mile for 25 years, I eagerly got together with him in Belgrade. He hadn't changed much, other than that he gained more territory – bigger bulk, and bigger presence. He lost most of his hair on top, and his temple hair and sideburns, white and silvery, gave him an aura of wisdom. White beard capped his chin, like an inverse mountain peak. He grew up without siblings near my hometown in Croatia, and perhaps because of that, he'd been extraordinarily quiet in our group conversations outside of high school. He disappeared in 1990, before the Serbian revolution in Croatia. According to rumours he may have joined the Serbian paramilitary, and anyhow, he had settled somewhere in the large Belgrade zone. As soon as I saw him, we resumed communicating as though we hadn't seen each other only a few days, starting with delighted smiles (his teeth were still good, white, and large) and a firm hand-shake.

Ah, there you are, old friend, he said. You are the same as before, same presence, aura.

Same aura perhaps. But you haven't changed, except for the better. You look calmer and more solid. And you speak Serbian ekavica.

Well, I live in Serbia, why wouldn't I?

Makes sense. But our friend Dule – remember him? – speaks Croatian, still. He says he's too old to change anything, and he has no ideology.

I had a lot of ideology, let me tell you, when we were chased out of Croatia.

Were you really chased out?

Let's not get into that. After what happened to Serbs in World War Two in Croatia – my grandfather and two uncles were killed by Ustashas – we were quick to respond to any sensation of threat. Both the Croatian locals and the Serbian army officers told us to clear out.

You didn't have to – many Serbs remained and they are fine.

That was unpredictable. Anyway, I like it here, and I belong. And I spent more than a year in the army here in the seventies where I fell in love with Serbian dialects.

I know, I visited you in the Zemun barracks.

Did you? My memory is not that good lately.

It was a quiet visit, and we sat on a de-barked log in the middle of the barracks. You sulked, and advised me to avoid joining the army at all costs.

Good advice.

Now we sat in front of a café aside from Kneza Mihajlova. After we covered many things in our conversation (mountain climbing, soccer violence, current elections), he said, You are coming to sleep at my place, aren't you?

No, I prepaid a downtown hotel. Pretty fancy. In Dedinje.

Cancel that. It's a boring bourgeois neighbourhood. Milosevic clan lives up there.

But it's elegant, and I have already paid. And Tito is buried there.

Of course I expect you to stay with me. What kind of host do you think I am?

Well, I need to be in Belgrade at ten in the morning. I am meeting...

No worries. We can easily make it back by ten.

I don't want you to cook for me. That's too much work. Let's find a good fish restaurant. I heard there's one on the Danube.

There are at least ten, but yes, there's a splendid one just on the other side, before Pancevo, on the way to my place. That's a great idea.

We walked down the streets, past the old *Politika* newspaper offices, and he said, Do you know it used to be only one page? You know, like *Abendblatt*, blatt meaning a page. And here's my car. Well not mine, but let's say it is for a few days.

Mile pulled out slowly. – I haven't driven in a year. My cousin lent me this one in Novi Sad.

Why haven't you driven in a while?

I had an accident and destroyed a Golf, made in Sarajevo, silver just like this one. Lucky I came out alive.

Your fault? Under the influence?

My fault. Didn't see that the lane disappeared and there was a wall instead, and I hit it and the car flipped and landed on the roof.

On the road, mostly rumbly cobbled streets, he didn't dare switch lanes, looked over his shoulder, not trusting the mirrors, and I looked as well. He seemed to drive in the wrong gear, the fourth up the hill, losing momentum, and then in the first down the hill, grinding, and he was aware of it. – The gear is not as important as the other cars and lampposts, I don't want to hit anything.

True, but you might not want to burn out the transmission either.

Don't say that, I am nervous enough.

I can see that.

Don't say that, I am!

He skirted the very edge of the road, nearly scraping the car against the knee-high sidewall.

You do have a bit more room on the left, you know, I said. Do you want me to drive? I've driven in Milan, Paris, Frankfurt, Budapest, New York, Moscow…

No, I am all right. It just takes a few minutes to get used to driving again. And I am self-conscious, you are like a driving instructor.

From the Pancevo bridge, I admired the views, left and right, of the Danube, the river I knew very well from my days in Budapest and Novi Sad, even broader and larger here, after receiving the waters of the rivers Sava and Tisza. On the left the white suspension bridge shone above barges with coal. Although it was early April, green colour dominated both sides of the river.

He parked timidly at Dunavski Pirat, and we both stepped out, and walked past lacquered red brick walls into the restaurant full of huge taxidermy masterpieces of catfish, pike-perch, carp, and even a shark. We chose a table outside, above the bank of the river, and next to a barky oak tree, which rose through the roof from the middle of the porch. The sides of the porch were all done in pine, with large open windows. We ordered fish paprika soup, and pike-perch and catfish, and shopska salad.

What kind of wine would you like? Mile asked. In this hot weather and with river fish, I think white would be good.

Oh, reds are always better. You don't have to listen to TV cook show recommendations.

It's common sense. Red wine can make you tense, and we both have high blood pressure, I assume?

Correct. For that, the best thing to do would be to eat a couple of apples now, and call it quits. But that's not what we are doing, is it?

You are right. Let's have a jug of red.

Soon the waiter brought us a large earthenware carafe as though we were in Georgia or Mesopotamia.

He slurped the red fish paprikash soup. For some reason I never liked the sound of slurping. He also slurped the wine.

The fish, also in large earthenware, was delicious, olive-oiled and garlicky and a bit oversalted: of course, oversalted, what food isn't, in the Balkans? The view of the Danube was spoiled and smudged because the plastic sheets used as a mosquito net had accumulated a sooty sheen from the river traffic.

You wouldn't believe the mosquitoes along the river, he said.

I would. I'd rather have a clear view and itch a bit, than…I mean, what's the point of sitting riverside if you can't see the glorious river?

You see it. You don't need to see all the details. Just imagine you are near-sighted and that's what the river would look like.

Good point. It's sometimes good not to see the details. Life is more beautiful without them.

Life, he laughed. What is life? Everybody talks about it, but it's too big to be talked about. He leaned back in his chair. I'd never paid attention to the colour of his eyes, and their blueness surprised me. With red cheeks, belying old-fashioned vigour, the blue stood out.

Yes, we live a cliché.

The restaurant is fine, but I see, they have raised the prices brazenly. I could run a better restaurant and my dishes would be more authentic and half the price. Anyway, let's go to my place, it will be nicer there.

How will I make it to Belgrade early in the morning?

I'll drive you.

But if we get drunk, as no doubt we will, we'll oversleep, and my meeting, one of the reasons why I am in Belgrade for the second time in two months, will not take place, and I'll never publish a book in Belgrade, which is a shame, considering I published in the zone, Budapest, Sofia, Warsaw, Moscow, Istanbul…even Zagreb.

Don't be so pessimistic. People will love you here. You kind of fit in with your temperament.

What do you mean by that? Anyway, I paid for a good hotel, and I snore at night, so it will be most peaceful if I go there and we can meet again downtown tomorrow afternoon.

Forget it. You still haven't seen my vineyard, and haven't tasted my wine. And I want to show you where I plan to make a restaurant. I have a whole building I am not using for anything.

That's amazing.

And I have 10,000 litres of wine, mostly white wine, first rate, organic, and all I need now is dishes. You know, that's easy. You just buy some meat and toss it on the grill and slice tomatoes and onions…a hot pepper here and there. But wine? That takes work and love, and time, years.

I can see that. With your robust body frame, you could inspire confidence as a proprietor.

Yes, I'd tell the customers I was the chef, but an unemployed elderly couple, my friends, would cook. They wouldn't charge much and they would be grateful.

Maybe in the beginning. Nobody is grateful in the end.

I am not planning the end. No exit strategy. It won't be Iraq.

So what's the theme? You have to have some angle for a new restaurant, especially in the boonies. How will you attract the paying customers from Belgrade?

They love going a bit sideways, and so we have the floats on the Sava, which are a huge success, even though they are far out in Zemun and Novi Beograd.

Yes, the theme is, floats. Wild stuff. And yours?

Staroslavenska kuhinja. Old Slavic cuisine.

Slavic? Are Serbs pan-Slavs? Maybe they used to be, but now, you've had a falling out with just about everybody – Croats, Slovenes, Macedonians, Montenegrins…not to mention your old friends Bulgarians, two fucking Balkan wars, when are you going to have the third one with them?

I know. Old Serbian cuisine.

What is that?

I am going to explore it. Maybe hire some ethnographic historian. But basically you know – mutton, pork, vegetable stews, beans, sour cream and garlic, lots of beans…

Blood sausages?

Now you are teasing me. Anyway, when we think ethnic cuisine, we usually assume only a few dishes as though our ancestors had no imagination and ate the same thing over and over, without experimenting, combining, and being inspired. I'll run the kitchen in the spirit of the old Slavic cuisine.

Ungaro-Croato-Serb?

Yes, naturally, cuisine was always fusion. Basically our ancestors cooked whatever happened to be around.

Our fish came in dark red glazed earthenware.

This is great, I said. And we ate, and hummed, and cleaned out the bones, and chewed more.

A black and white cat rubbed against my ankles, and stood on his hind legs, sniffing the catch.

He's well-trained, I said. Not jumping on the table, yet not afraid of people. The right amount of love and fear.

One thing, it's not safe to eat bony fish when drunk, he said. You might get needles in your throat.

Do you have a cat at home?

I don't feel good, he said.

What do you mean? Great food, good wine, mediocre company, you should feel great, I said.

By mediocre, you don't mean yourself?

Yes.

Yes means what?

It means no. I do mean myself.

Oh, we could play with words, but my friend, I don't feel well. I feel tension in my chest, not enough air, and pain around my heart.

Do you take pills for blood pressure?

Diuretics and something else.

A beta-blocker?

Not a beta-blocker. Ace-something. Not sure, I just believe the doctors and swallow.

What's your pulse like?

I don't know.

You measure it like this. Put two fingers on the radial side of your wrist, inside, gently, and feel for the beat.

I can't find it.

Or on the neck in front of the biggest front neck muscles.

I can't find it. Maybe my heart is too weak to beat right.

Don't be silly, I said. Of course you have pulse and your heart is beating. Give me your hand.

I found his pulse and counted 90 in a minute.

That's not too fast, though a large animal like you should have a slower pulse. Tell you what, I have a beta-blocker on me, a small dose, 50 mg of…Metoprolol. The usual dose is 100, and for a beast like you, it could be even 200. It will slow your heart rhythm and lower your pressure.

But I've never taken it. Isn't the first time always unpredictable? You never know what won't agree with your system.

It also works as a tranquilizer – it can eliminate physiological side effects of stage fright. Pianists use it. I think you had too much excitement today, driving for the first time after your accident, in the rush hour of freaky Belgrade! To tell you the truth, I'm impressed by how mellow the drivers in Belgrade are. You should try Moscow!

He looked suspiciously at the aspirin-like tablet.

Also, drink a lot of water, and breathe deep and slow.

He drank water, and breathed slowly.

You studied medicine. You learned something?

I dropped out before I could learn anything clinical but I would have made a good doctor, that's what my anatomy professor said. I do have the intuition and common sense of one …and I follow research.

You sure the pill won't do more harm than good?

Ninety-six percent positive.

Mile opened his mouth like a dog short of air and he looked redder than before. His massive hand with hairy knuckles stalled half way across the table. I guess he weighed between two fears – heart attack and the unreliable pill from an old Croatian friend.

He looked me in the eye, not blinking, like a huge St. Bernard puppy, in distress, at a bear. I could see he treated the pill as some kind of explosive, and he calculated, probably, which factor was more important here – that I was an old friend, or that I was a Croatian with resentments about the Serbian wrecking of Croatia in the '90's. Maybe he thought this was the sneaky assassination moment. Serbs kill their political opponents the old-fashioned way, with bullets in hotel lobbies, and Russians and Croats use radioactive drugs.

All such potential thoughts and doubts and suspicions only made him more tense and redder, and threatened his heart further. His own heart had become his enemy, and he could trust it less than me, I imagined, as we kept the gaze, and the fear in his eyes grew, black pupils pushing and thinning the blue irises into thin rings.

He snatched the pill and swallowed, his Adam's apple bobbing as though he were swallowing a whole plum rather than a 4-millimetre diameter.

Now I probably shouldn't drink any wine, he said.

It's all mine now!

He looked at me somberly and panted. I imagined that he may have thought about how sad it all was, that friends when tested could not be trusted, that our ethnic histories weighed so heavily between us, like the humidity in the air on this prematurely hot and muggy day, behind the soot-smudged plastic mosquito screen, which prevented fresh air flow.

Deepen your breath, I said. You need to calm down your system.

I don't want to calm it too much.

Don't worry, your heart won't stop, you aren't going to have a heart attack.

How do you know?

True, I don't. Most heart attacks take place in the morning, early in the morning.

The humidity messes with me.

Me too. It's normal. Once it rains, you'll be all dandy, this is just a bit of atmospheric pressure, you are right about that. You know what, let's not obsess or you will drive yourself insane.

I am insane.

Do you know any new Serbian jokes?

Even if I did, I wouldn't think of them now.

Let's keep eating. The fish will be cold.

And we ate. I gave the fish head to the cat and the cat purred and crunched the bones. Mile also gave the cat his fish head. Smart cat, he said. Chose the right place to be.

Yes, I'd say if I had a choice between being a bookstore cat or a fish restaurant cat, I'd choose the fish place.

Good fish, he said and chewed with his eyes closed, and a tear showed up in the corner of his eye.

Now tell me more about your restaurant idea, I said. Will you have fish?

Of course, only river fish as we are too far from the sea. And rabbit, goose, duck, venison, boar...

You know that the Papuk Mountain is now the best boar hunting area in the world. Even Russians come there to hunt.

I know. That's what happens when you lose Serbian hunters!

Yes, big mistake. Croatia went to pigs now. Wild pigs.

Sometimes I dream of hunting in those mountains, I must admit, he said.

A friend of mine does. After the war, he had a small rocket launcher in his garage, and he fired into a heard of boars, killing seven of them.

That sounds like a tall tale.

Wouldn't put it past Darko, you know him, the tall bony guy with a large broken nose, boxer style.

Mile kept chewing slowly, with his eyes closed.

I drank more red wine and felt it go to my neck and cheeks, clearly building up my blood pressure. Well, I said. It's been more than 20 minutes since you took the beta-blocker. It should begin to take effect. Do you feel any better?

I am dizzy. I think it would be hard for me to stand up. If I did, I'd probably fall.

And I thought, What if he actually gets worse, has a heart attack, goes to a hospital, and tells the doctors I gave him a beta-blocker, and it turns out that with his kind of heart failure, that's the last thing he should get. With an atrophied distended heart – if that's the case with him, probably is, since with his massive frame he tortures his heart climbing mountains in the summer and does nothing in the winter – a beta-blocker could actually precipitate a heart attack or even more likely a stroke, with the slowing of blood flow. Shit. So if he gets to the hospital, they will ask him what he took, and he could say a beta-blocker from a Croatian friend, and I could be arrested. And if he dies, I'll be charged with murder.

Now I felt heat in my cheeks, partly from the red wine and the hot air, but even more, from my thoughts. Mind can poison the skin, let alone the heart. What if my tension gets me? I'd forgotten to take blood pressure pills all week.

Would it be amazing, I thought, if we both had heart attacks in the restaurant at the same time?

Wait a second, I said, and took out 100 mgs of metoprolol and began to swallow it. I chased it with wine – not the prescriptive method – and it got stuck in my throat and melted there chalkily, and I poured more wine, and the bitterness sank down my esophagus, and I shook, as though I had swallowed a lemon with powdered aspirin. Anyway, this should take care of me. Now, what's to guarantee Mile won't have a heart attack? At the age of 59, with such a bulky frame, with certified long-term blood pressure history, isn't he the profile of a heart attack victim?

Do you smoke? I asked.

I did, until a year ago.

Are you better?

How could I be better that fast, in a hurry?

We kept eating in silence. We both had our thoughts spinning and affecting us. If he stopped thinking, I bet he would be all right. And maybe if I stopped thinking and projecting my anxieties, he would relax. I should definitely change our theme.

By the way, how was it to work as a bouncer in Zagreb?

Oh, it was wonderful, he replied. You know it was the late '70s, the American Sexual Revolution reached us, nobody worried about VD, people got drunk, and hot girls after dancing sometimes just led me into the dark passage on the side of the club, and we'd grope, sometimes have a quickie, some nights three or four, so it got to be exhausting. Oh, those were the days. He smiled happily.

You didn't seem to be interested in girls before going to Zagreb.

I was just shy. Didn't know how to express interest, but in the club, I didn't have to. Girls whose boyfriends passed out from Jack Daniel's would come up to me. Strange enough, before that, I never liked the idea of blow-jobs, but I got more of them than I could remember, and it was heavenly. I got addicted then, you know sex is a powerful drug. My mind is still diseased with it, but now it's all mental.

As you are not married, you can…

Actually I am. But to tell you the truth, this blood pressure, heart, and so on, well, I haven't done it in a while. Strange how life is – if I could have distributed the action I had as a young man over my life span, it would be just right. Now a few times I got together with a strange woman, I had to worry whether I could get it up, sometimes I did, sometimes I didn't, so it's no fun, it's embarrassing. It's like a medical exam.

You are married and you never mentioned your wife.

That's how it goes. Once you are married for a long time, what's there to say? I am not proud of being married. I wouldn't be proud of being single either.

So you are feeling better now?

Still a little dizzy, and tired from the atmospheric pressure, bad heart.

The bill came. Four thosand dinars.

My God, he said, this is robbery. This place used to be earthy and cheap but now…

Well, it's not all that bad, 60 dollars.

It's like one-sixth of many people's salaries.

Don't worry, I'll cover it.

You are my guest. I'll pay, of course.

No, I'll pay.

I expected a long and protracted battle which I would lose, because that is how things used to be in Belgrade 30 years ago. Serbian friends were proud and competitive hosts. I took out 4400 from my left jeans pocket and put the paper money into the little basket in which the bill stood, written in Cyrillic, in slanted blue.

Thank you, he said. You didn't have to. And now let's go to my place, and I'll treat you to some really fine wine, my labour of love.

I was a little taken aback that I had won this bill paying session just as I had a couple of months before when I had visited Belgrade as well. I won all the bill paying duels.

And I said, It's already pretty late, after nine. I'd rather go to my hotel, and maybe we can do the wine-tasting tomorrow or the day after.

As you wish. But it would be much better now, we are practically already there, only five kilometres away, and by now, almost 20 from your hotel.

Well, you know, I woke up very early to get here, and the quiet of the hotel before my work tomorrow would do me good. This was great, and to be continued.

But it would be better if you visited. Now is now, and who knows if we ever get a chance again. If our hearts last.

Oh how you talk. You are fine.

He drove unsteadily, his headlights short, illuminating only 4-5 yards of the black asphalt ahead of us, and he nearly hit the curb and then overreacted into the other lane. The asphalt was unmarked, freshly done, without the yellow or white edges.

What the hell? I thought. Is he having a heart attack right now? I reached out to grab the wheel. He steadied the driving, and I put my hand back in my lap.

We came to the main road, and he lingered at the stop sign, idling, the car sliding a bit back, and then, obviously in the third gear, he started forward to correct the backslide, and the car stalled at the crossing before he could turn left to cross the Danube back to Belgrade.

He hesitated a little, gasped, and restarted the engine, grinding it with the key turned too long.

You know how to find the address?

I don't feel well. Fuck it, I can't breathe.

You should see a doctor.

It's late. I don't know where to find one.

ER at the nearest hospital.

I don't know where… And I don't want emergencies.

He gasped, his thick eyebrows arched high, and he groaned.

I wondered: Is he just faking a heart attack so he won't have to drive to Belgrade? I thought it was his beloved town, and look how he fears it. Maybe he's been playing all evening long, just to get out of the chore of driving through the lively traffic? That's probably it, he's an excellent actor, and he wants to get his way, and what is his way? To get me to visit him at home, to show me how well he's doing, and what a great host he is. Now how bad is that? And why am I stuck on protecting my prepaid reservation of 75 dollars? It's done, and I can sleep at the hotel, and the 75 will be gone, or I can sleep at my friend's place, and the 75 will be gone. What's the difference? I should just count my losses, and fuck him, faking or not, he doesn't mean ill. Even if I were to lose 75 more dollars, who cares, is friendship a price tag?

Fuck it, I said. I don't want to jeopardize your health. This drive – even the thought of it – seems to be killing you. Let's just go to your place and I'll crash there.

Oh, good, thank you!

He turned to the right. His driving improved instantly.

Pancevo is pretty sleepy, I guess, I said. Where is the big glass factory?

It shut down.

Really? It was the largest one in Yugoslavia.

I think you are right. Anyway, those chimneys in the dark over there, that's where it used to be.

It's great to see it. My father did contract work for them. You have no idea how often I thought of this place, and how much, even as a kid, I worked to send wooden shoes here. Sometimes I stayed up all nights with my father, at the age of nine and ten, nailing leather onto wooden soles, and then I carted the large hemp sacks, fifty pairs per sack, to the train station before dawn, sometimes ten trips, to deliver to the cargo train, addressed simply, Staklana, Pancevo, SFR Srbija. The factory workers couldn't walk around the hot floors in rubber shoes, and the wooden clogs provided the best insulation, the workers loved them. Oh, this means a lot to me. I gazed into the dark and the still chimneys in the moonlight. Obliquely, I have more roots here than you do, I said.

No doubt, he replied.

We took another turn to the right – most of our turns, somehow were to the right – and in a couple of kilometres, he said, Here we are!

He pulled in the crunchy driveway. He showed me his bread brick-oven, containing two floors and windows, with the chimney five yards high, large enough to bake and grill sheep, pigs, and oxen, if need be, and then, he led me down the stairs into his dank wine cellar. We bent our heads, and I waved off a sticky cobweb from my eyebrows.

Here I have three thousand bottles of white wine. I have another cellar with 7000 more.

I met his wife – not quite as bulky as him – whose eyes shone, and she said, I heard a lot about you! – and mother-in-law afterward, a classic Balkan widow all in black, who immediately offered a walnut strudel. – I am so glad Mile gets to see a childhood friend!

Oh, thank you, you wouldn't believe how stuffed we got at Dunavski Pirat, I said.

But Mile, why? his mother-in-law asked.

Let's go to the porch and have some wine, Mile said to me. Riesling, similar to what we have in Western Slavonia, and Pinot Grigio.

I saw pictures of you hiking in Italy, I said, on your Facebook page. Is that where you fell in love with Grigio?

You got it. Now, tell me which one you like better.

I tasted the wines. They are both great, but it would be better if they were chilled. I think Riesling is more interesting, fruitier.

I've put a couple of bottles into the freezer to chill for half an hour, but for now, we'll make do with these. I put no additives, no sulfates, and you'll see, you won't get a hangover from this, no matter how much you drink.

We toasted. Zivili, and looked each other in the eyes, holding the gaze.

The clouds created a black layer above the indigo post-dusk horizon, and above the darkened fields. Black, indigo, and black, a rather soothing vision of the distance, with some rumbling in the sky. Why isn't there a country flag in such a colour combination?

Obviously, it has to rain soon, I said.

A yellow three-legged dog hopped by, below the cement porch.

He's bumming for food, but we are not eating. People sometimes drop off their puppies here. It would be better if they neutered their dogs like the Americans do. Go away, shhh, sss, he hissed at the dog, and threw a rotten apple after him.

Aren't you sorry for the poor creature?

I can't afford to feel sorry for them all.

It began to rain. We'd each already finished three glasses, and now he brought out chilled wine. We drank it, our throaty gulps clickety-clacking, almost like shoes on a sidewalk.

How is your heart? I asked.

You know, suddenly completely fine, he said. Yes, tension came and went. All good now. The rain has relieved the pressure. I really do react to the congestion in the weather.

Maybe the fact that you've had a litre of wine may have something to do with your sense of well-being?

We said, Zivili, to your life, once again. Our language, along with Hebrew and a few others, contains this toast, To Life, or Live! We also have Na zdravlje, for health! but Zivili is more common, and perhaps existential. Health, that may be too much to ask for, but as long as we are alive, it's good, let's live. That's all we can ask for. The toast may have been born out of bad history, who knows, but somehow I always preferred it to toasting health while damaging it.

So, no doctor tonight?

No, maybe tomorrow. I can't guarantee that we'll feel good after two more bottles.

I feel so much better! If I could be half-drunk all the time, I don't think I'd have any problems.

The rain became intense, and the air chill cleansed and soothed our skins, lungs, and hearts. Pine-needle smells and cypress aroma rode on the dispersed particles of water from the sky in a heavenly luxury. We went to sleep with our windows open, and sooner than I was ready for it, Mile woke me up. What kind of coffee would you like? he asked. He wasn't as ruddy as the evening before, but a bit ashen and pained. It's too early, he said, but I promised.

Turkish. What time is it?

Nine.

We drove over the bridge in a drizzle, and the greys dominated the greens on the banks of the river. Mile drove excellently, without any hesitant moves, and inspired so much confidence that I didn't look over his shoulder as he switched lanes.

During my meeting with a Serbian publisher, the publisher said, You think I am a publisher? There's no more publishing. People have no money, they don't read, or if they do, they borrow books from friends, ten copies sell, it's not a business, I now run an advertising agency and organize a festival, and primarily I write, I write novels now. And this is a horrible country, full of backstabbers and liars and thieves and fascists, I don't know what you want from us, fuck us, it's all gone to hell. I hate the place, oh, I love the city, but I hate what's become of it, the sheer vandalism, the death of book culture, I know, it's worldwide, but worse here. He gushed for two hours his resentment for his homeland, and I didn't have the heart to put my books in his hands, and I paid for our four coffees, and we shook hands, and promised to stay in touch.

And later, I stayed at the prepaid reservation hotel (this one downtown, down the hill from the Presidential Palace), and went downstairs to a jazz bar, and watched the tail end of Real

Madrid winning the Spanish Cup against Barcelona, and two tall, elegant girls danced and looked over their shoulders at me, somehow invitingly, but I kept looking at Modric passing the ball to Benzema, on the screen, and later when I went to my room, I wished I had the vitality and sprightliness and the courage to be with the young ladies, who looked too good to be true, but then, shouldn't the truth be good looking? So maybe it was all true, but I stepped out of the truth into my prepaid reservation room, and actually wished I were drinking with Mile on his ionized and cypress-scented porch.

But the rain that had started during our wine-drinking wouldn't relent, and it rained for days, until the whole region flooded, and people grew depressed, and so did Mile. I called him just before the Deluge, two days after our drinking, and he said, Eh, my friend, this rain is getting me. I have no will to do anything, and my heart feels heavy and crumpled. Let's bake a suckling pig when the rain is over.

All right, let's do that.

I boarded a blue bus for Zagreb during the rainfall, only three days after my getting to Belgrade, and thought, Maybe he was right, maybe that was our only chance to drink wine at his place. I ate an oily and sour burek as the bus pulled out of the terminal, spraying the passersby with bursts of muddy pot-hole waters.

Hugh Graham

AFTER ME

I was in the bar room of the Central Hotel, it was night and I cleared all the glasses off the end of the bar, smashing them. Someone said I was drunk and I hollered at the whole bunch of them, I said, Come up and fight. I said, Let any constable, Everett or any son of a bitch walk in here and try to take me, he won't do it. I was the only one in the room standing. No one would fight me, they never even said nothing. I told them I got one foot in the future, I know the future three genera- tions down, I've been there, and they will have horseless car- riages and buildings taller than a church spire and it'll all be machines. No one said nothin, they were afraid of me and my brothers, my family. Then Constable Everett come in. I knocked him flat and him and Constable Hodgins grabbed a hold of me, it took four of them to pull me outside and I fell. I hit the sidewalk on Queen Street, it was the damn doorman, another body builder with tattoos and a headset, I'd lost track of time, it had gotten dark. Then the cops from 52 Division, I was handcuffed, they knew me and put me in the cruiser. I didn't need this. I was planning to see Eve, I wanted to be clear of all of this for Eve. She hadn't returned my last couple of calls, my plan was to drop by her place, I had the feeling she was ready for us to be together, it was now or never. On the other hand, I didn't want to place too much hope in Eve because

I had nothing else. We'd met two or three years before, I was looking for an apartment and I saw one for rent, a two-bedroom, I had money then, now everything's tied up in bail. I went up and knocked and this woman opened the door, green eyes, a little strange, hooded at the corners but stunning, red hair and a beautiful, naturally smiling mouth. She said she was sorry, she'd just taken the place, I said, No problem, I was trying to think of more to say, I was too stunned, I managed a little small talk, she said her name was Eve. I said, Well, maybe we'll bump into each other. She smiled and said, Sure, okay. Bye now, and closed the door. So I was in the interview room, the cops were friendly, a little condescending, they asked me if I was still doing any art. I'm supposed to be an artist, I'd begun as a photographer, I've done production design on movies but mostly installation art, fragments, experiments with old photographs, for example a 60 X enlargement of Tom Donnelly's eye in the photograph from 1877, through the dissolving iris to all that was reflected on it, I used bits of cloth from clothing 130 years old and essences of lilac and mildew in plaster. It made me a living here and in Europe but the fact is I had no interest in art, the sole idea to annihilate the present for the past as if stepping through a window or a door into a field. The cops asked me if I was on my meds, I couldn't remember. Hodgins wouldn't keep me in the Lucan lockup more than a couple of hours because of what my brothers would do. Constable Everett come in, they were talkin about what to do with me and they let me out in the middle of the night sayin I was barred from Lucan. I was charged with drunk and disorderly and they said the Domino Club was getting a restraining order. They reminded me of my court appearance the next day on other charges and I was released. I went along to the hotel, the last of the old fleabag dumps on Queen Street. The room was small, the windows and ceilings very high, very old. I liked hotels, they were indeterminate just as I didn't mind common areas in jails and psych and hospital wards, at least for short periods. The room was almost bare, everything had gone into bail, my computer as well. The idea was to get a new start, motivation and so on by seeing Eve, just get up the nerve to knock on her door. I've never lacked for courage in anything, only this, I was very nervous about going to Eve's. I looked out the window, across the street, the old Victorian fronts forever there. I turned in early to sleep off the hangover for tomorrow and in case I saw Eve. I stayed in the Queen's Hotel to show I could. Walker's stage line had their coaches there, it was them shot my brother a month ago for tryin to burn the hotel. The clerk give me a room because he was afraid. I took a candle up and along the corridor and Sarah Coughlin passed me with a pitcher and basin, she was a maid there. I told her to get out of the hotel before dawn. I knew she'd never say nothin because she had a child off me, a boy, I always wondered where the little boy was, he'd have been seven years old. I got a bed for a few hours and woke up before dawn. I went down to the livery where Walkers had their coaches, I waited until the fire watch was round the other side and lit matches and paper to the mangers and the hay mow except the livery boy seen me, I told him, If you say anything I'll cut the black heart out of you. I couldn't find a horse, I walked out of town into the country, to the Roman Line. The sun was comin up, I seen behind me the smoke of the Queen's Hotel rising in the sky. I got up late and looked out, the southwest, the blue summer sky, the old fronts across Queen Street. I thought, I'm looking toward Lucan, time condensed, erased. I had to make a living,

I wondered if I could ever return to art, the problem was that art took you there but not all the way, not out of time like going through a skin, a membrane. The idea to navigate time the way you can navigate space. It's because of time that we suffer. It's a trap, like being a bound prisoner in a police car or bound to anything moving and condemned to move, bound to motion and loss forever. I went out and had coffee and a bite to eat. I'd been walking a lot to keep sane. I thought I might walk all the way to Eve's. I knew that once I'd decided to knock at her door, there'd be no turning back. But I hadn't decided. After the time when we first met, when I'd knocked at her door, I'd shop in the area or read in the coffee shops and restaurants in hopes of running into her. But it was in a bar that I saw her. I was having a late drink and she was with a woman friend. She was all smiles, even gave me a hug. I bought them drinks, and she jokingly introduced her friend as a chaperone. She was actually avoiding her boyfriend, someone called Tony. They'd just broken up. Eve's friend left and Eve and I joked that I was her chaperone now. She'd lived abroad, Italy, France, Brazil, everywhere, teaching English. Now she was back in Toronto teaching ESL, she'd been born here and she hardly knew anyone now. She asked me what I did and I told her about the art, making it sound plausible, accessible. She seemed interested. When she had to go I gave her my card, she didn't give me her number but said it would be nice to touch base. She left and I felt quite euphoric, so good that I was afraid. It was afternoon now and once again I decided against dropping by Eve's. I thought I'd see my friend Janis instead, I'd told Janis about Eve. Whenever I was at a loss, there'd always been Janis, so I continued up Spadina, the Roman Line was dusty, it was haying time, I was needed at home for haying. I was thinking the whole business, the troubles had started here in one fight over land, a neighbouring lot stolen from my father and because we were Irish it spread everywhere, to religion and the coach business, everything. Doherty give me a ride on his wagon, we talked about the fights I had when I beat Walker and I beat Simmons. Then I seen my friend Jim Feeheley ridin up and he stopped and says to me not to go home, that the constables are up around there looking for me. He went on and I thought, I'll stop at Merriweathers, they're Protestants, they won't look for me there. I went to where they were hayin and John Merriweather said I could give them a hand but I saw he didn't feel good about it, maybe because of the smoke in the sky from the Queen's. Later, I drove a load of hay into their barn and the daughter May Merriweather come out with water. I wondered if her family suspected me and her. The gang quit work at sunset and there was the whistle of the train comin across back of their farm, the Grand Trunk, that was how I'd see May, in by the tracks from the back. That night they give me the bedroom off the kitchen. I went on up Spadina. I hoped to hell my friend Janis would be home because the breeze and hard late sunlight of evening would soon give me anxiety, the light that could push me over the edge, even antipsychotics didn't help, all of it connected, backwards, to everything, even when I was three or four when we had a corner house and my friend Wendy, a little girl from across the street, pointed up at the wall of our house saying, There's a bad man, there's a bad man and I thought of a bad man in the wall. And then the first book I ever read was a pot-boiler about the Donnellys, a family of farmer outlaws in western Ontario who seemed mythical with a sort of dark grandeur, almost Homeric. Then I was about ten, it was 1960 or '61 when my father had pointing and repair done on the exterior of the house. There was scaffolding up and I'd watch as the bricklayer, a man called Jim Carlisle, broke out the old brick and mortared in another course. He was teasing and frightening, around sixty with wild pale eyes. He'd talk to me from up on the scaffold saying, Did you ever hear about the Black Donnellys? He'd say, I knew the men that killed them. I'm a Lucan boy, I'm from Lucan all right. When I was your age the gang that killed them still walked free, I seen them myself. They were old men but I knew who every one of them was. Then Carlisle would laugh. Janis was home, thank god, she'd had her apartment there on Dupont Street for years, it backed onto the CPR tracks. Her place hadn't changed, she did some sort of IT, online help from home. We'd gone out together long before. Years later we were friends. I'd told her all about Eve, about Eve admitting to being mildly obsessive compulsive. No matter where she was working or what her plans were Eve had to be at home around suppertime every day, even if she had to go out again. I said I'd left Eve a couple of phone messages and hadn't heard back. Janis said, Just go and drop by, nothing's going to happen, I mean nothing bad. She'd probably be glad to see you. Janis asked me about the episodes, if I'd been myself. I told her they'd been coming too often, Lucan, Tom Donnelly etcetera, which was why I was looking to get a solid grounding, get my mind on a relationship and I remembered my father having part of the dining room re-plastered by Carlisle's father, Frank Carlisle, at the same time as the brickwork, the old man plastering, he whistled as he did it, whistled beautifully. He was ninety and still did the odd job. He told me he'd helped build the house, he'd been a bricklayer on our house when it was built in 1895. My mother didn't like the

Carlisles but it only came up when she drank. My mother had a drinking problem. It was usually late afternoon when she'd be drunk and she'd accuse me of having caused trouble by talking to the Carlisles. And at night I heard my parents fighting about them being hired to work on the house. But I'd be outside with the old man Carlisle watching his son finishing up on the scaffold and the son started teasing me, threatening to say something about the Donnellys and the old man cut him off and said to me, My son remembers the men that killed them. Well, I knew the Donnellys themselves. I worked for them when I was boy, before they died. And for all that was said against them they were right fine people, they had the best clothes and buggies and ran the best coach line and the mother and daughter, they always gave me blackberry pie. Then the bricklayers were gone and my mother would be fine and then she'd be drunk again and telling me that I'd caused irreparable harm by talking to them. Then she'd accuse me of bothering the people upstairs. We owned the house and had the ground-floor apartment and my aunt lived on the top floor. I never knew who lived on the second floor. But sometimes I'd hear footsteps above my room at night, I thought they were ghosts. Janis asked me about my the court appearance tomorrow but I was looking out though her back porch, the train tracks in vicious blades of strong, late bad sunlight and Janis was calling Hello? Hello-o! I'd walked those tracks with my back to the train just to see how quickly I could get off. By a millimeter. I was getting leery and Janis said I could stay over if I wanted and the train came by, the soporific rush and hum and clackety-clack loud against the back of her place, the whistle now of the night train back of Merriweathers, I was half asleep in the bedroom they give me off the kitchen when May come down quiet and got into the bed. I told her about how I knew the future after my death and she lay with me, we lay with each other and then in the dark she says, We shouldn't of. I says, Why? She says, The wrong time of the month, I says, Don't worry. Again she says, We shouldn't of, I was a bad girl. She touched my face and I now know that was when the seed took, July, 1877, because she was in the family way a while later and they sent her away to have it. I heard it was boy. I never loved any girl as much as I loved May and then I hardly saw her any more. It was the same with all my brothers and my sister, no one local would marry us because of who we were, even friends like Merriweathers, like they knew what was going to happen. At dawn I decided to go back into Lucan. The sun wasn't up when I left Merriweathers' by the tracks that curved straight into town, there was still a gap in the chain-link fence in the parking lot and I got through and up onto the tracks, it was just dawn. I walked west on the westbound tracks to see how long I could go on hearing the roar and the horn coming up behind me as if to knock you through time forever as through a membrane, an event horizon. I thought Eve would probably see me now. The first time she phoned, I'd given up on hearing from her, and then we talked a long time. She was forty, I was in my early fifties. I wondered how much we could have in common, I mean someone like me, the way I am. But she was interested in art because she'd had so much of language teaching, she was curious. Except she was back again with Tony, the boyfriend. I could hear the train behind me. Still, we'd meet for coffee up on Bloor and she'd talk about Tony, he was younger, thirty. She had rules and he kept breaking them. They were off again, on again. I took her out to dinner, she'd ask about the art and I'd tell her about the power of the senses to invoke the past, the train horn was blaring up fast behind me, I told her nothing about the meds and the psychosis, I always steered the conversation back to her and anyway she was always happy to unburden herself about Tony, it was deafening and I stepped off and the wind was incredible, the cars howled by. Eve suggested email by which time I'd sold my computer to cover the legal costs but she never cared about me not doing email. As to her not returning my last couple of calls, she'd told me her landlord had allowed her to redecorate and she was busy stripping wallpaper and repainting. So tomorrow would be good. I was all the way out at The Junction and I realized I had the court appearance back at Old City Hall. And I had to be there. My brothers would be out on Main Street, we had to show that we were free, that nobody could touch us. We'd often wear our suits, double-breasted with double-breasted waistcoats and we'd loaf while we had the new coaches built, to show we were still in business. So my brothers were there, the Queen's was burned to the ground and I told them I'd done it. It went on into the fall, the fighting and burning and they were burning us out and our friends too. The whole township, Biddulph, was flat and at night you could see where every fire was burning but by winter the stage coach fight had wore itself out. The railroad killed it off anyway. It wasn't until the next year, March, that it all started up in a different way on account of the run-in me and Jim Feeheley had with Ned Ryan. I left the tracks now with the damn evening light threatening to come for my court appearance, the same evening light that bothered my mother. My father never talked about it, never told me why she drank until after she'd died and he'd sold the house and we moved to another place along with my aunt. He brought it up apropos of something. He told me that before I was born my mother and her mother, my grandmother Quinn, had had a fight. Her mother had said something terrible about my mother's father, my grandfather Quinn. My mother idolized her father and she was outraged. My father wouldn't say what she'd said but the whole thing, the argument, had actually happened in the corner house, our old house, on the floor above us. Before I was born. I'd never even known mother's family had lived there. So anyway after the fight, my grandmother got fed up and went out for a walk and right then she was killed by a drunken driver. At around the supper hour on a bright summer day. My mother was destroyed by guilt and by what her mother had said about her own husband, my mother's father, and my mother began drinking especially on evenings of hard sunlight, the light when her mother was killed. I decided to catch the subway at Dundas and I met Jim Feeheley. He was with Ned Ryan. Ryan had just sold his farm and Feeheley had gotten Ryan drunk like we'd planned. It was on account of the land next to ours. Land my father had cleared and claimed and even killed a man over. In self-defence. That was how it all started. Because the law gave the land to cousins of the man my father had killed and the farm passed on to Ned Ryan, another cousin, and my mother bawled out Ryan telling him we'd cut the guts out of the next man to make a dollar off that property. Then Ryan went and sold it to the Cains who were part of the same faction. They all wanted to drive us out. So it was March 1878, me and Feeheley were walkin Ryan home up the Roman Line and at dusk we threw him on the ground and I hit him a few times, I'd knocked him out and I took the cash off him, five hundred for sellin our land. We just walked on, I paid a taxi, I could hardly afford it but what the hell. Once I was with Eve

I'd really have to get myself in shape. The money, the legal problems. I got to Old City Hall, Court Room Six. Everybody was there, my shrink, my lawyer, the social worker, the Crown. My lawyer liked the fact that I was an artist, if he only knew. I could hardly even remember the offence. Until it came back, wild parkland near the mouth of the Humber on the lake in March of a year or two ago and a man walking ahead of me, maybe a hiker. With glowing athletic footwear. I got up very quietly behind him, Feeheley had him distracted and I got him down, beat him hard and got his wallet for the sale of the land and I looked up and Lake Ontario was as flat as Biddulph township. I caught a cab, then changed my mind and went to look for the guy. I felt terrible, I wanted to return his money. There was some blood there but he was gone. The lawyers and the judge and police witnesses went on a long time about my diagnosis and medication and then the cab driver didn't show up and there were technicalities. My lawyer noted I'd never tried to abscond bail, my father and Keefes and Feeleheys stood as bondsmen for me on the Ryan robbery, anyway I'd stay and fight it until it was dropped. The whole feud was centered on the Ryan thing now, they'd even gotten a vigilante committee up against us with this new constable named Carroll and a lot of drummed-up other business. I'd paid restitution for this guy, for robbery and assault causing bodily harm by the Humber. I thought maybe it had been thrown out but my lawyer said we had to wait so all my money was still tied up in bail. But it felt good to be out on Queen Street, it felt like it would be over and done with soon since they'd found no true bill on Ryan and I was out and free and there was a row and Feeheley and Constable Carroll went at it in the mud and ice outside the court, tearing hair and gouging eyes and hammering each other bloody 'til Feeheley bit part of Carroll's nose off, there was a crowd of about a hundred. Me and my family went home and I decided once and for all to go up and see Eve the next day. It wasn't just infatuation. I really did feel we'd gotten to know one another. Her problem was Tony, off and on, and I accepted that, I also knew, though I didn't remark on it, that it had to do with her mood swings, what she called, My own issues. I called them problems. I certainly had problems. We both had problems and opening up about them would bring us closer. I went back to the hotel, the room where the view southwest over the roofs and cornices became the grandeur of Lucan, the terrible winter sun over Lucan, the railroad tracks curving into town over snow under nights of green stars. I wondered where my little son with May was, adopted somewhere, it made me sad because I wanted someone to live after me, but only by May. And because it didn't feel like there was a lot of time, our days were numbered. I was trying to quit drinking then, I steeled myself and resisted going down for a drink. I took my meds and went to bed early. I wanted to be in shape for Eve. She still hadn't returned my last call but I knew she'd be at home around seven. I began to sleep, recalling my studies in art and photography. New books had come out on the Donnellys and I'd pass by our old house, the corner house, and wonder about the old man who'd helped build it and his very eyes having seen the Donnellys and their killers and scanning the courses of bricks on our house fifteen years after the massacre in Lucan. And the thousands of bricklayers and labourers and maids who had built and served in all the old brick houses in Toronto knowing those times, times of great dresses and ribbons and suits with sabre lapels and double-breasted waistcoats and watch chains, the photographer's linoleum, the muddy Arcadian backdrops and the side roads and violence and blood and the wild bare bush, the ice and mud of March. And the portrait of Tom Donnelly and his brother Bob, vicious and sartorial, hands held in fists. Who had known the hands that had built the walls of our house, the wall that my friend Wendy had pointed up to, saying, There's a bad man. And my mother's family there after the war. Upstairs. Before I was born. I wakened, it was sunny, I hoped it would cloud over. I rested and read most of the day. I made a point of dressing well. I set off for Eve's around six. Recalling what my father had finally told me. What my grandmother had said to my mother, in a moment of spite or carelessness, that my grandfather was born out of wedlock, that he wasn't a Quinn like his brothers and sisters, like the brother who was a judge and who had had the house built in 1895. My mother had a sensitive pride in her father and even if he was only a salesman, it was important to her that he was a Quinn like his brothers who were lawyers. But her mother told her that my grandfather was brought into Quinns by his mother, my great-grandmother, May Merriweather Quinn of Lucan. That my grandfather's real father had been Tom Donnelly. I went up the long straight blocks of downtown, old North American fronts and facades the same everywhere as the morning fronts of the main street of Lucan, the mess of galleries and verandas, pitched roofs, the whole violent ramshackle outside the court when I was found not guilty a third time. They gave up and instead their vigilance committee and their so-called constable Carroll tore our farm apart and insulted our mother and father looking for anything they could charge us with. They said they were the law but it was about the land and about Ryan. My father had said to me, we were living in a high-rise by then, he said, You are the great-grandson of Tom Donnelly by your mother. To my mother it had been a blight. But to me and my father it wasn't. My father had liked the bricklayers who made my mother so nervous and he learned that old Frank Carlisle had been born in 1870, the son of Tom Donnelly by Sarah Coughlin who worked in the Queen's Hotel in Lucan. And Carlisle knew that he and my grandfather were half-brothers. My father joked that my uncle had hired Carlisle and then his son to keep them quiet. The house was up ahead, the house built by my mother's family, by Quinns in 1895. But of course the sun was getting bad now. It had been a grey evening long before when I'd asked about renting the second-floor apartment but I'd been mostly curious to see what it was like, my mother's family's apartment, there on the second floor. The place where Eve had answered the door and told me it was rented and she'd smiled. Where Eve lived now and I went up the stairs to knock. My heart in my throat. I had no idea if I'd survive it because their vigilance committee kept getting bigger and bigger and there were wagons full of them with shotguns and scantling going round the side roads. Even then, nobody would fight me, they knew nobody could. But now the thing was death. What had got me to drinking, I was addicted to drink by then, on and off it, even my mother and father telling me not to cause trouble. The knock sounded odd. I knocked again. The door was open. I pushed it. The place was bright and bare, there was no furniture, nothing. There had been a rental sign outside, I'd thought for another unit. There was nothing but dusty sash windows and bits and layers of wallpaper stripped through to the bare plaster and workmen's graffiti and signatures scrawled with 1895. I lay down on the floor, I thought I can sleep now. When I wakened it was night and I was at the Keefe wedding when Ryder's barn went up on fire, we saw it in the distance across the snow, burning across from our place and everybody knew what it meant. Me and my parents were in and out of court for arson and it didn't go nowhere. And then one night, they all come in to our house, forty of them, faces blackened, some in women's bonnets and clothes, they had clubs and axes, they'd handcuffed me but still I fought them. They killed my brother at another house and now they killed my mother and father and my cousin and set the house alight and I run out still in handcuffs in my stocking feet, I was bleeding all onto the snow and Jim Ryder stuck me in the midriff with a manure fork, I seen the blood firing out of my belly and I fell and they threw me in the house, everything on fire, and broke my skull with a spade but I was over Biddulph by then, high above the snow, I was in fields of stars, the towering needle of fire into the night sky where I'm still on my way to Merriweather's and I still dare you to laugh when I say I know the future, I live in it, I am my own great-grandson. And you tell me, Which am I? Me looking forward or my great-grandson looking back? I am either and both and you can never tell me no different. There is no way you can say I am insane or mad. I am sane and I will stand and fight any son of a bitch who says different.

Nicholas Ruddock

MARIO VARGAS LLOSA

There are cobras in Peru. They could be anywhere but usually they're in the long grass by the river or in dried-out arroyos. They sway to their own rhythm, to the rhythm of the wind, to the slow quotidian rotation of the earth. They hug the dampness of loam, the chalk-dry dust. They regurgitate the bones of mice and feral dogs. Born in deep holes in the ground, they are several centimetres long at birth and have hundreds of brothers and sisters fighting for space, writhing together in seething balls, clustered, seeking sustenance from their overwhelmed mother. Most inevitably die, but one or two survive and leave the nest and thereafter live on their own. They are quick and merciless and, we assume – by measuring the size of their brains – that they react instinctively. That's anthropomorphism, however; perhaps they calculate every move at a speed beyond our own abilities or reasoning.

Why do I tell you this? Because of Mario Vargas Llosa.

I was born in Lima, as he was, twenty years before me. So we share a birthplace, and, of course, that singular locale bestows a similarity to our early years. But ultimately it is the divergence in our lives that commands attention. Well, it commands my attention, not his. He became world-famous as a writer and I did not. He entered politics and rubbed shoulders with dictators, I did not. He won the Nobel Prize, I did not. Should I go on? He etcetera and I etcetera, our lives so different, more so as the years advanced. But we forged a bond once, on the night he struck Gabriel García Márquez in the face with his intemperate fist, and since then we have had a connection, of which he is unaware. No blame can be laid at his feet for what happened much later, in Toronto, Canada. A famous man can become, unwittingly, a mentor to violence.

I shall explain. At the age of seventeen, having led a normal youthful life, I was accepted to the Universidad Nacional Mayor de San Marcos, in Lima. There I met and became enchanted with a dark-haired girl named Estella. At that time, she accentuated her equally dark eyes with half-moons of mascara, and she was a fledgling member of the Communist Party. Her father, a banker, and her mother, a dressmaker, were not enthused with her politics or with me, her new boyfriend. They were distantly polite, that's all. But at my house, things were different. My parents were shocked and frightened and said directly to us, "What can you be thinking of, Eduardo? And you, Estella? By now the secret police will have your name and therefore Eduardo's by association, and it is our money, earned by what you would call *bourgeois labour*, saved over the years in the safe banks of capitalism, that have allowed you to waste your time in cafés, both of you, to skip classes, to foment class warfare." Estella and I stood together, holding hands, trying not to respond in an inflammatory way. "Eduardo," they continued, "you say you are in love with this girl, against whom we have nothing but whose parents must feel the way we do – betrayed. Look about you, both of you! You do this from the comfort of our large home in a neighbourhood of affluence from a bedroom with lace curtains and high ceilings, in which, by the way, you seem to have no concept of restraint."

When Estella was not present, my mother and father continued to harangue me, at our table, over roast pork or beef or fish from the sea, saying the two of us would inevitably be targeted and punished by the state, that Estella was bent on self-destruction, that she would take down those in her retinue with her. They had seen it often, proud and ancient families ruined. My mother also said that she had heard, through the grapevine of mothers and grandmothers, that Estella Sepulveda had many lovers before me, taking them indiscriminately. I should be wary of transmitted disease, she said. I shuddered at the thought but knew it was not true. In many ways, in her intimacies, Estella was shyer than I, more innocent.

Our parents took action against us. They joined forces at the end of the school year and, for the summer, she was banished to Paraguay and I to Mexico. Before we left, we met briefly at a café by the seawall to say goodbye. Pigeons ate disconsolate crumbs and gulls stalled overhead. Poets in chairs tilted forward, their hair slicked back, their chiselled faces, and anorexic were the women, bearded the men.

"We are to be exiled like Trotsky," she said.

"I'm the one going to Mexico, therefore I am Trotsky, not you."

She looked at me with those sad mascaraed eyes.

"Trotsky was killed in Mexico with an axe. By an assassin. He was targeted. The same could happen to us," she said.

I laughed. I was nothing to the world of intrigue. My life was not in danger and the facts of Trotsky's death, the details, were news to me.

"Estella! I will not be axed! For two months I shall work in my cousin's cinema. Then we shall be reunited."

"We are being torn from our roots."

"Estella, do you think this café is under surveillance? My parents say it is."

She looked about, her eyes moving from the street, to the waiters, then to me.

"Of course," she said.

Our life was thrilling then. Estella, the café, the sea, the birds, the secret police. But we were also children of our parents, and obedient, so our summer separation became a fact.

"We should not write," she said. "Our letters will be opened. I am unable to prevaricate or dissemble. It does not matter, our love is inviolable."

We leaned across the table and kissed in full view of the dozens of spies.

Moving on: In Mexico City I was given a room in the house of our cousins, on the second floor. My window overlooked extensive gardens. There was perfume in the early morning from dahlias and jacarandas and from flowers I could not name. A slow breeze shifted through the curtains, soft and pliant. I did not notice the notorious smog of the city until I was out in the street, mornings, walking to the bus stop. Then my throat would go dry as it never had in Lima, where fog smoothed the edges of rush hour, where the traffic lights blurred like watercolours, as though they were subaquatic, in yellow, green and red.

I thought of her, the way she looked up from her books, her manifestos and her pamphlets, and even more so the way she threw her clothes to the floor saying, "Now our bodies are in service to the state." "What do you mean by that?" I had asked her and she said, "Eduardo, this is how the proletariat is formed." Then she laughed, which in my heart made me wonder, as I touched her, if I should question her sincerity. For, in private, I admit, I questioned my own. Society had been under siege for so long yet nothing seemed to change.

Those mornings in Mexico, I alighted from the #52 bus between 8:58 and 9:02. I passed a kiosk, an apothecary, a bakery, and then I opened the door to the theatre, which was situated on a busy corner, using a large key, heavily toothed, cumbersome. It required some hand jiggling and subtlety before the tumblers gave way to the lobby, the morning hush.

"Show up, be groomed, take tickets, nothing could be simpler, Eduardo, my friend. Check the washrooms, there's a mop in the closet."

Those were my instructions. My uniform was of simple grey material with red piping and there was a hat, fez-like without a tail, which I was shown how to wear.

"Like this, Eduardo, see? This angle? Jaunty!"

I was given a bobby pin to use in case it slipped.

"Tear tickets in half like this, usher them in, use this gesture with your arm – like so! – welcoming!"

Two gold stanchions were joined by a scalloped rope, the rope as scarlet as the lipstick of the Hollywood actresses portrayed on the posters outside, who were pouting, smiling fetchingly or knowingly or both, and every one of our tickets had five digits stamped onto it in the same deep red. Also scarlet-red were the carpets and the heavy curtains and the wallpaper, though the wallpaper was decorated with gold filaments in an abstract pattern, meaningless.

"You are the eye on the street, Eduardo, and, as you can see, the neighbourhood is in decline, there is random violence, but in our cinema we are left alone, as a general rule. Crime outside rarely touches us. We portray magic, how the world should be, even for criminals. They are some of our best customers."

The outside world was a hectic twenty feet away. Inside, the reels unwound and the soundtrack rose and fell like waves of a distant sea, muffled, foreign. The voices of the actors – this I would have written to Estella had she allowed it – "were like syrup or castanets, smooth and desultory then staccato amidst laughter false and true," and there was shouting and the firing of guns and a crying or crying out, most often in English, a language I did not understand.

If you had told me that I would meet Mario Vargas Llosa there, that my life would be changed, I would have laughed. How ludicrous.

But one day my cousin said, "Eduardo, my friend, economic necessity dictates that our movies are fluff. You can see that. We pander that we may eat. However, for the upcoming Festival, I have arranged to show films only by the Swedish director, Bergman. Once a year we have this opportunity to show cinema as it can be, as art. But he can be depressing, Bergman, even as he strikes to the heart – some would say the breaking heart – of love."

"Yes, cousin."

For the Festival, the clientele changed. Men in dark suits arrived with young women in gowns, and smooth was the silk caressing the bodies of these ladies, tempting the whimsy of thin cotton. Estella, Estella, my thoughts were of her. The scarlet rope and the gold stanchions were pressed into service for the first time, for crowd control. Cigarette smoke filled the lobby, spilling from the throats and tongues and heads tossed back. Small cigars were ground down and bent into white sand, into pedestal ashtrays we had rented and polished for the occasion. Banks of flowers appeared too, erupting from vases of coloured glass. The background music changed into something more sombre, off-key and northern.

"May I have your tickets, please," I said again and again. "Thank you."

I fancied myself, for those few days and nights, as Hermes, conductor of souls to the underworld, as gatekeeper to an inner sanctum where truth, for once, stumped artifice.

These very words I wrote to her, in a letter, breaking our pact of silence. To which she replied fondly, ignoring the censors, "Eduardo, you are learning so much about inequality from these socialites. And the quality of your writing is ever so much better. I love you."

Then it happened. On the second night of the Festival, before a screening of *Cries and Whispers*, there he was, Mario Vargas Llosa, a latecomer. Unmistakably him, and alone. I took his ticket casually, as though this happened to me daily, evincing no surprise. But I did say – and here I quoted from Herman Hesse – "Price of admission your mind, Mario," and the writer laughed and stopped in his headlong rush. We compared our Peruvian accents, our neighbourhoods in Lima. Then a reedy note from within, the expiration of a solo accordion in E minor, and Mario Vargas Llosa said, "Excuse me, but Bergman…" He shook my hand and in he went and the lobby was empty.

The ticket seller from outside left her booth, smiling at the take. She was holding a thick sheaf of pesos.

"Eduardo," she said, "soon the bosses will be even more millionaires."

Together we stood looking into the street at the rising quarter-moon, the passing kaleidoscope of cars, buses, sirens and heat. Her shoulder touched mine then moved away. I thought again of Estella, wondering where she was, and with whom. I declined a cigarette.

Intermission came. The second film was to start in twenty minutes, *Shame*, from 1968. I saw Vargas Llosa in a knot of conversation by the outer door when "Mario!" came a shout. Everyone heard it, a greeting with such pleasure yet command, and all turned to see a shorter man, moustachioed, in a white linen suit, picking his way through the crowded lobby, his arms held open for an embrace.

But no welcome came from the Peruvian.

"You! You son of a bitch!" he said.

Then Vargas Llosa struck the still-smiling and totally un-suspecting newcomer with his right fist, delivered straight from the shoulder in the classic stretched-out boxer pose, and a cracking sound like eggs or bone jumped out of either the fist or the face and, quivering now with his own violence partially spent, Vargas Llosa watched his victim fall backwards to the floor.

"García Márquez!" he shouted that all could hear, "how could you do this, to me, to Patricia! Get up, you blowhard egotist!"

Then, laughing at some fiction or fact that only he could understand, he drew back his polished boot and kicked the already dazed man, whose flapping hands were splayed out in front in useless supplication, in the ribs. Once, twice, three times.

"*Hunghh-humph,*" gasped the Colombian writer, for it was certainly he, also unmistakable, also apparently alone.

Vargas Llosa looked at me.

"Strike like a cobra," he said, "This is how it is done."

I stepped up. I pushed my fellow Peruvian respectfully away and knelt to the wounded. From his nose came a slow snuffling-pulsing ooze of dark blood, viscous, falling to the floor, and here the floor was tiled in a picturesque mosaic a century old. The shed blood dripped down upon a jungle tableau of green and yellow snakes seething in concert, upon parrots squadroned across a muddy river, upon a jaguar's face black with jewelled eyes, supine upon a branch. Márquez's suit coat was now smeared with red tenacious mucous, as was the collar of his open shirt, his moustache, a small gathering pool of it at the base of his throat.

"No more, no more," said the guttural voice of García Márquez.

By then other theatre-goers had intervened. Vargas Llosa had been pulled or pushed away and it was over and done with. Lights in sconces flicked off and on, beckoning all to the inner theatre. The intermission was over. By then I had helped the beaten man to his feet. His left eyebrow was already swollen and abraded and he held a shaky shirt-cuff muffled to his nose.

"I'm okay, I'm okay."

Smiling then as though nothing had happened, a brave face stunned, concussed.

"Can you go back in?" I asked.

"Of course. I am here for the art of Bergman, not for this."

I held him, he was wobbling. My hand was fast to his elbow. By then the house lights were dropping and the word *Shame* leapt subtitled to the screen, and that simple word, so apt under the circumstances, resonated with all of us. People shifted to give García Márquez room, so he could sit on the aisle. Faces of concern looked and looked away and then looked again. Handkerchiefs passed his way in gestures of universal sorrow.

As for Vargas Llosa, he had disappeared, gone with his devils or his angels, gone with his intemperance, his cobra strike.

Afterwards, as I emptied the ashtrays and vacuumed the carpets and mopped up the drying blood from the tiles, what I remembered most of this extraordinary night was the power of the Peruvian writer's anger, the no-holds-barred attack, the spontaneity, the no-shame of it, the fierceness and the fire of his eye, the violence he loosed without restraint from what must have been the adrenaline-fused beating heart of madness, of revenge. For revenge is what it must have been, the only explanation.

The patience of the cobra, the knowledge of coiled strength, the passive waiting, his confidence that his time would come. The recognition of the moment.

The rest of the summer of our banishment passed quickly. Then we were back in Lima and Estella was waiting at the airport. We kissed and went straightaway to a meeting of the Marxist League. I moved from my parents' house and with our summer earnings we rented a small flat near the university. Now we were free of criticism and we lay together in joy and fascination every night in a bed with a cool breeze that felt its way over the rooftops from the sea. It wasn't long before she was pregnant because, Estella said, "the concept of birth control is foisted on the poor by the rich, strength is in numbers and the ruling class fear us, they wish to maintain their wealth undiluted." She wrote pamphlets on this theme and distributed them on the street. When our child was born, we were forced to leave the university, the cost of books now prohibitive. We took jobs to support our little family. She wrote articles for her magazines while I found work happily in a library, whistling under my breath as I stocked the shelves, looking quickly at new books, especially those for small children. I stopped my own writing endeavours as I could see that my style was old fashioned. Better I should stick, I thought, to the simple honesty of labour.

Then the government convulsed and changed direction and looked at her, at Estella, more carefully. They did not like what they saw. Men without uniform stopped her on street corners. They advised her to mend her ways. Our small and beaten-up car, upon which we depended, caught fire for no reason. We were denied proper insurance. By then we had three children but Estella could still not be silenced. To bend her knee, she said, was anathema. I thought of Vargas Llosa, what he would do, but my hands were tied. Any cobra strike of mine would soon be traced to us, to the children, and we all would suffer. I stayed my hand, I bowed my head.

"Eduardo, we have no choice but to leave."

Thus came the first sign of our eventual supplication, her desperation. It took months for our paperwork to be processed, considered, rejected, processed again, reconsidered, stamped, reviewed and finally approved. During this time I was discharged from my job at the library and bile rose in my throat, bile that could have been venomous but, out of fear, was instead pathetic, innocuous, harmless, a burning dagger in the chest only to me.

"Never mind," she said, "soon we will leave. Things will be better in Canada."

Canada had been the only country to accept us, but still we had to wait. During this time the children were expelled from their primary school and therefore spent time only with similarly carefree children of other radicals. All of us had been treated the same. I watched our children in the parks running through fountains shirtless, kicking balls into nets. Meanwhile Estella took in laundry and rode a bicycle up and down the humid streets, delivering newspapers. This allowed her to say goodbye to her friends without compromising them, but her so-called friends were slipping away.

"Eduardo, no longer do they invite me into their apartments. They look past me, up and down the hallways, they look everywhere but at me."

"Times have changed, Estella."

"It is sad. They say goodbye but they say it so awkwardly. They're not sorry to see me go."

Then she rode her bicycle down familiar hills for the last time, over rain-slicked cobbles less treacherous, she said, than the words and sentences and paragraphs she had written in her manifestos, in her political papers that had brought our coming exile to pass.

Everything we could take with us fit into three suitcases. Unseen by the neighbourhood, we waited for our cab in the shadowy vestibule of the apartment building. Dust motes in yellow sun canyoned down from the transom, and the children cried.

At the airport we saw mirrored sunglasses on the faces, implacable, of the security police. Their reflections multiplied in the polished glass of vast windows. We spoke not a word and walked out onto a tarmac vaporous with jet fuel. A drizzle from low clouds mocked us, but the children were happier now, hand-in-hand, skipping, singing in rhymes. It was a lark for them at last.

"Airplane, airplane!" they said.

In Toronto, snow bristled in the air. We had no resources and the little money we'd saved vanished into two months' rent for a small upstairs flat on Markham Street, south of College.

After two months of numbed paralysis and worry, Estella was hired by an employment agency.

"Eduardo, so it has come to this."

"Yes."

"This is democracy? Eduardo? Nothing is different here. They keep us down with words, with platitudes, with poverty, not with car fires and guns and helicopters."

The employment agency dressed her in blue-grey overalls, wrote her first name only, *Estella*, in yellow script above her left breast, gave her a plastic bucket and a mop, and she left home as dusk descended upon the unfamiliar northern streets. Down went the sun, slanting from a more acute angle, and earlier in the day. Dark shadows jutted over curbs. Rarely did Estella raise political questions or pronounce on the obvious inequalities we could see at every hand. It was as though she were now half-beaten. On Dundas Street, the children and I watched her climb aboard the streetcar, adjust her mop, shift the empty bucket at her feet. One of a crew of twenty in a skyscraper of metal and glass, she started every night at the fifty-sixth floor and descended, one paper-strewn floor after the next. It could be peaceful there in the hum of the fluorescent lights and, for the most part, she was left to her own devices. And she was proud, she told me – as she had been in Lima with the news-papers and the bicycle and the laundry – to experience first-hand the life of a working woman, after being raised in such comfort. She worked hard. She was praised by her supervisor for her fastidiousness, for never scuffing or chipping the legs of expensive furniture.

Then I was hired by the same company, but on a different shift. One of us was always at home with the children, walking them to school, watching them play on swings in the park, even in the ice and snow.

But I did not thrive as well as she did in the heart of capitalism. I found myself indifferent, even resentful as I scrubbed the porcelain bowls of toilets with cleanser and a bent-wire brush. Here the water in toilets was a false blue colour, from a cylinder in the tank, as though even our most natural functions needed a mask, a disguise. As Estella had done, I hoovered conference rooms and Lemon-Pledged mahogany until I could see a blurred version of my face reflecting back. I looked tired and older and my supervisor upbraided me, "Faster, faster, Mr. Ariza, or whatever your name is, faster!" and he pushed me, slightly, between the shoulder blades, towards the public washrooms on the thirty-second floor. Just a push but I felt the bile rise in me again and in my helplessness I turned and pushed him back, not in the fashion of Mario Vargas Llosa, but saying to my supervisor in an injured voice, "Don't touch me like that!" as delicately as a child in a schoolyard. Tears filled my eyes. Then I turned away from the confrontation and stood alone for five minutes, ashamed, outside the empty washroom until my heart stopped beating its fandango.

I was terminated the next day and so was Estella.

"Guilt by association, Eduardo. We need to learn better how to channel our personal discontent," she said.

I admitted to her how embarrassed I was by my passivity, how different my action had been from the crack of fist on face, in Mexico City, ten years before.

"I should have punched him hard. Better to be hanged as a wolf than a sheep."

"No, Eduardo. Here, if you do that, you will be arrested. Remember, we have children. And look, to be practical, we need milk from the store."

I tucked my shirt into my pants, picked up my wallet from the kitchen table and took to the stairway. On Markham Street I saw pigeons head-bobbing, beaking up whatever they could by the curb. Invisible scraps, pebbles. They appeared to have no responsibilities, certainly no children. At the store on Dundas, I didn't have enough change.

"Twenty-five cents short, what do you know, I'll be right back," I said, embarrassed.

The clerks rolled their eyes.

At home, she counted out what was left in her purse, turned out her pockets and I returned to the store, to the eye-rollers. Later that night for the first time, my little Marxist cried. She no longer wore mascara. She held her fingernails knuckled into her hand. I stood and put my arms around her and held her head to my chest. I leaned down and kissed her hair. She was worn out by her labour.

"Those bastards," she said.

Now we were even recycling tea bags, squeezing them in our fists, marinating them in water to make them last, until there was no colour, no discernable taste.

"Oh, Eduardo," she said, "school books, crayons, binders, boots, coats, mittens. I'm going to talk to Juan Antonio up the street. Maybe he has something."

And Juan Antonio said, "Yes, actually, Estella, if you don't mind driving and you don't mind evening work and you don't complain about social injustice, I do have a job for you."

"I will do what I must to make ends meet."

"Good. Then you take my car, you deliver pizza, you get five dollars a delivery."

"Five dollars?"

"In this relationship of ours, Estella, I am the capitalist and you are the underclass because I am the one with the means of production. The car. Which is capital. Every pizza you deliver, we split the take which is ten dollars. Oh, you have to pay for gas. Even your friend Lenin would have to pay for gas. There's a Shell station around the corner."

She reached out her hand and caught the keys to the Kia, which Juan Antonio threw in an easy loop across the kitchen table. He was fond of her despite his jibes.

At this juncture, depressed, I stayed home full-time with the children. My English was so much better than hers, and they needed help with their homework. I put on a jolly front to fool them. They were as happy as clams. I remember their teacher saying to me, "They are as happy as clams, Mr. Ariza."

Her borrowed car was a small blue Kia with a plug-in sign glowing on the roof. But, as it turned out, delivering pizza was a tough job, even tougher than cleaning office buildings. There was no down-time at all. After she left the tiny bakery, its windows misted up with yellow light, heat from the ovens pumping in waves out the door onto Clinton Street, after she slid the pizzas into their insulated boxes, she didn't have time to amble along. Far from it, she had to race against the clock. Twenty minutes or the pizza was free. What? This was a shock to her, this unfortunate fact that Juan Antonio had forgotten to mention despite his enthusiasm for the market economy which he had said "provides us with a ladder up, Estella," and the cost of the pizza, should she fail to deliver it on time, was, to her, twelve dollars from her pocket. Plus the wasted gas. Thus, inevitably, did the humble worker pay. There was a clock which glowed green on the dashboard of the Kia. She told me how she knuckled down on the steering wheel, stick-shifted her way through the narrow streets of downtown, accelerated through green lights and amber lights, revved impatiently at reds, double-parked, flipped on hazards, jumped out with still-warm boxes against her hand, raced up and down sidewalks checking out the numbers of the houses which were hard to read. Porches were hooded and poorly lit. Meanwhile the minute hand on the dashboard moved into warp speed, malignant.

So far so good, she was gaining experience. But on her tenth night a headache slowed her down, aching from all the neck turns, the clutching, the brakes, the quick decisions. Streetcar tracks tossed her left and right. Someone thumped the passenger door with his fist and shouted at her. She drove on. Pepperoni and double cheese, this one. Construction on Bloor Street, a detour and then, believe it or not, at ten o'clock at night there was a marching band blocking the roadway. No way through the tubas, the snare drums, the top hats, the sparkling batons that the skinny white girls in skirts and stockings were twirling high into the night air.

Oh Jesus.

She reversed the Kia, almost stalled, the car trembled and shook and jumped but she cut her way back through a fearsome alley and turned right. Wrong way down a one-way street. A ticket would finish her. But the clock still said, okay, okay, three minutes to the good. Couldn't see the house numbers though. She pulled into an open spot, got out and started to run until there it was, number 37. Up the steps she hurdled but the porch was full of cast-off boxes, cardboard, orange crates, two tricycles askew, a garbage can, piles of newspapers. A metal pipe or something caught her ankle. A jab of pain. She leaned for a second on a discarded barbecue tipped up against the front window. Heavy curtains with no lights on. She knocked on the door, the knocker a death's head, an iron skull with eye sockets shadowed, heavily ridged. Then she waited, she listened, she shouted "Pizza! Pizza!" but her soft Spanish voice died at her feet. Okay! She hammered *one-two-three-four* again with the knocker, put her ear to the door, bent down and flipped up the mail slot and peeked inside and saw a leg in blue jeans slide out of the way. "Pizza!" she shouted through the slot. Then the door was yanked open and a hand grabbed the front of her coat and pulled her up and inside.

A large bearded man, a dim vestibule.

"You're late with the pie, buddy. Oh, wait, hey a girl! Well, this is something new. Something better."

He let go of her coat but his hand moved down and touched her breast and stayed there. He pushed her against the closed door. With his other hand, he took the pizza box.

"Free, this pizza," he said, "and free the feel too."

A black T-shirt over muscles and belly and tattoos running wicked to both wrists. His hand where it was.

"You made me wait at the door."

"You gotta knock, that's what the knocker's for. Now get the fuck out."

"The money, please," said Estella.

Three more men came out in a phalanx from what might have been a kitchen. It was too dark to know.

"I was here on time, I knocked."

"You know what *fuck you* means? You stay, you'll find out."

He opened the door and pushed her back onto the porch. "I'm doing you a favour. Thanks for the pie."

He slammed the door, the death's head jumped. She looked at the mess on the porch for five seconds, walked back to the flickering roof light of the Kia and drove away.

At 3 a.m. she told me how the bearded men had cheated her, how she'd been there on time even though the parade had slowed her down, how the first man waited to open the door then dragged her into the house, how he'd touched her on the breast, rotated his hand slowly, left his hand there, rubbing her, pushing her against the wall, how they threatened – what did they say? – to "fuck me." Maybe she misunderstood, maybe that "fuck" word didn't always mean sex?

I said she hadn't misunderstood, it was a direct threat of sexual violence and a death threat too. Because what would they do with her, after?

"Oh, Eduardo," she said, "it's more the money, the money we lost, after all that work."

I lay helplessly beside her. Over and over I imagined the assault. Then I asked her for the address of this house of cowards.

"No, I will not give you the address. They are too dangerous."

"We are Peruvians, we cannot accept this, " I said.

"We need to be smart Peruvians. Revenge cannot be a reflex."

I reminded her of what had happened years ago, how I had seen Vargas Llosa deliver a blow of revenge apparently in defence of a woman. "Patricia," I had heard Vargas Llosa say.

"Eduardo, you are not a violent man."

"The address, that's all I want."

"I tell you what we shall do," she said. "In the morning we will fill a wine bottle with gasoline. Then we will wait. If ever I am called again to deliver to that house, I promise, I will call you, Eduardo, and then you can be your Mario Vargas Llosa, just once, for us. If I am not called, then we will accept this as a learning experience, which we will not forget. We will not forever eat cake, I promise you."

No, she would not quit her job. Every other customer on every other night had been polite to her, and the tips more than covered the gas. She hadn't expected that. Once she was given a twenty-dollar bill, extra, on top of the usual.

So we settled into a routine. Friday and Saturday nights she drove Juan Antonio's Kia and in came thirty or forty or even fifty dollars. I found a job myself, a bit like the library back in Lima, stacking shelves, but now it was with cans and packages of rice and sugar and condiments at the grocery store just three blocks away. The children began to speak English with ease. Snow fell every day now, then it was Christmas, then New Year's.

In January, at midnight, the phone rang and it was Estella from work, saying "Eduardo? It's time. I'm supposed to go there again, to the house of the bearded men."

I checked the children. Sound sleepers, deep in their own worlds, far from ours.

From under the front porch, I extricated the gasoline-filled bottle of Rioja we had sequestered out of sight and I ran the five minutes to Clinton Street.

Already she had the pizza prepared.

"Stay here," I said, "I will do this run."

"No, we are in this together. Here, the address, look."

"Two cobras then? Let me drive."

Ten blocks away, we pulled up in front of the house. There was a parking spot wide open, an omen of good fortune.

"Here it is, one free pizza," she said.

I was calm, I was under control. I knocked at the door and the death's head rattled up and down for me as it had for her, and one of the bearded men came to the door quickly, smiling, pointing to his watch.

"Late, damn your eyes."

I shrugged.

"I know," I said. "What you get tonight is free, with our pleasure. I am sorry it has come to this."

I handed over the box and the door closed and from within came raucous merriment, male laughter receding decrescendo as they moved deeper into their lair.

It was far too dark on the porch for anyone on the street to see anything. Estella's face a pale moon. I took the wine bottle from my jacket, unscrewed the top and opened the hatch of the ramshackle barbecue which had been left up against the front window. Nasally, the sharp vapour of the gasoline.

"You will enjoy this vintage, it's Shell Regular, it goes well with pizza and cheese," I said.

I emptied it *truckle-truckle* into the black heart and belly of the beast. Streams of thin fluid ran invisibly, gurgling, overflowing from the barbecue, running down onto boxes and newspapers clumped below. Seeping to the semi-rotten floorboards that were sagging, creaking under my feet.

"Next, my friends, the cobra strike!"

I cupped my hands, lit a cigarette, dropped it into the grill and walked briskly to the neighbours, first on one side, then the other. I hammered hard on their doors, a warning, but I didn't wait for them to answer. Then I walked back to the Kia and already there was a quiet but distinct crackling, an orange-red glow starting up from the recess of the porch.

She was turned in the passenger seat, away from me, watching, saying nothing.

We drove around the block. We made it to the top of the one-way street in less than a minute, and there we waited, blocking the roadway. I checked my watch, 11:00. But the alarm was slow, 11:10 when the first siren came from the distance and by then we were out of the car, standing like lovers between two darkened houses. The fire truck couldn't get past the Kia. The men jumped out, they leaned on the klaxon, pounded on the car. I ran to them, covering my face with my hands, waving as if to say, "Sorry, sorry."

I pulled the car up onto the sidewalk and they blared past me, one truck, two. Then I parked the car and Estella was there and we ran down the street and by then there other people running, calling to their friends.

Already the burning house had turned into a bonfire gone halfway to hell. The firemen were everywhere, they'd jumped off their trucks but the flames were bottom to top, porch to roof, licking from the upper windows. Neighbours on both sides had their garden hoses on full blast, as best they could, soaking down their trees and bushes, the side walls of their houses. Then it got so hot they had to give up, they ran across the street, joining us.

"Christ, look at that," one of them said.

We were all devils then, our faces lit by dancing flames.

Whoosh, the front window blew out. Glass shrapnelled into the yard, a wind-sucking roar. Tinder-dry for a hundred years, now this, an *infierno*.

"Back door's nailed shut," said one of the crowd, "padlocked, iron grilles on the windows, the place is a fortress."

So upstairs was the only place the men could go. Pitch-black the smoke, crackling the flames. Coughing, wheezing, overweight and out-of-shape, in full-out panic mode they were scrambling to the third floor.

Then there they were, for all of us to see. Climbing one by one out of the high casement window where there wasn't much room, a ledge. They looked down, confused, then they scrambled half-over each other up to the pitch of the roof. By then the ladders were getting into position, stretching out, telescoping, but it was too late. The scorching heat, the toxic smear of gases. Desperate, all they could do was jump, so they did. One by one, three of them off the roof into the flickering orange and black, into the confusion, and it was a long way down. They pinwheeled their arms then hit the ground *thump* like sacks of grain. Or beanbags. The firemen were on them in a trice with oxygen, pulling them across the road into the relative cool but there was nothing they could do. Covered them with tarps then turned back. There was the fourth guy, crazy by now for sure, hanging from his fingers from the eaves then dropping, turning, *whump*, right down onto the wrought-iron fence that ran between the houses, spiked, skewered on it, his chest and abdomen heaving, impaled there like a medieval warning.

"*Madre de Dios*," said Estella.

Coils of his intestines fell to the ground, glistening, and whatever breath he had was going *chuff-chuff, chuff-chuff*, inaudible over the racket of the hoses. Another tarp was placed over him, out of kindness, until the fire was more or less under control. Then the ambulance men were there and with power tools they cut the whole section of fencing down, the biker-beast with it "like shish kebab," as one of the guys beside us said, smiling.

By now the street and the sidewalks were awash, slip-sliding with newly formed ice and slush. Water spilled from slackened hoses. Smoke drifted, a haze in the chill of the night. Charred remnants of the house lay jagged, a shell, smoldering. Now just two placid fire hoses arced into the grey frying-pan-sizzle of what was left.

Arm in arm, we watched as the firemen cleaned up, tilted back their hats, gathered by their trucks, The neighbours' houses had survived, they even had lights on inside.

I was trembling, seeing what we had done.

"This is how Vargas Llosa was, afterwards. I remember, shaking. Look, my hands."

"It's a hormonal reaction, Eduardo, it's adrenaline, it's natural. Those men should never have stolen our money, or touched my breast."

"I don't feel good about this. Not entirely."

"Snakes have no feelings."

"No."

"Let that be your guide. Their blood is cold."

She stood on her toes and was just able to kiss me on the side of my neck.

"You are not cut out for this, maybe. Let me tell you one more thing," she said.

A fireman asked us to step back as he rolled and coiled a hose just in front of our feet.

"Thank you," he said, sweating under his hat, his heavy coat.

"Eduardo, I spelled out the English words FUCK YOU TOO on the pizza. Out of pepperoni. So they'd know it was me. I wanted them to know. What would be the point, otherwise? I even checked a dictionary for the spelling. FUCK YOU TOO, I wrote, in pepperoni, FUCK YOU TOO, the perfect slogan for predatory capitalism, the kind those monsters practised. It could even be their motto."

I imagined the bikers reading the message spelled out on the cheese, upon the succulent mozzarella, how they would have said to each other, "What the fuck is this? What's this?" before the distant crackling of flames came to them, the slim tentacles of smoke undercutting the kitchen door, then their saying, "Oh Jesus, the delivery girl!" before they ran up the stairs, dropping the cardboard box to the floor just as Gabriel García Márquez had dropped, poleaxed, to the tiles of the cinema, in Mexico City.

"This is the only violent political action I have ever undertaken," she said.

"Estella, I love you. I have always loved you."

"We have done ourselves proud, we have exceeded our wildest imaginings."

Before us lay a wasteland.

"We should get back to the children," I said.

There was not enough heat from the embers for any warmth now. The two hoses played on, quietly shimmering. Grey ash had settled on top of the slush, a strange thick consistency under our feet.

"Rub your boots off like this, on the side of the curb," I said.

College Street was empty except for a taxi or two. No streetcars at this hour, the tracks of steel reflecting the cold. On Markham Street, a thin cat jumped through powdery snow and disappeared behind a garbage can. I pushed open the small gate to our front yard. With my foot I adjusted the wooden lattice under the porch, where I had taken out the gasoline.

All the houses on Markham Street are joined together in a row. No lights were on in any of them.

I turned and latched the gate and found the house key in my pocket.

"Eduardo, in the morning, I almost forgot, there's a sale on light bulbs and sundries at the big capitalist emporium."

"Honest Ed's, you mean?"

"Yes. It would be smart to be there early, before they open the doors to the masses."

We stayed up for a cup of tea, we reached across the table to hold hands. Then we went to bed. She folded the length of her body against me as she fell asleep. Of course it was still the deep darkness of winter and the sun would not rise for hours.

Here in Canada, I am told, there are animals called wolverines. They walk silently over the crust of snow, their fur is pitch-black yet they cannot be seen on the retina of the human eye. They have no pity on what they find. Pound for pound, they are the quickest and most ferocious killers in the world.

Bart Campbell

SLIM AND THE HANGMAN

When he sees the little girl in denim overalls lurching gun-slinger style up the weedy east side lane, the teenage boy puts down the shammy cloth he is drying Terminal Town's perpetual morning moisture from his Tin Lizzy's carburetor with, and watches her coming.

Enormous grey eyes and a small freckled nose beneath the brim of her red straw cowboy hat stare back at him. She is swinging a conker back and forth in front of herself, one of those horse chestnuts with a couple feet of string pulled through two holes bored in its skin that every Canadian child once played with before television was invented. As usual her well-groomed collie is at her side, and you can tell by the way he's grinning at her that dog and girl are inseparable soulmates.

The teenage boy has seen them before, always watching him when he is mechanicing his truck. Once he hailed, "Hey!" and she threw a stone at him. Hit him in the mouth and chipped a tooth because he was too surprised to duck.

But this time he's ready for her. He reaches into his hip pocket and pulls out his own conker.

The little girl smiles wickedly and pulls the rim of her red cowboy hat down lower over her bright eyes and begins swinging her conker one-handed, just to show off.

Her dog barks "Go!" and they square off several paces apart. Swinging their conkers back and forth, they begin shuffling slowly towards each other, their chestnuts whispering threats as they swing past each other, back and forth, across the diminishing space between them. Until at last the conkers collide, and the young man's chestnut cracks off its string and bounces into the weeds beyond.

—Wow! No one's never beat me in one draw before!

The little girl beams. Her dog barks and wags all of himself from pride for her.

—Would you believe me, Mister, if I told you my conker has been in one-hundred-and-three-eighty duels and never lost yet! My daddy makes better conkers than anyone.

—No way! What can I trade you for a champion conker like that?

Her big grey eyes flash. She polishes her conker against her overalls and holds it up close for him to inspect. —It's a beaut, Mister. And you can have my champion conker for keeps if you'll drive getaway for me and Rags when we bust Daddy out of Oakalla.

—Um, huh? You mean like a prison break?

—Cork it! Here comes da screw.

Somehow the teenage boy is not at all surprised to see a uniformed prison guard approaching them. Everything about this little girl is more melodramatic than the cowboy movie serials.

—I was thinking I'd need to knock and make sure I had the right address, the guard tells them, But bejaysus but yer da's a very crafty man, lassie.

The girl already knows that, and tells the man so. Her wonder dog sniffs him once and then ignores him.

—Yer da's asked me to deliver yer birthday present, lass. Duz yaz think yers boyen here can lend a hand?

—O-my-gosh! O-my-gosh! O-my-gosh! The girl and her dog both spin like tail-waving squirrels when they see the doghouse in the back of the guard's truck.

It is an exact 1-to-8-scale replica of their real house, and as it is carried around to the backyard to where the girl wants it, the guard tells how amazed he is by its resemblance to the house before him because he knows her daddy built it completely from memory, without even seeing a photograph of the original.

Mommy laughs when she comes out onto the back steps, drying her hands on her apron. She is a short, sturdy woman with dark woolly hair —I'm sure there's a heck of a story about how the nut managed this one. Would you pleasure us by sharing a cup of tea and telling us how our Arthur's doing, Mister…?

—Logan, Missus Evans. Jake Logan is my name. But your husband calls me Dog Face. And I would love a hot cuppa wit yuz and tattle tales about our Slim. Yer mister's quite the character, ain't he?

—You don't know the half of it, Mister Logan. Not the half of it.

⁓⁄ᵢ\⁓

Just before Warden Owens slams the thick iron plate down on top of the dark hole they've shoved you in he informs you that you will be serving all your incarceration in solitary confinement because he is aware of your bad reputation for previously organizing prisoner strikes and riots. Looking up at that bastard in his natty green suit you feel like a crab in the bottom of a bucket watching a fisherman licking his lips.

SLAM! falls down the thick iron plate. There is no light but what drips through those three dime-sized air holes of your thick lid. Your dark, dank hole is just tall enough for you to stand up in. Four steps long. Not even wide enough for you to turn around without brushing shoulders against the cold stone walls. No light, no sounds, no smells except your own stink. No door, no window, no views but inner ones. Nothing but darkness so profound that every feeling you ever held back drips from every pore, clammy emotions leaking, leaving you defenceless and alone with yourself, your worst enemy.

Always a practical man, Slim, you immediately begin from where you are, and start pacing up and down your dark hole in quick figure eights. Three steps, left about-face spin. Three steps, right about-face spin. Repeat until you can do it with your eyes closed. Repeat until you shall cross this wide, salty desert of time and loneliness. Three steps, left about-face spin. Three steps, right about-face spin. You march yourself stupid, march the miles back and forth across your dark hole. Three steps, left about-face spin. Three steps, right about-face spin. Until you are panting, sweating from your hair roots, running for your life and worrying about how your wife and kid are going to survive without your pay packets. Three steps, left about-face spin, you march forth seeking the oblivion of total exhaustion, three steps, right about-face spin.

The hardest part is feeling cold in the dark all the time because the pricks even make you give your blanket back every morning before passing down the breakfast gruel, lest you be warm.

To save yourself from going completely nuts from loneliness and despair you begin building a toy sailing schooner for your girl's seventh birthday present from several cigar boxes that Dog Face gave you as payment for a trick-bottom milk crate you made for him. You whittle and shave and join by feel in the darkness, make rudder and masts and tongue-in-groove decks with one tin spoon your only tool. You make portholes from the eyelets of your lace-less boots. You finger-twirl wool threads pulled from your diminishing blanket into rope, block, and tackle. You make sails from the tails of your prison shirt.

And you find that separate peace you were hoping for from your work until the iron lid of your dank hole swings open and Warden Owens himself is standing above you, or at least you think it's him, because he's hard to make out in the bright light after your blinking eyes have lived in darkness for so long. Looking up at that bastard you feel like a bug from under an overturned rock watching a kid going to squash you beneath his big boot.

And you sure don't like the squeaky way he tells of his "little bit of carpentry work," and you make Owens say it thrice, you are so daft from living immersed in your dark hole for so long that you can't believe you are hearing his indecent proposal right.

Building an extra-large coffin, you have no problem with. You've made enough done boxes in your carpentry career to fill a graveyard, knowing as many poor people as you do, and you never declined a request or charged for one yet. But you've never built a gallows before, double drop doors and all, and you're not sure if you want to, let alone do it for free. Building a man-killing machine has got to be bad for your soul, and probably if you wasn't going nuts from darkness and loneliness and clammy cold misery you'd never consider taking on such ugly work.

But poor bargain though this probably is, you are smart enough to make Warden Owens write it up like a tendered work order contract and sign it before you agree to begin. In exchange for being moved to an aboveground cell with an out-side looking window, and the lumber and the time for making your own special woodworking project you have in mind for your daughter's seventh birthday gift, and its timely delivery to her, you will build Oakalla Prison's new gallows, and one extra-large coffin, made to measure. (What hard things won't some parents do, trying to trick their kids into believing they are hav-ing a happy childhood?)

Dog Face and Crackers have to get down on their knees and hoist you from your hole when you don't have the vertical strength to climb out on your own. How long has it been since you raised your arms over your head you wonder? When that simple action hurts like hell when you try.

With blinking mole eyes you deduce you must be the war-den's last minute desperate choice for this dirty job because you find the hangman waiting for you in the hallway outside the iron gates of Solitary Row.

—Good sir! he says, You must be the master carpenter whom is lending his skills for our important work for human justice. I am William Hitchens, High Hangman, at your serv-ice, sir.

He's a tall, portly old bugger, with stringy ginger hair and a flat, ruddy face. He's dressed for work, you notice, in well-worn overalls, his flannel shirtsleeves rolled up to his elbows, an anchor-and-rope tattoo on his forearm.

You shake his hand.

—Arthur Evans. But most people call me Slim.

—Well, shall we go and meet our client, Slim? Lead on, Warden Owens, if you please.

You don't know how many brick hallways (left and right), and concrete staircases (up and down), your gruesome crew traverses before you finally arrive at the Death House, but all those electric lights shining on white-washed brick walls have you dizzy enough that Dog Face must steer you by your elbow.

Your dizzy mind spins quicker when you find you know the Death Row prisoner. Valentine Pointe is a great big Sto-Lo Nation Indian you've worked with on a bunch of building jobs around town. Val is that big and scary size of Indian like they breed them up the Northwest Coast, six-foot-six and wide as a door, handsome and strong as a killer whale.

—Val-Man! What the fook happened to you?

—I killed a cop, Slim. And now they're going to hang me.

Now you really regret taking on this shitty job and you have to sit down on Val's bunk, you feel so dizzy from that cold fact and all the white lights.

But woozy as you're feeling, you appreciate how the hangman visits with Val first, and politely passes the time of day, even if he is obviously looking him over with an experienced tradesman's all-seeing eye, his black leather satchel already open on his lap with some of the tools and equipment of his gruesome craft.

Eventually Hitchens asks Val to stand, and he measures him with a tailor's tape and enters all Val's vital statistics into a thick black leather-bound ledger with his sharp pencil. When Hitchens weighs the condemned man on the scale in the hallway, Val says this is the first time he's been outside of his cell in two months.

—Don't they ever let you out into the exercise yard, Val? you ask, incredulous, and give the warden the stink eye.

—No, they never let me out, Slim. All I do is sit in my cell and worry about what's going to happen to Shayna and the kids without me.

—Two hundred and forty-one pounds! Hitchens announces with a low whistle and writes Val's weight into his ledger.

Hitchens takes his ugly business business-like, you appreciate. He'll get his job done the right way and probably won't be too bad a boss to work for, you can tell.

Hitchens thoroughly examines the contours of Val's neck and feels down all the muscle cords. Measures its circumference.

—Twenty-two inches! He whistles. You'll be my biggest yet.

He makes copious notes and some drawings of Val's neck.

—Experience has shown me no two necks are the same.

He asks Val to stick out his tongue and gently employs a physician's balsa wood tongue depressor to examine it thoroughly. Hitchens peers down Val's throat and asks him to say "ninety-nine" three times.

"Au revoir," Hitchens bids Val with a respectful bow after he's repacked his satchel. Then he hands Val a page of religious tracts.

Val lets the page drop to the floor without a glance and gives you a most woeful look. —Build her good and strong for me, Slim. Same as you know I would for you.

—I will, Val, and you shake his hand on it, You know I will, pal.

Outside the Death House the hangman and you walk side by each down a short gravel pathway with Owens leading and Dog Face and Crackers coming behind, and you consider kicking the warden hard up his skinny ass. Why the hell not let yourself feel some joy? When it's been so long! When all Owens can do to you is throw you back in that dark hole you just crawled out of. At very worst, another session with his punishment paddle. At least it will get you off this shitty job you are deeply regretting taking on.

—I hope you don't take me wrong, Slim. From me last bit of showiness back there, Hitchens is telling you, I'm not really a believer. Giving the condemned man those biblical quotes back there was just for showmanship and style's sake. "An eye for an eye; a tooth for a tooth," and, "Who so sheddeth man's blood, by man shall his blood be shed; for in the image of God made He man." Because really I don't believe a word of that clappity-clap, Slim. When you're dead, you're done, as far as I've seen, and I've seen lots of dead men.

—How much time do you estimate you shall require to complete the work, High Hangman? the warden asks, as this unholy work party passes through some wide iron gates beneath a big sign: GALLOWS HALL.

Inside is a big, high, open space, large enough to play floor hockey in. The row of barred windows near the roof are at least thirty feet up the concrete block walls. You walk directly over to the thickest puddle of sunshine in the room and breathe deeply like a shipwrecked sailor just clawed up the beach from the dark, desperate sea.

—Two weeks, I expect, Warden.

—I shall inform the prisoner, High Hangman.

Owens leaves, and Hitchens says to you: —But really two old master craftsmen like ourselves could have her done in three days. I only told him so long because I am receiving a per diem and the longer this job lasts, the more profitable for me. But also because there is nothing quite as spiritually bracing as knowing you have exactly one fortnight to live, for to focus a man's soul. Truthfully I envy our Mister Valentine Pointe, his fourteen day interlude!

You shudder involuntarily from hearing such cruelty. When you go, you hope to go fast. Sudden! Struck down by a fast car, or something that way.

—Now let us set up our kitchen space first thing, shall we, Slim? Tea first! That's my motto. Er, but maybe you should just sit down and let me take care of everything, Slim. Because you don't look very well.

—⁓⁓⁓—

It feels good to be sitting on a pile of good lumber again, and this gabby Hitchens certainly knows how to run a job site, you decide, with your belly full of the rashers and eggs the hangman just fried you both on his nifty kerosene camp stove.

You look over the blueprints for the gallows Hitchens gave you. The essential parts of the simple scaffold are fewer than you expected, only a couple extra cross beams to support the gravity drop doors.

Hitchens mumbles happily to himself as he studies his notes and works out the correct "drop" with the algebra of his trade.

—Two feet seven inches! he states irrevocably, Because I've had to makes some adjustments so our weighty Val's drop isn't so long that his head might gets pulled off and frighten those sensitive bishops that attends my every execution in Terminal Town. Better to err on caution's side that way I always say, and anyways if my client does not take the drop effectively, I'll just climbs down into the pit and gives his legs a sharp tug and it amounts to the same thing.

Hitchens sits down beside you on the lumber pile and lays his ledger on your lap and points at his calculations on the open page.

$$\underline{\hspace{2cm}}\ 412\ \underline{\hspace{1.5cm}}\ =\ \text{length of drop in feet}$$
(weight in stones)

—His weight in stones because our equation has developed from the collective experience of nine hundred years of continuous English practice. No country's hanged more than our Merrie Olde England, and why all the best hangmen are English born and trained, like me.

Hitchens is certainly a chatty man you've noticed already. Probably because he's so lonely, you guess. Who would want to be friends with the hangman?

—Our Mister Pointe weighs 17 stone 3 pounds and I've had to makes some adjustments because of his remarkable neck girth and his extra-long spinal column, so I'll gives him a drop two inches longer than our equation makes her, but that still means at least four feet of Val will be twirling above the deck so our hood shall not be optional. That angry look some of them throws you when it's not instantaneous is hard for me to bear. Because I am not ashamed to admits it, Slim, that the older I gets, the more sensitive.

Hitchens takes his ledger back and stows it neatly in his black satchel.

—If you want, I can brings some of my best press clippings to show you tomorrow. The missus scours all the local and national newspapers for weeks after me hangings because I intends to one day write and publish a treatise upon my craft. The missus is hoping my little pamphlet's sales will supplement our pitiable retirement savings. If only.

You set to work picking the straightest boards from the pile for the corner posts. You appreciate the sweet smell of the cedar and rub your hands along the furry lumber and know that if there is such a thing as reincarnation you want to come back as a cedar tree.

—Because it's a crying shame how the office of hangman don't receive its rightful due in our Dominion of Canada! Is not the hangman just as much the loyal servant of the state as any other occupation of law? But we receive no state salary! No pension! Only the insult of piece-rate contract work with not even a dozen murderers sentenced to death any given year in all of our so-called civilized country! Because let me tells you, Slim, if not for the journeyman hanging work I picks up because of my long, solid reputation in some of those more appreciative, so-called backwards States United of America, why the missus and myself would have starved to death long ago.

You look inside the tool chest over in the corner and are pleased to find it almost as well stocked as your own at home. You take out the three-foot crosscut saw and test the sharpness of its steel teeth against your thumbnail. Sharp as shark teeth! Makes your tail bone shiver with anticipation.

—I blame it all on the liberal legal attitudes of our times, Slim. Only a hundred years ago there were more than two hundred offences for which a man, woman, or child woulds be hanged. But now there are only three crimes in Canada still punishable with death. Three! Murder, high treason, and piracy. Pswoshh! Why two of those crimes are practically obsolete! And so there is really only murder for which our country's supreme punishment is even considered. Only murder! And even then they don't sentence murderers to hang nearly enough. Dids you know, Slim, that they haven't hanged a child anywhere in Canada in more than a generation? Is it any wonder our society grows more amoral every year? Because the sooner our legislators draws up a much more supplementary list of offences punishable by death, the better for our public safety, Slim! And the better for my retirement savings.

You've stopped listening to Hitchens babbling and seek the mesmerization of your trade. You measure, T-square, and score cut-lines into a deliciously pliant cedar plank with a nail.

—I say the neglect of my profession comes from how we treat hanging like some hole-and-corner job to be done in big secrecy, as if it were something to be ashamed of! In the good old days of public executions, the public was able to judge for itself my craft and naturally that increased the popularity of my profession and the public demand for more. Oh, I've seen it for meself, Slim, because they still have public hangings in some of those States United below. Peoples really enjoy getting out with their kids and the neighbours on a sunny afternoon and watching someone die for them. Oh, there's nothing like a good public hanging to fascinate a mob.

You enjoy feeling the push and pull of your saw through the strong heart of the cedar plank. You pause to lick sawdust from the back of your hand. You can't resist and suck your knuckles clean.

—It's a tragic waste, Slim! Whens there are so many public spaces around this town suitable for a good hanging! Where one and all may enjoy a fine view and contemplate the hangman at work and see for themselves what a great patriot he is, fulfilling an unpleasant but necessary social task in the most estimable and entertaining manner.

You're listening to what the rasp of your saw says, not Hitchens: Last! Task! Save! Self!

—And think of how much revenue could be made from that kind of crowd, Slim. Peanuts! Popcorn! Balloons! Binoculars! Of course it would be necessary to employ a really competent impresario to oversee the sale of vendor permits and maximize the public profits and arrange those important little effects like pipers piping a suitable lament for the assembled.

The butt end of the post you are sawing drops crisply Plonk! and you caress the freshly exposed wood as sensuously like it was your wife's luscious breasts slipping from beneath her nightie during lovemaking.

—Of course to do complete justice for my profession they should makes a film of every hanging so the whole world can watch over and over again! Think of the dramatic possibilities. The pull of my lever. The sudden drop. The loud crack of doom. The close-up of the condemned's face as their neck snaps. Then the slow pull back revealing their last kicks and paroxysms. Every hangman a movie star!

You lick sawdust from the side of your saw and shiver down to your toes. You hear the hangman's voice muffled, like it is coming from a radio playing in a down-the-hall apartment.

—)|(—

Your new cell is the empty one across from Val's on Death Row. It's a cage not that much larger than the hole you just climbed out of, but it's got a small barred window looking out at a tall brick wall that lets some sunlight in. Sometimes you get to see the shadow of a bird across the bricks and feel something resembling hope for a couple seconds.

Val definitely enjoys having your company across the narrow corridor, all the other Death Row cells except his have been empty until now. But you've grown accustomed to living inside your own solitary thoughts and find Val irritating, keeping you up all night asking you questions without answers and telling long anecdotes without endings. But you try to be kind because you probably would be just as needy for companionship if you had less than two weeks to live, and was locked up alone in a cell, with no visits from your loved ones, ever.

Val always wants to hear about your day's carpentry. How high the scaffold deck? The distance between joists? How thick the frame boxing those heavy gravity drop double doors?

—Why nineteen stairs, Slim?

—I don't know, Val. Hitchens never told me why.

At least you don't remember the hangman saying why nineteen black steps. ("Not too steep and freshly tarred and sticky lest the condemned man should slip and fall and hurt himself climbing those steps he'll never climb down," is all you remember Hitchens advising, and you won't share that with Val.) —Tradition, I suppose, is what you do say to Val.

—But there is always a reason behind every tradition. I wonder why nineteen, Slim?

—I'm going to sleep now. Ok, Val?

Because what's the fucking difference? Nineteen steps or thirteen? Broad or narrow? When you have already built enough staircases by now to make a stairway to heaven if ever they were laid end to end.

But Val won't let you sleep. He wants to spend all night guessing why nineteen stairs.

—Why did you do it, Val? you ask, to change his fucking subject, and because you've been wondering, Why, Val? Why did you kill a cop?

—One of the neighbours called the cops after I went on a tear one payday. Every shitty thing that ever happened to me happened when I was drunk, Slim.

That makes you wince, it sounds so familiar, and you are wishing you never asked him. But Val tells all the ugly details, sour wine stink and all, about how he passed out on his couch and woke up hearing Shayna screaming and saw a cop raping his wife on the other end of the couch.

—I pulled him off Shayna and his neck bones just kind of crushed between my fingers like a turkey neck, Slim. But you know I'm glad that bastard is dead and I'd do the same all over again. Some things you just can't let the bullies get away with.

~/|\~

It feels good to be doing some honest carpentry work again. Nothing feels more trustworthy than a T-square on a plumb line, and a few licks of your hammer can fix anything. You are loving the carpentry and try not to think much about what you're building, though practically as soon as you set the bubble on the first crossbeam, Hitchens begins stretching his rope between your vertical posts.

When you complain he's getting in your way, Hitchens says: —But our rope is why we're here! It is the very substance

118

of law and order. And my rope is of the best possible quality, of course. Fine, soft, pliable, and strong. And I need to stretch my hundred feet of rope for careful study to determine the best thirteen feet for our purposes.

You tell Hitchens to shut up about his sacred rope, you don't want to hear the details of his gruesome trade, but he can't seem to help himself.

—I'm not a monster, Slim. I tries my best to be kind and quick for all my clients. I treat the despicable and pitiful the same. You'll see, Slim, from how I place my Jack Ketch knot just so below our Mister Pointe's wide, manly jaw. The brass ring forward, just behind his left ear, so it will rupture his jugular vein and make things kinder with a sideways jerk to dislocate his vertebral column and rupture his spinal cord so he'll hardly feel a thing, with hardly any jazzing in the air, some squelches of strangulation and then only the eternal peace of nevermore.

—Just shut up, for Jake's sake, Hitchens! I don't want to hear about it.

But for all the hangman's chatty ghoulishness, you really don't mind Hitchens. He's better than most of your previous job-site bosses. At least he has a sense of humour, and he cooks a hot lunch for you every day.

—You'll want to do a better job than that, Slim, Hitchens jokes when you make a rare mistake and cut one plank short, Because who knows but our apparatus might be used on you one day coming.

And that jars you. But then you glance over at his hundred feet of good rope stretching between the scaffold posts, and then up at the barred windows thirty feet up the brick walls, and then you wink at him.

Hitchens laughs heartily. —Go ahead and try, Slim. I won't raise an alarm. I dare you!

-⁓\|⁓-

Warden Owens makes a surprise inspection of Gallows Hall and announces he wants some bleachers built because they are anticipating more spectators than originally expected.

—Well, that's not in our contract, you tell him. You've got to give me something extra for that.

—What do you want now, Evans?

—I want Val to have his thirty minutes in the exercise yard every day, the same as all the other prisoners get.

—Impossible! The exercise yard is too far from Death Row and I can't spare the manpower for the necessary daily escorts.

—Well, Val can have his thirty-minutes exercise here with us in the gallows room then, can't he? The Death House is next door, for fuck's sake.

Owens pales. His thin lips quiver like a snapped plumb-line for some seconds. —Fine, have it your way, you bastard.

-⁓\|⁓-

Hitchens further proves he's a decent boss by putting on a fry pan full of bangers and squeak every day for Val. He even mostly keeps his trap shut when Val's around, though you suspect that's because of some rule of trade against becoming friends with his "clients."

Val loves his daily thirty minutes out of his cell (you knew he would) and he spends every second doing carpentry work (you knew that would happen too, and so you save all the joins and risings for Val's help). And you two master carpenters make a magnificent man-killing structure from that pile of fine timber.

Val is fascinated with the many challenges with building the dropping doors – three-inch thick oak doors rigged with thick steel bolts and hooks that must fall open at exactly the same moment, and their great weight caught by spring catches screwed into the scaffold posts to prevent rebound.

You save all the scrap ends in a neat stack in the sunny spot of the gallows room and use it to build Rags' doghouse for Jeanie's birthday present. Val wants to help but you won't let him. —No way, pal. This job is all mine. It makes me feel a little bit closer to my daughter.

Because sometimes you start feeling that shivery way you do when you're back at home working in your basement woodworking shop and sense your wily Jeanie creeping cat-like up behind you, going to pounce on your back and cover your eyes with sticky little fingers, shouting "Guess who?"

—/\\—

Warden Owens navigates the labyrinths of whitewashed hallways on his way to Gallows Hall to watch the High Hangman test the drop doors, and as always Owens enjoys watching his guards leap to attention when they see him approaching. Every day Owens makes at least one surprise inspection to keep his staff on their toes, never knowing when "the prick" is going to appear around a corner. Owens enjoys how he is hated by his staff, thinks that it means he's doing his job halfway right, because he would prefer to be feared, and will be eventually, after he's fired another slew or two of them for any excuse, so the remainder of his guards will "get" how truly scary their new warden is.

As Owens walks his prison's halls, he keeps glancing at his photograph in the newspaper he is still carrying, and has not put down since he first picked it up yesterday. *The Vancouver Sun* published a great gushing profile of him. The headline:

WARDEN OWENS AND HIS PADDLE
DO MORE WITH LESS!

He thinks he looks handsome and determined in the photograph, holding his blood-stained punishment paddle across his chest. Owens is very pleased by how the article speaks very enthusiastically of his many administrative changes, and the subsequent budgetary savings coming from the reduced manpower requirements for ruling the Oakalla Prison Farm that he has achieved since he put the fear of swift corporal punishment into his prisoners by reinstating the leather whiffle punishment paddle.

Warden Owens' prolonged pleasure over his good publicity is snuffed quick as a candle when he enters the gallows room and sees that their testing effigy has his newspaper photograph pinned to it, and that the condemned man himself is pulling the drop door lever.

Boom! The burlap sack of straw and sand snap tight, and then Owens hears Slim Evans laughing at him, while he watches his own face twirling in a noose. Then Owens finds himself speechless, as if laughing Slim has cast a voodoo spell on him. He coughs and chokes but can't speak the words he wants to shout: "Paddle his ass all the way back to his hole!" And the worst part is how none of the three guards there even offer to get their warden water, but only stand rigidly saluting him, prepared to watch him choke to death.

—⁄ι↖—

As Val pounds flat the last spike into the stair railings, the High Hangman says: —Well aren't you two going to carve your names and the date somewhere in the drop pit so someone knows who made this beast?

You hadn't considered it until Hitchens mentions it. You usually do leave your names carved on the underside of some board, but you don't think you want to on this job, or even admit doing it.

—Wel,l I'm going to write my name on a post, Val laughs at you, and takes up chisel and hammer and chips on the showing side of the front corner post:

Valentine Pointe,
Second Carpenter and First Served.

—⁄ι↖—

The day before Val's scheduled execution, High Hangman Hitchens insists upon having a dress rehearsal for the grand performance, with you playing the part of the condemned. Hitchens wears a top hat and claw-hammer tail suit and polished boots with big brass buckles.

—We all must know our duties, and the other fellows' duties, and do what needs to be done well and quickly, Hitchens tells the six guards and the warden as he walks them through their parts.

Hitchens even insists the guards take off their boots and practice tiptoeing in stockings so they take the condemned man by surprise when they rush into his cell to pin him.

—Tie him well, lads. Or else he might hit the platform on his way down and tear his nose off.

Hitchens has the guards practise binding you with his leather contraption a couple times. It is a broad belt with many straps and buckles for fastening your elbows and wrists to your sides. Another belt straps your knees together. Being bound makes you struggle and pant.

—This is the part when our warden shall tell the condemned, "You must be very brave."

—But I don't want to say that, Warden Owens protests, I hope he soils himself with fear.

—But you must say it, Warden! Hitchens insists, It's tradition that the warden says thus. And where would our English empire be without our English traditions, Sir? God save the King.

The hangman stares the scoff from Warden Owens' face.

—You must be very brave, Owens mumbles finally.

—And thus commences the condemned man's final walk, Hitchens leads his unholy crew through their dramatic marks. Down the corridor the chaplain shall read the burial service but don't think we need to be polite and let him finish, because just as soon as Mister Pointe arrives at our gallows it's quickly up our nineteen steps with him, and into the noose, at galloping speed. It is cruel to prolong these things.

And, pinioned as you are, you find that you are actually agreeing with something Hitchens is saying for a change. Famous Last Words are for the movies, and not a real execution.

Of course the guards drop you painfully onto your bum knee halfway up the nineteen steps.

—Well, mistakes are what rehearsals are for, Hitchens says.

—Get me the fuck out of these straps!

—Soon, Slim. We're nearly done.

And then fucking Hitchens slips his evil noose around your neck and pulls it very snug. You look down at the double drop doors beneath you, and feel fearful.

—And I shall set my knot "just so," Hitchens says, and then I will nod at you, Warden. And you must toll that brass bell once. And please try to put some snap into your wrist, Warden. Make our bell ring.

Owens rings the brass ship's bell loudly and seems very pleased with himself about it.

—Then I shall tug my lever, and you watch Hitchens place his hand on the lever. You try to hop off the top of the drop doors but it's impossible to shift but an inch with your knees bound together. You almost fall over, and only the tug back from the noose stops it.

—The bolt is drawn. "Boom!" goes the trap-doors. "Squonk!" our body falls. The sudden jerk! Some kicks and wheezes, and then it's all over except for paying the hangman. Any questions, gentlemen?

—Can you take your fucking noose off me now? you glower.

—Yes, of course, Slim.

And Hitchens does, but leaves you still bound upon the drop doors.

—The custom is to leave them hanging for at least half an hour, Hitchens explains —But that's completely excessive and unnecessary. Once the physician signs the paper our man is lowered directly into his coffin.

—Fucking unbind me, you bully.

—⁄ı∖—

You can't sleep knowing Val's scheduled to be executed in the morning. And for the first time since you've been bunking in the Death House, Val doesn't keep you up all night with his questions and long anecdotes. He sleeps deeply and didn't seem at all afraid when he said goodnight. As you stare at Val's sleeping face behind the bars of his cell across the way you are feeling more lonely than you ever did in solitary confinement. You stare at him so long Val begins to resemble the innocent, peaceful baby he probably once was, and you hate yourself for building the gallows that are going to end him.

Then you must have fallen asleep because you find yourself waking in a panicked start from hearing a loud, long sigh. You don't know if it came from Val, or yourself, or some Death House ghost because how many hundreds of men have wasted their final days here in Oakalla Prison's Death House since it was built in 1878, you wonder? And how many gallows worn out before you built your version? And how many good men will your gallows kill before it is replaced? You can't believe you built this monster for those bastards. Especially for so little! Only fourteen days respite from your solitary confinement hole which you are probably going to be thrown back into directly after Val's execution.

You can't fall asleep again, from listening to the silent darkness for another eerie sigh. Then an hour before sunrise Hitchens has you out of your cell and in the gallows room to test the drop doors. You are surprised the sound of his whispering and your cell door sliding open doesn't wake Val, but he doesn't even stir.

—Sometimes the planks can swell with rainy weather like we're having, is Hitchens' way of explanation, but you can tell that really he's only feeling lonely and wants your company in this dark blue hour before dawn.

As Hitchens helps you lower yourself into the drop pit to oil the lever works and hinges, it occurs to you that what he really wants is a private moment to say goodbye to you, now that your job together is done and the gallows built. But he doesn't know what words to say for a change.

Dog Face brings "der carpenter and der hangman a cuppa tea" and neither of you speaks as you slowly sip, side by each sitting on the bottom steps of the gallows. You sit silently together for an hour watching the big empty room. Hitchens doesn't fry up bangers and squeak and rashers for breakfast like usual, which suits you fine, you wouldn't touch it if he did.

Apparently nothing brings a crowd out early like a reserved seat at a hanging, and all the bleachers you built are full a hundred minutes before the ten o'clock execution time with many standing in between. You consider the couple hundred people gathered and know they can't all be news reporters. You recognize many rich men from the society pages and wonder how much Owens is charging them to witness his novelty act.

Naturally, as you are watching this macabre crowd, you get wondering how best you might begin mingling with them, and start subtly "borrowing" articles of clothing from a few of them, so you might walk out of the prison gates in the middle of the crowd when this big show is over. But Warden Owens must have been having similar thoughts about you because he orders a guard to handcuff you to one of the drop-pit posts.

You watch the couple hundred expectant faces from a crack between the canvas curtains making the gallows skirt. They are a festive crowd, blowing lots of cigar smoke and sharing pocket flasks. Gallows Hall hums like many beehives from so many conversing voices and it's disconcerting for you because this big inside space has always been quiet as a tomb for you previously, except for Hangman Hitchens murmuring soliloquies. Or perhaps it's because you haven't seen a crowd for so long? Not since that afternoon you were arrested.

Both those hanging-obsessed bishops that Hitchens talked about are here, sitting side by side in the first row. One Catholic, the other High Anglican, but you couldn't guess which is which from both of them looking so the same: fat, bald, and fingering the gold cross bobs on their watch-chains. Behind them sits Mayor Telford and Premier Pattullo. You are surprised that no one is trying to say a sermon or make a speech or sell $1 bottles of snake oil.

—Watch that Val don't kick you in your head on his way down, Hitchens warns you when he makes his final inspection of the drop pit, ten minutes before ten.

—Do me a favour and test your rope on fucking Owens, first.

—Can't, Slim. That smart prick hasn't even paid me yet.

Then Hitchens briefly rests his hand on your shoulder and looks you straight in the eye like he wants to tell you something, but he doesn't speak. Neither do you. What can two men who have built something evil together say to one another? Except I won't tell on you, if you don't tell on me.

Val and his escort enter the gallows room and the crowd falls silent and you can hear Val telling the prison chaplin:
—Fuck off and go pray for yourself, you weak-as-shit loser.

From beneath the gallows you watch Val climb his last nineteen stairs, two at a time. Apparently the guards hadn't got the belt around his knees and you're glad you warned Val. You watch him between the deck slats. Val refuses the hood, just like he said he was going to, by doggedly shaking his big head back and forth when Hitchens tries to slip it over him.

—Suit yourself, Mister Pointe.

Hitchens slips his noose over the condemned man's neck and adjusts the brass ring against his jugular vein as he tightens it.

—Forgive me, you hear the hangman say to Val.

—Just do it quick, man.

Hitchens nods at the warden, and you notice how Owens rings his brass bell with a wide smile. And Boom! the drop doors fall open above you, Val's legs come down kicking, the rope coughs tight, and with a loud tear Val's headless body smacks the concrete floor you are standing on, spewing blood up your pant legs.

You watch Val's head swinging from the noose, his eyes wide open, his lips moving over his gritted teeth, as if he's trying to speak to you. His grimace like a smile makes you jump back as far from "it" as your chained wrist will let you.

Screams and loud wails come from the crowd on the other side of the curtain and you can hear Hitchens shouting on the platform above:

—What do you mean you won't pay me, Owens! He's dead, ain't he? That's what you wanted!

And you sob, knowing all you can do, chained to your post, is to watch Val's grotesque face twirl and wait for Owens to send a couple of guards to drag you back to that hole you wish you never crawled out of.

Priscila Uppal

BED RAIL
ENTRAPMENT RISK
NOTIFICATION GUIDE

I had just embarked upon one of those embarrassing, unexpected, and all-consuming affairs, when the diagnosis arrived.

My husband had been going full throttle into a Percocet addiction that left him flaccid and unconscious in the afternoon – bathrobe untied while the cat licked Bloody-Mary-flavoured potato chips off his hairy knees. Truly, Moses was in such bliss we felt him ill-named. Perhaps Byron or Poe or Lady Gaga would have suited him better. Nevertheless, his early onset kidney disease was momentarily appeased by the mix of canola oil and three-day-old sweat.

I believed the house would stand in its place as it had always stood, regardless of the hooded eyes of equally distressed neighbours with their ungrateful and oddly ill-proportioned children. What else could one hope for in life besides three bedrooms, a gas stove, and a wooden deck partially protected from one's mediocre neighbours by a hedge too unimportant and yet too intimidating to be controlled by anything other than Weed Man?

Believe it or not, my affair began on a hospital bed. Vintage model. In a museum exhibition my soon-to-be lover had helped curate. His area of expertise is the history of medicine whereas mine is book illustration. I was submitting some text for an upcoming exhibition on Christmas book illustrations – an overt attempt to entice families in search of something to do over the holidays to patronize the flagging museum. I wasn't even supposed to be on his floor but the elevator was broken and I must have thought I could will my floor to lower itself once I'd struggled up five flights of stairs and was weary of doing more. I was slightly flushed when I opened the door into my soon-to-be lover, and perhaps the flush was giving off pheromones as he immediately acted like we'd once had a tryst in the stairwell.

Where would you like to go for lunch?

I…I don't think I know you.

Then all the better reason to go for lunch.

I'm sorry…I think I'm lost.

No, I've been waiting for you.

I think I giggled. Probably like a schoolgirl. He had good hair, brown with a bit of curl. He was a good thirty pounds overweight, but I have to admit that I like a man with an appetite. I also have to admit that I like a man who won't take no for an answer. My husband was like that once but over the years had surrendered to the aimless purgatory of compromise. I like a man who will beat down your door to bring you a bouquet of roses – as long as that's where the violence stops, of course. Just enough to get your blood pressure up, to make you feel like a prize worth working hard for, but not a treasure to be kidnapped at gunpoint.

What's for lunch?

Anything your heart desires.

I knew that was a lie, of course. A pick-up line. But it was the one I wanted to hear. I wanted to be picked up. I hated walking all those stairs. They spoke of the monotony of my daily existence – I was itching for a little excitement. In fact, I had been toying with dyeing my hair a bright crimson red or trading in my loafers for some funky Fluevogs – the kind of thing that makes the other members of the department suspect you've come into some money.

I'm having a bad day, I said. *Well, a bad week, a bad month, to be honest, maybe even a bad decade when all is said and done. I could…I could use some…lunch.*

Let me show you something.

And he gave me his hand. And I took it. I felt light on my feet, like I was on promenade, and it didn't seem strange to be walking by all these glass cases with various medical instruments on display.

This bed, he said, *used to belong to the sick-wing of a convent in Quebec. Nineteenth century. It's in beautiful condition. The mattress is new, of course, but the frame, the frame is just as it was first made. Look at the sturdiness of these railings. An earthquake wouldn't break them. Long ago, things were made to last.*

I was about to make a joke about my husband's field, that the 19th century was practically post-post-post-modern in our house, but then bit my lip as it seemed very ridiculous to mention a husband at this moment even though my wedding band was in full view, and at a certain age one must always expect to be dancing around unmentioned spouses. My husband's field is Anglo-Saxon poetry, which is why he is on Percocet. No one cares about dead white poetry from fifty years ago let alone one thousand years ago. I fell in love with him because it seemed so strange, this tall black man from Nova Scotia who was passionate about some antiquarian language no one even knew how to pronounce and with less authors than one could count on a hand. He told me that's what he loved about it. Anonymity amid acute pain and fear. The Anglo-Saxons were people who believed if they sailed on the ocean they might fall off the edge of the earth, who converted to Christianity when they were promised presents and an after-life, who when their husbands left for work might never know what death befell them. He used words like befell. At first he was feted, the only black in his field, but then enrollments for all literary courses, let alone literature you needed a special decoder to read, dropped in favour of terrorism and globalization studies. The university had given him an admin job, on the top floor of the library where no one else went and where it was easy for him to stay at home and no one was the wiser.

His right hand patted the new mattress on the old steel-frame hospital bed. I have always found it hard to sit on a bed – whether in a hotel or a friend's cottage – and not imagine who has had sex on it. When visiting my uncle who had a heart attack in the hospital, I had flashes of the head nurse and one of the residents doing it doggie-style, blue scrubs about their knees. I didn't have the imagination to conceive of patients doing it, although I now know that they do. Nobody has less dignity than the sick. If they want a fuck, they have a fuck. You can leave the breakfast tray by the door.

Later on, he said, *hospital beds came with warnings, like everything else.*

And he pointed at a pamphlet at the side of the bed in a glass case. Of course, my eyes went straight to the illustrations. All of men – medical illustrations of women would be considered pornographic for some time to come – simple line drawings, all of men pinned or caught in unusually freakish positions on a hospital bed.

I caught a chuckle in my throat. It seemed in poor taste to laugh at these men, and yet they didn't look like bed martyrs but more like bed fools.

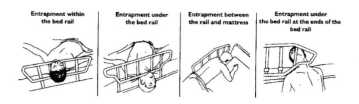

Bed Rail Entrapment Risk Notification Guide, I read aloud. He shrugged. *It's human nature to try every position possible. These men are idiots.*

They took a risk, he replied, patting the mattress again. *How about you?*

I must have made some feeble gesture at modesty, as he laughed lightly and said, *Don't worry, we are the only ones here. The museum is practically a cemetery on weekdays and this section is under construction.*

I laughed. I was thinking, how lovely to be under construction, rather than in process of demolition. So, without any further gestures at modesty, I joined him on the hospital bed, and we did make use of those sturdy 19th-century railings, mimicking some of those idiots in the illustrations – can you guess which ones? – with the hubris of our unentrapped bodies.

Later on, when I pressed him about his confident proposal, he told me he was getting too old to care about shame. *Women are like doors,* he said. *They are either open or closed. I take the chance that all are open until the door is shut in my face. Why live like a lonely man when there are other lonely people out there who can, for a time, make the loneliness take a back seat?* He patted my pudgy behind. *Until the crash?* I added, hoping he wouldn't notice the missing hooks while I struggled to clip my bra. *Doesn't need to be that dramatic*, he replied. *Even a little bump can sometimes set the air bag off.*

For the next six weeks I was either full and light, or completely deflated and disoriented. I went from home, where I underwhelmed my husband, to the university, where I underwhelmed my students and colleagues, to my new lover's condominium – the exhibition now open, our hospital bed was no longer available – where we removed our clothes and revealed our underwhelming bodies to appreciative eyes. I had bought myself two new bra and underwear sets and two pairs of Spanx and a perfume endorsed by a buxom celebrity, and felt almost invincible during those stolen hours. We did it in his bed, of course, but also in his closet, in his shower, on his kitchen counter, and in the laundry room. I thought I felt parts of my body coming alive that had been dormant for years – like taking a yoga or a spinning class, I was sore and tired but also invigorated and defiant, and unlike at yoga or spinning class, I had orgasm after orgasm without having to imagine myself lapping up the waves on the sands of St. Lucia. I knew this new-found pleasure did not have much to do with my chosen lover – I'd had affairs before, if intermittently – but this time it felt more urgent, more necessary somehow, as if my body had chosen it rather than my disillusioned heart.

I returned home sometimes in the most foul mood, and revelled in it, slamming the doors and banging pots and pans while I overcooked pasta or undercooked chicken. It didn't matter, my husband either ate every crumb on his plate and threw up or stared at the pepper mill and didn't bother to lift his fork or spoon at all. I considered him sick, and therefore tolerable if non-contributing. I put out his bowl the same way I put out Moses's. And he thanked me the same way, by rubbing up against me at strange hours and drooling on my arm. Both were also losing an alarming amount of weight. And yet, I can tell you, with perfect sincerity, I never stopped loving him. I just loved him from a distance. It had been that way for a while, Percocet just made the measuring easier. I also learned it's very easy to get Percocet if you can dislocate something. My husband had dislocated his shoulder when he played varsity soccer and could now do so at will. We all have our talents. He seemed to think he'd found a good use for it. And how could I blame him? I wasn't going to find him a reason to embrace his admin job. I wasn't going to fill the void of the unpronounceable Anglo-Saxon world that was being replaced by hip hop and video games. Despair befell him. All I could do was my best to keep him afloat before he floated off the edge of the earth.

So along with Moses, the three of us lived like this – inside our own skins playing our own private games with our bodies – until the day the tests came back from the lab. Is it after the age of 35 (if you're lucky 40) that the calendar is marked with tests? Like a throwback to high school or university but without the keen giddy energy of moving towards something, a welcome completion. No, these tests are intrusive reminders that your body is only on lease and one day the landlord is going to staple an eviction notice to your door. You may have ten years or two years or two months to vacate the premises, but the day will come when the moving trucks will be idling outside and the minutiae that once comprised a life is now junk in boxes with nowhere else to go. I had been having tests for years now, for various reasons – back pain, or fatigue, or dizziness, or mandated yearly exams – nothing had ever turned out to be serious, a virus here, a vitamin-deficiency there. My abdomen was sore. Tender. Ultrasound non-conclusive. Likely fibrous tissue. But to be on the safe side. Biopsy. Then wait.

I've been waiting for you. I didn't know this when they took the biopsy. I was nervous, yes – who isn't when undergoing a biopsy? – but I honestly didn't think it would turn out to be anything. Nothing in my life had really turned out to be much of anything, so why would this be any different? I would be given some sort of antibiotic or menopause aid and book a follow-up appointment with my GP.

Sarcoma cancer. A rare soft-cell cancer that grows in connective tissues that support other types of tissue in the body. I thought I'd never heard of it but was then reminded that Terry Fox had sarcoma cancer. That he died of complications related to sarcoma cancer after collapsing from his marathon across Canada. Then on top of the fear of acquiring a disease, I felt guilt. I was not good enough for this kind of cancer. I was an adulterer and a mediocre academic. I gave expired canned goods to food drives. I never made a donation to charity without a receipt. I had never donated to the Terry Fox Run. What was I doing with sarcoma cancer?

I wasn't superstitious or religious enough to believe that I was being punished for using my body. I was merely being punished for having one. And, like everything sooner or later I suppose, it had decided to let me know how disappointed it was in me. After turning my PhD dissertation into a book, I'd never managed to write a second one. I wrote catalogues and museum collection notes, not original academic treatises. I'd never had children, something my mother, dying of lung cancer in hospice, never failed to mention when I visited her – *why would you marry a black man if you didn't intend to have children? Those mixed kids are the most beautiful in the world.* Yes, the nurses would acknowledge, it was a racist comment, but when my husband deemed to show up with a Pot of Gold truffle box or Licorice Allsorts for the staff, they would sigh and look me over like I was some ungrateful fool who had won a trip to Caribbean and refused to book it because the cat didn't like to be boarded.

I had the distinct impression the doctors were less than impressed as well. This cancer usually strikes the young and fit and while I was pretending to be younger than I was, I was nowhere near young – I've always thought middle-age should be just that, the projected middle-age of your life, so 40, not 50 or 60 the way people kid themselves – and I don't think huffing across the street to catch a streetcar or swaying to Elton John's *Greatest Hits* after an evening of drinking too much wine constitutes fitness. But they duly informed me that there was nothing I did to deserve this cancer, that it was simply one of those unfortunate things, dumb stupid luck, that made it choose me, so I tried to believe them. They also told me the cancer was of an aggressive type, my favourite type of suitor, and we would need to book surgery right away.

My husband was so flummoxed by the news he forgot to take his Percocet for five days. It was awful. The worst week I can remember of our marriage. He followed me around the house like I was in continual danger of fainting, picking up my coffee mug if I left it in another room, fetching my slippers, trying to button up my blouse. I found him one afternoon, head in his hands, praying. I didn't think I was going to survive his urgent concern. Moses protested this stupidity by peeing outside the litter box.

I tried to let him off whatever hook his emotions were dangling from.

Maybe I'll be on Percocet, I joked.

You can't die, he said to me.

Nobody said I'm going to die.

Nobody said you wouldn't.

I paused for a second and realized that what he said was true. They told me a good deal about the surgery they were going to perform to get rid of the cancer – how they were going to have to remove my abdominal wall and replace it with biologic mesh – a hush descended whenever the words "biologic mesh" were used because, I was told, only two hospitals in all of Canada had it – mesh made of real animal and human tissue rather than synthetic fibres – and it was quite expensive and therefore saved for specific circumstances – but they didn't tell me what they were going to do if the cancer wouldn't leave, if it broke down the door of the next fascia wall and threw me like a limp cavewoman onto its back.

Trust me, I said, *when this cancer realizes I'm not the pretty young thing it thought I was, it'll split and find another woman at least ten years younger.*

I'm the one who's dying slowly, he said, and burst into tears. I put him to bed and placed the Percocet bottle beside his alarm clock so he wouldn't need to get up to rummage through the bins in the bathroom.

I didn't want to tell my lover – I'd even toyed with the idea of telling him my husband and I were on vacation in Jamaica while I was in the hospital – but once the surgeons explained that I would require an acute pain unit and be on enforced bed rest for at least eight to twelve weeks and afterwards would likely be on a walker, then crutches, then a cane for the next many months, well, not telling him about the surgery seemed almost impossible, as you couldn't disappear entirely from the world in this day and age without someone finding out what's happened to you. So after the pre-surgery MRI, I sent my husband home in a cab with a six-pack of beer and take-out burritos and met my lover at one of those free-trade coffee shops where no one pays attention to your suffering as long as you sprinkle a little cinnamon or nutmeg into your cup.

I gave him the facts of the situation. Cancer. Rare. Aggressive. Operation as soon as the three surgeons could clear their schedules on the same day.

I'll visit you at the hospital every single day. I'll bring you anything you need. Anything.

I was shocked by his words, I think, but shock was already becoming an ordinary emotion. *I don't want you there.*

I've been through this before, he informed me. *My wife – ex-wife – she didn't want me to go with her to her treatments. At least that's what she said. Then when she got better, she packed her things up and told her lawyer I'd abandoned her when she had stage 2 breast cancer. It's true I didn't know what to do, so I did what most men do, I just let her tell me what to do. She said to stay away, so I stayed away. And like most women, she didn't mean what she said, so, I'm going to assume you don't mean it either.*

I mean it. I love my husband. He loves me. I don't want you to see me in pain. That's what marriage is for.

You're right. I'd forgotten.

The next thing I know I am awake, nauseous, and in acute pain, and am introduced to my acute pain team – a slew of nurses and surgeons-in-training and social workers and psychiatrists and students who rotate in and out of my schedule like different food groups the entire time I am in hospital. I get poked, answer some questions, get poked again, and then get bumped out of my private room for someone else in acute pain.

Then the next thing I know I'm wheeled down to our car with a slew of prescriptions – including the blood thinner injections that ache like bee stings and a morphine derivative that I wish made me loopy and ethereal but at best only makes me sleepy – and an order for a hospital bed to be delivered to our home the following morning.

I laughed when presented with the pamphlet. I laughed so hard I nearly pissed my pants. It was almost identical to the one in the glass case that my lover-in-limbo had shown me on that day when I had no idea what was growing inside me, plotting to overthrow my less than ambitious plans. The history of medicine was quite a different experience than the reality of medicine.

I spent the first two weeks of enforced bed rest tracing this particular figure:

**Entrapment between
split bed rails**

It had been a long time since I had picked up a charcoal pencil, or a pencil of any kind for that matter, and it felt alien but sturdy in my hand. I had spent most of my career interested in lush manuscript illustrations, the kind I used to hope I would one day be able to draw before I realized I did not actually have talent but only a workman competency, the kind that made a children's book a magical landscape of moons and ghouls and haunted castles and rescued princesses. This booklet was an insult to a talented artist, probably something that paid the bills, and likely not even a very grand bill, two months' worth of hydro or dry cleaning a rug your cat pissed on. And yet, the lines of this figure appealed to me: his outstretched arm and pinned chest, how his ear was now in a perfect line with the middle point of his chest.

My husband bought me a new sketchbook, but never bothered to look at what I was drawing. Perhaps he was afraid that I was drawing my new rearranged body or some abstract ode to the pain I was feeling, a type of pain he could only imagine as it was so concretely associated with my distressed flesh, ironically much harder to conceive than the mental anguish of crushed dreams.

My husband returned to his old habit of muttering Anglo-Saxon riddles. But on the Percocet they all became even more jumbled, answers paired up with the wrong questions. On a good day, the old language would flow from his mouth like an ancient chant, but on most days he stuttered and sputtered the strange symbols out into the air and could have been mistaken for a schizophrenic. I would calm him down like one, repeating the answers to the riddles back to him for comfort, several of which didn't make sense at all in a modern context: inkhorn or garlic pedlar. Still, my husband would turn soft and sad and take my hand and we would both forget for a moment that time for me would not be as kind as it had been for the Exeter Book where the original riddles were housed.

And then all of a sudden my lover, or now ex-lover, or so I had thought, appeared. He rang the doorbell and my husband let him in. He was holding an outrageously large houseplant that I immediately had no intention of watering.

I'm a colleague of your wife's, he said.

My husband replied with the Anglo-Saxon word for Moth, but my lover would only have heard a grunt. If he wasn't so completely disoriented, I might have thought he was being affectionate. The Moth riddle is my favourite one. We used to recite it together during the first years of our marriage whenever we bought a new bookshelf or moved our precious papers from one cabinet to another. *To me it seemed a remarkable fate, the worm had swallowed the speech of a man, a thief in the night. Though he swallowed the word, the thieving stranger was no whit the wiser.* Moth. Book Moth, in particular. I liked to imagine the Anglo-Saxon squires chasing those winged creatures, desperate to preserve their painstakingly created gilded manuscripts.

Undeterred by my husband's lack of hospitality (a word I have ceased to understand since my hospital stay), my lover carried the already burdensome houseplant to the corner of the living room, where I happened to be in the middle on a modern, built to be temporarily erected and then dismantled, hospital bed. I thought I would be livid, but I was in too much pain. Instead, I just felt confused, as if my lover had jumped from an illustration in a children's book into actual flesh. My husband picked Moses up, very gently as Moses's bones were now very brittle, and went upstairs. I had tried to give him the eyes that would say, don't leave me with this stranger, but his gaze was buried in the cat's matted marmalade fur.

How are you feeling?

I didn't reply.

Are you comfortable?

I didn't reply.

Can I get you anything?

Not a plant, I can tell you that, I said, and then regretted it. What did this poor portly man do to me? And why was I all of a sudden annoyed by his portliness? *Sorry, but I wasn't expecting any visitors.*

I thought maybe I could bring you lunch sometime.

I don't think so.

Why don't you want me in your life anymore? Now his voice turned to a whisper. *You've always meant more to me than sex.*

I wanted to say: If I only meant sex to you, you must have the lousiest sex life in history. Instead I said: *I don't need any more complications.*

I want to make things simpler for you. I just want to help.

You're not going to make things up to your wife by helping me.

Ex-wife.

Right now the only relationship I'm trying to fix is the one between me and my body. It's in shambles. In fucking shambles, do you understand? Even though we had a prenup, it's trying to take me for all I'm worth. Do you understand, you useless fat fuck?

My lover, or ex-lover, was so taken aback that he picked up the gifted houseplant and hugged it, hiding his face in its leaves.

And then I heard Moses wail. My husband ran down the steps with Moses wrapped in a yellow bath towel. The vet would later say that although Moses was declining at a faster than normal pace, this was the regular course once kidney disease sets in.

I stopped drawing. Forced to submit to the therapeutic numbness of daytime television, I can tell you two things: One, *Family Feud* is the greatest game show ever (a massive sociological study of white and black America – the surveys will be a much better anthropological tool than Anglo-Saxon riddles – think of the implications of *We asked 100 people when you hear noises in the basement, what are you most frightened of finding?* And one family says my ex-wife and ghosts and the other family says burglars and broken furnaces. Or *We surveyed 100 married men and asked when money is tight, what is the first thing you give up?* And one family says eating at restaurants and the other family says my mistress); and Two, Dr. Oz is a fucking asshole. I thought I might find his show comforting, that his recommendations might make for interesting and useful additions to my growing health food store list. But that man is a health whore, jumping on every study or cellular bandwagon with the same amount of patronizing enthusiasm to titillate his studio audience. Apple cider vinegar saves lives. Mammograms save lives. Broccoli saves lives. Tylenol saves lives. Hugs save lives. And everything, absolutely everything causes and cures cancer.

The only place on earth that felt safe was my electric hospital bed with the adjustable rails. As long as I was in the bed, I knew no one else could join me there. Only sometimes Moses, if I lowered the bed as close to the ground as possible and lifted him up onto the mattress. Then we would sit together and watch *The Price Is Right*, or *Let's Make a Deal* – all the oldies with new comedian hosts. We couldn't watch *Family Feud* together because I laughed too hard and it scared him. When the survey *What might break if Grandpa and Grandma make passionate love?* came up, I was shouting the answers: hips! glasses! beds! Poor Moses shook uncontrollably until I lowered him back down. Then he went straight to his own cat bed. But my husband had beat him to it and was lying with his head on the hairy cushion, passed out in narcotic bliss.

That's why we have benefits.

I don't want to leave you.

You're going to have to go on disability, like me, if this contin-ues. Better to take care of it now.

I don't want to leave you.

You're barely here as it is. I mean you're here, of course, and I appreciate it, I really do, but you're not here, you're off somewhere trying to run away from your pain, and I can relate, I really can, I wish I could do the same, but I'm not running anywhere right now.

I'm scared of rehab.

Me too, but you can't keep doing this to your body or it's going to break.

I really love Percocet, he said, and started crying, then sob-bing like a little girl whose favourite boy band has broken up. *But I, I suppose, I mean I know…I suppose this is what I need to do because…I love…*he paused…*I love you more.*

It no longer mattered to me if he did love me more than Percocet. It wasn't a competition. And if it was, I was not addictive and could not ease his pain as quickly, but we shared two decades of memories and meals and body fluids and some-times loving words.

I'll be waiting for you.

And so my husband was shipped off to be cured of his afflic-
tion while I would lie in limbo to find out if it was even possible to be cured of mine. I assured him that I could handle
all the day-to-day routines: I had microwaveable dinners and
could run my own baths, and I had graduated from the
walker to crutches and could even get down to the corner store
for any items that hadn't been delivered from the grocery store.
And this was all true, but I spent most of my time in my hospital bed, still consumed by daytime television, now adding
even the horrid hybrid gossip-cooking shows with theme days
like "Pumpkins and Spooks" or "The Perfect Meatball." I was
still even watching *Dr. Oz*, though I stopped taking notes and
started to cheer for the Styrofoam re-enactments of bowel
obstructions or chronic inflammation.

My ex-lover had dropped by twice after the first visit, the
second time with a bouquet of daffodils and the third with a
vanilla-scented candle, but you could tell his heart wasn't in it,
and neither was mine. It wasn't just the sex between us, but it
wasn't enough. And I'd had enough of whatever this affair had
been meant to give me. Our space had been dismantled long
ago. A new exhibit was certainly under construction.

So when I heard the doorbell ring for a fourth time with
the accompanying plump shadow against the foggy glass, I
yelled at the top of my lungs: *The answer to the fucking riddle
is Moth! Moth! Moth!*

And I thought back to that first time on the 19th-century
hospital bed. The frame was built to last, but the mattress was
new. Of course it was new. Mattresses can never last. And I felt
an ache inside my body the likes of which I've never felt again

– like I could finally feel the holes, the holes that would never be filled because there were always going to be more holes and more holes and one day there would simply be too many holes and this body would be deemed unsalvageable.

And then I was brought back to the Technicolor of the television as that man's face rose up and took its hallowed spot on the screen. Dr. Oz was having a special show devoted to the Emperor of All Maladies. *The C word no one wants to talk about, that no one wants to pronounce.* And that was the final straw.

The C word no one wants to talk about, that no one wants to pronounce? I'd counted at least 100 mentions of the word cancer on his show in the last week alone. Flyers came in the mail for lotteries and bike races and naturopathic clinics all spelling the word out in bright red and yellow letters. I could no longer have a conversation with anyone without the word coming up. Cancer. Cancer. Cancer. Fuck you, Dr. Oz, and your colonoscopy scare. It was just a scare. Pre-cancerous. Like, Pre-view in the theatre. You can still make changes to the show. Shut it down if you want. And he didn't even go back for the next screening after three months as instructed, but waited until nine, even though his doctors kept calling him to remind him to book the appointment. Hypocrite. Pre-cancerous hypocrite. I'd had enough.

But my rage was too fresh and when I pounded on the channel key of the remote, I lost my grip and it fell to the floor. At first I breathed a sigh of relief, since Dr. Oz's smug sallow face had been replaced with the grey glory of a hippopotamus taking a bath in the African jungle. But after a couple of minutes, when the segment switched to a focus on birds of paradise, I saw the orange spot out of the corner of my eye, and I saw it one last time in all its feline glory, just before it pounced.

Entrapment between split bed rails

Entrapment between the end of the rail and the side edge of the head board or foot board

Entrapment between the head or foot board and the end of the mattress

Remember, I had laughed when presented with the pamphlet and yet it is exactly in one of those positions that I was found. I laughed so hard I nearly pissed my pants – before I truly understood the term – an instinctual bafflement at the gross incompetence of humankind to find itself in such incomprehensible and tragic positions. Can you guess which one?

In his long ago outdoor days, Moses had been a bird hunter. In fact, it was one of the reasons we forced him back indoors. The newspaper had run several articles about how cats were decimating the city's bird population. It had probably been years since Moses had seen a bird, even a virtual one, and regardless of his kidney disease had opted for one last catch.

I had tried to do something – nothing concrete, nothing helpful of course, since my dear cat was completely on his own risky adventure – but my body had reacted, as had my heart, and now I could not hear Moses crying, nor could I even smell his wet fur. I had a feeling, though, that his pain was now over.

The angle of my face, where my right eye opened, could look no further than the fallen booklet with its Notice to Patient, Patient's Family And/Or Primary Day-to-Day Caregiver, that stipulated, no, that contractually obligated, one to follow its directive: DO NOT use this product without first completely reading and understanding this Bed Rail Entrapment Risk Notification Guide. Reading was not necessarily *understanding*. I pondered this for a while in my entrapped position. What optimism. I certainly did not *understand*. Life did not make it easy for one to *understand* the risks of living. I had spent the majority of my life thinking and feeling and doing and acting – but could I ever say I spend any time understanding? Does my cancer understand the risks of being inside my body? Maybe it does. Maybe it is the only thing that understands my hopeless desire.

The thought calmed me somewhat as I surrendered to the realization that I had lost control over the situation and could no longer help myself. I would have to coexist with this new pain. I would be stuck in this uncomfortable, but ultimately non-terminal, position until someone came to rescue me.

Leon Rooke

SARA MAGO ET AL

A fat man and a thin man and a woman who was in between came into the café, in the afternoon this was, around three, with another hour left in the day shift. They passed up the cleared tables in front, and sat – odd, I thought, but live and let live – at the unwiped booth in the back where the staff and the regulars, what few there are, sometimes assemble, all the cups and crumbs and crumpled tissues still on the table along with a deep spread of salt in which Sara Mago, now dozing at a counter stool, had fingered in her name down to the yellow top, and the words "Hereby Looms a Tale," with cartoon balloons dripping from the letters that were meant to represent her tears, all her morbid life up until this hour. And mine, I guess, as well. All our fallen yesterdays, our gloomy tomorrows, no relief in sight, not today, not ever, though let's not be overly dramatic, if you don't mind.

Not a word, not a nod from these three as they entered, the woman who was in between sitting between the other two, all on one cramped side – odd, I thought, but live and learn – and moving aside coffee mugs and the like to make room for their elbows, then all three solemnly studying the vista, though no news there. This vista being a seamless vista, the same desert scrub through two days journey, coming or going, until you hit the rugged Pecos on the one side or scaled Edwards Plateau for Austin on the drab other.

I said, "What will you have?" calling this out to them from my spot at the cash register – "What'll it be?" – as I rung up a No Sale on this ancient chatterbox just to see was it still into free enterprise. "A cold drink," I said, "a menu, a meal, a snack? Here at Doc's Place we aim to please, service like a shot, reasonable prices too, check and compare."

Their three heads turned as one and regarded me warily, defeated by the heat, I would guess, not so much as a nod of civility in the way they kept looking, as I hit the keys I like to hit on the old machine and rang up $999.99, the most you can ever buy at Doc's Place, according to the old machine.

"Soup de jour?" I said. "Vichyssoise, special today only? Ice water, beer, our number one deluxe milkshake?"

Outside I could see tumbleweed skittering along all in the one direction like squat little musical signatures, emblems of runaway time midst the rueful space, a thick scrim of ashen dust coiling four or five feet above the desert, and above that layer upon layer of rubescent, dormant haze stretching far as the eye could determine, the sky crowning this wizardry an endless stretch of limpid blue, which would be the colour of Sara Mago's eyes, of Sara Mago down at the counter end if ever again she opened them. Sara's love had run out, leaving only the last vestiges of charity to limp about on hobbled legs. She's endured the daily broken heart, the breakfast jeers, met death face to face, yet retains the innocence of a starved child, all of which combines to make her sleep-headed daylight through dark, the most dreary company imaginable. That white uniform she was wearing, why am I only now mentioning this? To begin with, it was dirty. I mean, before all the savagery started, or perhaps before it was so much as thought about, that uniform was filthy. She has two. The other was torn, likely in a fight. She had not yet had time to sew up the bodice, if such was intentioned, nor yet time to wash its replacement. So the soiled one was the necessity. And that one had not survived the ordeal without becoming – what might be the word? – besmirched. More besmirched. In that it was now spotted, smeared, with Doc's blood. She'd fainted, or fallen, slipped, maybe wallowed in his spewing – would I know? She claimed his last words were *I don't know you!* but who this *you* might be is up for conjecture and in any event she could not have heard his last words, being elsewhere, and I have serious doubts that old Doc, a man of unsound mind so solidly entrenched such had become his vocation, would have thought any act, final or otherwise, deserving of last words.

"Highly recommended, homemade," I said to the three sojourners, "best you'll find any place on this road, good for what ails you, that's our soup de jour."

They shook their heads, these three sojourners did, each in slow and considered denial of need, the woman hunched low between the men, her spine curved, chin all but resting on the table, their shoulders overlapping hers, one bent finger poised above Sara Mago's name engraved there in salt as though she would smooth out the grains and exchange a stranger's name for her own, though let's hope for her sake she imbibes not one dram of old Sara Mago's morbid news. I set the tape going, not the Brahms, not the Chopin, but a yippi-eye-o cowpoke tune, with a Ry Cooder man stroking the backup strings.

The woman's eyes momentarily locked with mine and what you saw there, in the livid aftermath of her musical dis-taste and before some residue of inherited politeness made her swallow it back, was melancholia deep as a fever, the way the heart works from within to burn its insignia upon your face as resolutely as hot iron on the skin of a yowling calf.

She then took to picking up the coffee mugs, glancing into them, sloshing the leftover coffee around though not spilling any, and speaking in some secret code to the other two, a quiet drone of observation perhaps, with no particular expression of grievance or sorrow in her expression, commenting, perhaps, on nothing more consequential than the shade of lipstick smears on the cup rims, the cigarettes heaped in the ashtrays, the tattered, crumpled field of napkins, messages you might compose in salt the way you scribbled a name in sand on a lonely beach – and the two with her whispering back their odd consent or notice of same, nodding, and looking away at this and that, yes, at this and that, the lean one by the window now saying with crisp authority to her, "Don't go haywire on us, Dobe."

Don't go haywire on us, Dobe.

Though I could have got that bit wrong: not Dobe, could be, but not Dale or Doll or Dole, only something within that range of sound, the woman at that point snapping out a quick beat of code, spoon rapping the table, spitting out a quick response – "… haywire dot-dot haywire your dot-dot self!" – as she squirmed her shoulders clear, her head darting up like a chipmunk from its catacombed depths – "dot-dot your frigging dot-dot asshole self…" – before subsiding with a deep pull of breath, her shoulders now further sagging, curve and slide of backbone, and clasping her hands and fluttering them restlessly over the table, just one eye and the top of her head about all that was visible now, as my yippi-eye-o cowpoke mounted his mustang and clippity-clopped off into yippi-eye-o land.

"Why isn't she here?" the woman moaned. "What time is it?" – and all of us, Sara Mago excluded, slammed our eyes onto the remorseless clock.

No movement there, nothing going on with that clock, that clock has gone into other zeniths of being. New batteries required, that clock no longer bound to its earthly quest.

"She'll be here. Said she would. Just hang on."

Sara Mago groaned, brushing at her rear-end as if to disrupt the flight plan of swarming bees.

I put on the Brahms and watched to see would the woman in the booth unclench her fists, lose her grimace, make peace with the world.

Outside, the tumbleweed continued their pilgrimage. The dust field was lifting, allowing the yucca bushes, creosote, mesquite, and like plumage to say hello, we are back from our vacation, hope you did not miss us too much, it's a bit dry out here, for god's sake could you not grant us a nice rain.

"Look," the older man said to me as I arrived with wiping cloth, with glasses of water. "Flap on off, okay? We've been cooking in the car all day, we want to sit here for a few minutes undisturbed, family matters to discuss, okay?"

Hoekay, I thought, by your leave, amen, let's put the working man in his place.

"No charge for that water," I said, "though it might interest you to know we had to drill through hard rock to get that water, an aquifer, you know, yes, by god, a giant ocean existing mere miles beneath your feet."

"Buzz off," the older man said. "Hoof brain," added the other.

I looped back into the hanging cove off the kitchen, a warren of rooms each the size of tea biscuits – warped floors and joists, cracked low ceilings, a leaning, afflicted place, with doors that opened to other doors, windows that opened to walls. A dark, rustic, unswept maze, our No Where place, its Fix-it times come and gone. Sara Mago and me, come and gone, yet holding on, god must wonder why.

Because who else will keep the vigil, command the post?

The air conditioning didn't reach back here and the heat was breath-taking, lapping at my face the way would an eudemonic dog. I sat down a minute on the creaking bed. An eye for an eye, I thought, tooth for a tooth. I could smell the burn in the thin, gloopy mattress, charred black bowl there where a thousand buttocks over the years had tossed and turned. Scant nights ago, under the flat-iron hand of drink and swimming in the afterglow of good times, Sara Mago had leapt from the perils of restless sleep, banging her head on the ceiling, screaming, *"Oboe, you dumb fuck!"* Rousting me from the flaming mattress with a bucket of cold water over my flanks. *"Now move, you sonofabitch!"* Up on the wall a defaced yippi-eye-o calendar, marked the year, but which year?

I peered at my face in the broken mirror over the cardboard sink. You could see the years, that was about all there was to be said. Where had my dimples gone? My rosy cheeks? The throbbing halo this young fellow used to wear?

"Okay," I said. Flap, flap, flap.

As a crow would flap. As a lone, scheming vulture might.

I took the back way out. Up the path to the ancient trailer sitting in warped disarray on rotted tires. Scene of the crime. Home sweet home. The screen door was still down on the ground, kicked aside and trampled, the lock on the main door wrenched loose of its screws, a jagged hole and peeling slithers in the weathered surface where Doc had put his boot through the flimsy wood. A patient man would have mounted the single step, turned the knob and entered, to be greeted by an empty nest.

A radio was playing somewhere, static mostly, blur of Wichita country and distant el espagnol.

Olé olé
Love came through my door
and I did not know her name

I upended the mangled bed and removed the blood-stained sheets before heaving the hinged side back into the wall. I plopped the seat-side back to its favoured position. Shattered vases, tables, glassware. The radio under the bed.

Olé olé
I was your Mr. Right
Who could do you no wrong

I yanked the plug and the static died. The pole lamp in which one bulb yet flickered was overturned, that bulb ghoulishly displaying the trampled pages of Sara Mago's slew of floor-strewn books, *The Siege of Lisbon, Baltasar and Blimunda, Ricardo Reis*, etc etc, the wherefrom Sara Mago had petitioned for and secured her name change with a total no-hassle outlay of $29.95 not including postage and the wrath of a newly-minted Poppa Doc.

The sheriff's crew had removed the knives, the pistols, the rope, the body. They'd left behind the suicidal chair, surmising that it had splintered under his weight, "well, my gosh!" perhaps being his final thought.

I opened the small, thumping refrigerator and guzzled back a spot of homogenised. I looked in the aged freezer to see if she still had it there: the tight wad of dollar bills bound by rubber bands and encrusted with ice inches thick, as everything in the unit, and the unit itself, was.

Still there: Sara Mago's secret *bicycling through Portugal* stash.

Sara Mago had come howling through the trailer door after discovering Doc's body. She'd trampled daisies and thrown pots down the well. Then she'd flung herself into a zigzag course onto the highway with me trailing. Don't ask why. Do not ask why.

In the sky two white lines were soundlessly writing themselves, miles up from the floating horizon, and through all of this the heat rippling like the flesh of horses on a race course.

The highway, for the whole of its dusty, wavering length, coiled through the plains like snakes climbing a frazzled rope.

Perched on a leaning saguaro a hawk squared off in contemplation of its sun-baked kingdom.

Sara Mago's head remained down on the counter, not much to see except a pile of honey-strewn hair, pale, thin arms encircling her head and one tight fist marooned over a sugar bowl.

The woman was looking at the twin jet tracks up in the sky, her eyes hard, more than a little mean, feet pressing the booth's opposite seat, the muscles straining in her legs, her throat thickened too, a whole heap of knots up in her brow, and all the while addressing her companions in some code hard as timber.

I went over to their booth with my wiping cloth and cleared their table, saving the salt for last, scooping that into the palm of my hand, scattering the salt over the floor and wiping my palm against the apron.

"We close in fifteen minutes," I said, an outright lie.

"Creep," she said.

Sara Mago stirred. The older man turned to regard her, not overly interested, the younger one staring out the window and muttering "Jesus Christ" under his breath with a look on his face that asked why in god's name would anyone choose to live out here. Sara Mago looked like she'd been walking too many miles on blistered feet with a noose around her neck waiting for someone to hang her. In a slurring voice she said, "I think I took too many pills, I feel birds have been nesting in my hair, in my mouth, watch your language, you," and her head plops back down.

About this time the door swings open and in stride two officers of the law, johnny-come-latelys to the desert patrol. One carries the wreath he's lifted from the front door. "Surprises me," he says, "to see you'd put up a wreath for that miserable bastard."

"That's the Eternal Wreath," I tell him. "It gets passed along."

"Seen any suspicious characters today?" the one says, and I think about that as I'm watching the other one down beside Sara Mago, stroking her hair, his face up at her ear and her hair half-covering his face, patting his holstered pistol too. "Nothing today," I said, "not a peeping soul, nada, no suspicious persons crossing our parameters today." The one I'm saying this to squints at me, wrenching his head, squinting all over, a small welt of pink skin in that fresh cut beneath the left eye.

They settle onto stools a space removed from Sara Mago, giving her serious study, the one saying, "I see old Katsky's taking it hard," the second one saying, "Two to go, we're onto something hot now, no time to chitty-chat."

"Water," the other says, the one with the cut under his eye, "for the fire-eater in the cruiser. Fact is, you could take it to her, she's not going anywhere without that dog."

"That damn dog," the first one says, and the two of them smile, obviously sitting on a story they are eager to tell.

Over at the booth the woman is trying to wedge herself free, she's flapping an arm at the lawmen, but there's a hand clamped over her mouth, both men are pressing against her, pressing her flat, or so it seems, she's fenced in so all to be seen of her is a pile of hair, one eye, the nose, that big hand over her mouth. You'd almost call it assault, a trespass of the living temple, someone should intervene, but this is yippi-eye-o country, maybe Dobe has gone haywire again, could be such is her natural state, maybe she's only saying hello, what business is this of mine, there's such a thing as an entitlement to privacy.

And the troopers are telling their tale.

"It's like you say it was with Katsky running wild on the highway after she finds Doc jiggling from a rope off that hotshot chair, except this was daylight not an hour ago, we spot this figure weaving on the road. I'd say not exactly running, going in circles, more like, thrashing this stick, which turns out to be a walking stick, except not exactly a regular walking stick, laminated tip, you know. She's screeching to high heaven, drugs, we figure, alcohol, a runaway war bride, another one of those. But it turns out she's blind, a legitimate one-hundred percent blind person, a teenager for god's sake, and she's lost her Seeing Eye dog. Some sonofabitch, you could say, has struck her dog with his automobile, probably intentionally, she thinks. She's berserk, it takes us a while to learn that. Yes, so she thinks. Though, now listen to this, an accident or intentional, this didn't kill the dog. She hears the *blam*, all these sundry noises, maybe she even heard a blaring horn, tires chewing on gravel, then *blam, crunch crunch crunch*, that dog whining. Whining. Moans. She hears that. Then nothing. Silence. Silence like the universe has ceased operation, has closed down. Her dog. Where has her dog got to? So what we compute is that wounded dog, delirious, has dragged herself off. That Seeing Eye dog's mind is not functioning. She's out in the scrub dead or dying. We harness the girl, we zigzag each which way over the terrain, miles and miles, the binoculars busy. We search high and low for that goddamn irreplaceable dog, well, insofar as there is a high out here in this goddamn place which I for one wish the Mexicans had retained."

Maybe you guys hit that damn dog your own selves is what I'm thinking.

Outside, in blinding sun, a jeep and two trucks lumber by, digging for the army depot fifty miles up the line. The girl in the Dodge Charger is maybe thirteen, sitting bunched up, a dusty, shrivelled rag, like she's been rolled in spined prickly pear, has wrestled with cacti, her face and arms spotted with dried blood, though what I mostly notice are her eyes, those sightless eyes, she's looking somewhere else, she's blind, no doubt about that. "Who's there?" she asks, a stricken voice. "Did you find my dog, those troopers, they said they were looking for my dog, who are you, are you looking for my dog? Something happened to my dog, a car hit her, I think it must have swerved right into her because Pozzo would never never have walked on the road, Pozzo is an exceedingly bright dog." She would not shut up about that dog, Pozzo had the heart of ten thousand dogs, she was a dog of priceless merit, a saint was dear Pozzo, I was getting nowhere at all with my questions,

What were you doing walking that road, where were you going, where do you live, only drunken idiots and hapless soldiers ply that highway, here, drink this water, it's a furnace out here, forget that damn dog, How dare you say that, go away.

The vehicle the trio inside had arrived in, boasting Oklahoma plates, was a tired-looking heap with little to say for itself. It was pocked with rust, dotted with dirt and insects, but I didn't see anything indicating it had slammed into a dog. Boxes on the backseat seemed packed with baby clothes.

The troopers were leaving. It's vamanos time, they said, another search for that dog and we are done around here. As for Doc, they say, his body is ready for release, you can pick up and bury the bastard anytime you like.

The sky is a stagnant unknowable blue.

Sara Mago, waking up, groans, "I dreamt someone was nuzzling me." She stretches those arms. "The men in my life," she says, "beep-beep, and they're gone. After I've drunk all the liquor in this world, after I've smoked all the cigarettes, after I've gone to bed with all the men in the world, then maybe I'll be happy. I dreamed I was in a big field containing nothing but empty sacks. I opened one of those sacks and a dead man jumped out shouting in a strange language. Then all the other sacks opened and out jumped—"

"Don't tell me," I said.

Sara Mago can feel in her haunches the smallest shudder in the earth's core, the smallest shift, plates rubbing together, teensy rupture fifty miles beneath the earth's crust.

"I need to wash my face," she says.

Beep, beep, she's gone.

"We will have that soup now," the booth woman says. Her voice is bright and cheerful, a marvel to behold.

Out in the desert wastelands a solitary figure was on the move. Not fast, and not without difficulty. It seemed to be coming our way on three legs. Now and then for long moments it tumbled over and disappeared, becoming as one with the rippling heat.

A dog. It would be needing water.

Maggie Dwyer

CHIHUAHUA

Paul Boudreau unlocked and carefully opened the door to his bachelor suite. The small square of cardboard he had placed in the jamb fell to the floor. Good. No one tried to bust into his crib. He unpacked the contents of his plastic bag of groceries: a litre of 2% milk, a loaf of day-old, sliced white bread, two apples, a box of Kraft Dinner, small jars of strawberry jam and instant coffee, and six eggs, and set them on the narrow wooden shelf that served as a counter. That stuff had eaten up most of the ten bucks the padre loaned him. Things cost more at corner grocery stores than at the supermarket but he'd wanted to check out the neighbourhood. With a flourish like a magician, he smiled a small happy smile and pulled a package of bologna and another of tea bags from inside his bomber jacket. Presto! It was easy to lift things from Mom and Pop stores. That old Chinese guy didn't see nothing. Paul would lay money on it. He made sure he told the chink he was renting a suite from the New Path Ministry people.

~~~

The New Path was an inner city congregation whose members were among the city's most disadvantaged. The pastor offered counselling, a map of the path to eternal salvation and low-cost housing. The housing was in an old building bequeathed to the church by a long-departed congregant; a dark brown brick three-storey block that had the words "Maple Leaf Apartments" cut into the Tyndall stone lintel over the centrally placed front door. It had looked fine when the original tenants took up residence in June of 1940. The building was set back from the street behind two spindly elms, each surrounded by a parched square of browned grass. The pastor had the building cut up into bachelor suites and set up his office in the bedroom of a large suite on the first floor. His assistant, Martha Wiebe, managed the building from her station in its former living room that did double duty as a meeting room in the evenings.

How do we deal with the world, asked Pastor Martin Kroeker. Straight up, answered his congregation. Okay by me, thought Paul. He was good with New Path. He always worked out the rules on the first day at a new place. Found out right away who to suck up to. His story this time was that he was a construction worker, had been up in McMurray where he got messed up; he was off the booze and pills for a year and a half. Told the padre he needed to take a meeting right away. He liked the way you could drop in to the Double A. Any place, any time. It was a good way to get connected in a new town. There always were a few rounders in the crowd. You could see their shaky hands trying to hold the Styrofoam cups of coffee steady.

He couldn't get his issue from welfare for another three days so Martha Wiebe gave him the address of a food bank where he could get help if he ran short after using up the pastor's ten dollars. She got him to sign for the keys to his crib and handed him a copy of the New Path rules.

She was about the right age, he thought, as he watched her fat white fingers write down all his fake info. Over fifty. Plain face with a tiny squashed nose that looked as if it had been stuck on to her round face in a hurry. Her blue eyes were soft behind thick glasses and her dull thin brown hair that she tucked behind her big ears had no curl. He looked at her hard, wondering if he would see the sign he searched every older woman's face for: a flicker of recognition, an acknowledgement that, yes, she was the crazy one who bore him. His own Mommy. He belonged; he was claimed. He hated all of them.

Sucking up to the good folks at the soup kitchen on Hargrave was easy for him. That's how he'd met up with the padre. He was trawling for lost souls at the soup kitchen and Paul didn't mind pretending to get reeled in. He did need the safe comforting arms of Jesus. He had to keep a close watch on his cash and he was feeling pretty low in himself. He wanted to move on but he had no ride now.

～

The old man's classic '66 Dodge Polara was his inheritance. Paul's sole earthly possession. His last foster dad, Charles Hardwick, told him that he would give it to him, when he was sixteen. So, when the old guy up and snuffed it, he went back to Nanaimo for the funeral. Ha, ha. He got into the house and took the keys when she was away at the church. He left that punk-ass town in style. The widow so upset that she did not even report the car stolen. The old tea bag didn't have the nerve. The old man had told him at least a hundred times that the car was going to be his. He couldn't take it over when he turned sixteen 'cause he was already inside for setting fires. And that was no accident. Stupid sorry ass little fucker Brad Weston ratted him out.

Charlie was the only one who'd believed him. Patricia Hardwick didn't. That's why he always went back when he got out. To see Charlie and check up on the old bitch. After Charlie had a stroke, he didn't trust her to look after him good enough. And he was right. What he found the last time made him mad. She should never have left Charlie sitting out for hours on that crappy little glassed-in porch tied in his chair. It was grey and rainy every fuck-ass Nanaimo day. And that made the porch cold and dark as the hole. He swore he would have carted Charlie off with him right then but he knew he couldn't change his diaper. They'd both hate it. Besides, she had an orderly come twice a day for that.

And he was so pissed with her whining that he didn't go to Charlie's funeral. Why would he, after the way she kept on ragging that it was him coming back into their lives that sent the old man into the hospital where he croaked. That was a lie.

He wasn't sorry to leave Nanaimo. It was the armpit of the Island. Forget parole. Fuck that shit. He did his time and he was a free man. The Dodge had flown along the #1 highway like Charlie said she would. Only took him two days to make Winnipeg from Vancouver. He really poured it on until he got here. She was rust free, a two-tone beauty. Steel-blue top and sky-blue bottom. Winnipeg seemed safe enough. He didn't know anyone and no one knew him.

He heard about Winnipeg from Pedro Fehr, his cellmate from his last bit. It had been Pedro's idea; he'd said it would be easy to cross the border there. He drew Paul a map of a place where he used to cross the border near Gretna and gave him a phone number to a cousin in Altona. Pedro said then you drive straight south to Dallas, then turn west to San Antonio, and keep on a-comin' to the Mexican border on the Rio Grande. He said the police aren't looking for people trying to get into Mexico; it's the other way round. And once you're down there, it's easy to, like – disappear. He'd snapped his fingers. Paul was going to hook up down there with Pedro who had some good plans for them. They talked about it every night when they bunked together. Lots of people there working with the Mexicans and getting pretty rich. Pedro had cousins there and these cousins had a farm where they made cheese way out in the boonies that they could stay at between jobs. These dudes called themselves the Fehr Trade Dealers. Besides the cheese, they were dealing coke and had good connections. Pedro said it was near Chihuahua where they invented those cute little big-eyed dogs. Maybe he'd get one. Paul always wanted a dog but none of the foster homes would let him. If he had a little dog, he could take it with him all the time. Call him Mickey the mouse dog. Carry it in his pocket. Mexico. He was going to see lots of different shit there.

Nobody'd told him that this flood was coming and it fucked him up. He had to sit tight. He still had 583 of the 800 dollars he took from Patricia Hardwick's secret hiding place behind the glass-fronted case that held Charlie's war medals. Served her right. She was the reason that Charlie never adopted him. He heard them quarrelling about it. That's why he'd never said the name Dad to Charlie out loud.

WW II. That war was about the only other thing they talked about. And Charlie didn't say much about that. You don't know what it is to kill a man, he'd say. Charlie had been a gunner and was lucky enough to survive. Almost intact, except that, as he would say, he could no longer live up to his name. Couldn't get his wick hard anymore due to unspecified damages. Gave my all for King and country, he'd say. That's why they took Paul in. Always wanted a son. Got a lot out of the war, he said. High blood pressure, trouble in the water-works, and the France-Germany star for his trouble.

Why did that girl refuse? He'd thought she'd wanted a hot sexy time. All her talk about vampires. He didn't fuckin' get it. She started off real friendly at the coffee shop and, like, she talked so wild. Sitting close with him in the back seat of the Dodge, she traced the outline of the small triangle of beard he left unshaved below his lower lip with her round silver tongue stud. It felt cold and smooth. She said she liked doing it. He was cool. Like the Beats, she said, naming Kerouac, Cassidy, and Burroughs. He had no clue what she was yakking about. He didn't give a flying fuck. He'd just wanted was to get into her pants.

After he got rid of her, he'd started driving east again on the old Canada #1. He didn't even know why. He freaked out when he saw a RCMP cruiser that stopped a pick-up truck on the shoulder near the turnoff south to Steinbach. He'd tightened his grip on the Dodge's big chrome steering wheel. Fuckers'll have me down next, he thought. There was nothing but the CBC coming in on the old AM radio and he couldn't stop thinking what a fuck-up he was. No wonder old Patsy wouldn't agree to adopt him for real. Seven years he lived with them. He hated every one of her tight grey curls.

He'd never meant to do the girl like that. He picked her because when she smiled she smiled a little like Linda who was his first. She lived two streets over from the Hardwicks in Nanaimo. She was pretty and a hot little thing at seventeen and she took him into her bedroom any time she wanted it when her fat mother worked evening shift at the hospital. Linda was nice to him. Sometimes, after, she made him some food or they went for pizza. They planned to go to Vancouver as soon as he had his sixteenth birthday at the end of December, but by then she'd died from meningitis that got in her brain. Pedro told him that in Spanish *linda* means beautiful and that's when Paul started thinking of her sometimes again.

Why wouldn't she open her legs and get it on? He wouldna had to hit her then. He didn't want to hit her. He didn't mean to hit her. Only when he saw she was afraid, he'd got mad. Now he was in for it. If they got him for it, he'd be back in the joint in the range with the heavy dudes. Lifers. Some fucker was gonna want his pretty ass again. Or the Native guys would get to him. No way. No fucking way.

He was sweating heavy now and tightened up inside himself like a spring. Same as when he first got in the joint. Trouble could come from any side. He was watching everything along the highway. Snow was bad. Coming thick and fast, whiting out everything in front of him. And he was tired from being up all goddam night hiding that girl. Why'd she go with him if she didn't want it? The weather forecast said it was going to develop into a blizzard. He couldn't see for the white shit. Had to drive real slow. He had the map spread out on the seat beside him. He saw that where the highway widened out close to a place called Richer, there were old roads leading off from the wide median. He followed one in and found some gravel pits and parked beside an old metal gate. He got out to stretch his legs and breathed in cold, fresh pine-scented air. The heavy snow cover muffled all sounds from the highway. He saw a red-tailed hawk circling widely above. Didn't it know that it was too early to return from the south? He thought of sitting it out there but he was hungry and right pissed off. The cold was too bitter for his thin old leather jacket and the Stampeders cap he lifted in Calgary. He had on his Western boots and leatherwork gloves that were some better for snow. Not good enough but he hadn't planned to stop anywhere this friggin' cold.

He hated to leave his wheels behind, but now the back seat was covered with a sickening mess where her blood froze on the upholstery. He had chipped away at it and a fair bit of the frozen stuff lifted off. It was like pale pinkish ice. The outline of the stain was faint. He wished he hadn't made such a mess getting her onto the tarp. He'd never get it all out. Charlie would be furious if he knew the original upholstery was ruined. He always kept his ride in mint condition.

He dug a crescent wrench and a screwdriver out, removed the British Columbia licence plates, and hid them in his toolbox. Maybe he'd get a chance to come back for his Dodge before anyone else found her. How else was he going to get to Chihuahua? He wiped his hands and his hammer off the best he could, using the snow beside the car to scour them clean the way he and Charlie used to clean their dishes with sand when they went camping. He scooped up more snow and scrubbed his face. The cold sting was good and Paul felt more awake and freer than ever.

He picked up his toolbox, walked out to the westbound side of the highway, and headed into the blowing snow. It was a goddam cold hike and there wasn't much traffic. Lucky for him, after twenty minutes he came to a crossroad with a gas station that had a café. He ordered a hungry-man breakfast plus coffee and a side of fries with gravy.

He remembered the girl had asked him what he liked for breakfast.

"Special K," he answered.

"Yeah." She felt his right biceps. "You like to lead a healthy lifestyle. I could tell that from your great build. I bet you work out every day."

"Yeah," he answered. There was lots of time to bulk up in the joint.

She didn't know that his "Special K" meant kentamine. The cat tranquilliser. The breakfast of champions at Oakalla. He was one more a-hole in the k-hole. He did a lot of drugs there, everybody did, to cut the boredom, shorten the time. As a good-bye present, his bunkmate, Pedro had given him some of his stash of special little white pills. He said to slip a couple in some bitch's drink and you'd get a piece of ass real easy. Said it was way better than booze. They don't remember nothing. Not your name. Nothing. So you never have to pay for it. And pork her once for me, Pedro said. In five weeks he'll be out, getting his own.

Paul paid for his breakfast with some of the money he'd stolen from her little purse. Thirty-two dollars and 83 cents she had. Besides her wallet, he took her driver's licence and university I.D. card, because it had a photo of her smiling nicely, and the keys to her apartment.

Paul had been sure he'd get to screw her. They'd left the coffee shop and he drove them out to the ruined monastery she wanted to see. He got her into the wide back seat of the Dodge. No problem. But she didn't seem to get stoned the way Pedro said she would. Maybe she hadn't drank enough of her spiked coffee. Or he didn't wait long enough.

She'd said it was too early for sex and giggled in a high-pitched nervous way. It was still daylight. She started to fight back when she felt his hard bone. He tried holding her down but she was a wildcat. Tried to bite. He got her tight by the hair with one hand. She was screaming and kicking with her feet at the frosted-over windows. He was the only one who heard her. He slapped her hard on the mouth, then reached down to the floor for his toolkit and got his hammer out. He wanted to show her he meant business and she had to give it up. She looked really scared and put her hands up over her eyes like the old bitch, Patricia. Cryin', whinin' no, no, please, no. His eyes turned a hard blue metal. All he remembered was a brief steely flash, a glint that barely registered. She saw it coming. She had it coming.

He pulled open her clothes and looked at her. Red blood was running out of her ear, down her neck and onto her chest. Her brownish pink nipples looked soft. He touched them. He sniffed at her bush. She smelled pretty clean. A little tangy from the fresh piss that she wet in her panties. The hair was way lighter than her black head hair. He liked her smell and her warmth now that she was quiet and he came all over her cunt hairs. He had his mouth over one of her nipples when he did it and he bit down hard. Then he bit the other one to even the score. He remembered it all real clear.

He was way lucky to get back to Winnipeg on only the one hitch. Right outside the café he got on with a big old motor-mouth dickhead trucker in a Freightliner who was on his CB radio the whole way. If he wasn't on the radio, he was yakking about the storm coming up out of Colorado. Ever been through the States? I been to every one of them at least once, 'cept Hawaii. They say the roads are bad going south today. You're not dressed for it, is ya? The guy looked over at Paul's leather bomber jacket and ball cap. It's not too bad now, the guy said, but the temperature's going into the toilet again. She's going to blow hard. Damn hard. I can't hardly believe you're out here on foot. And all's ya got are them cowboy boots? You sure lucked out when I come along. I pulled outta Thunder Bay at eight this morning. Knew I had to lay the hammer down to get to the 'Peg before night. We are in for a good blow, I can tell. Our house got swamped in the 1950 flood and I know what a bitch Mother Nature can be. She's goin' on one hell of a tear today. I'm taking my rig off the road. Gettin' on home to hunker down.

Paul didn't have to say much. He had him a chance to think about his next move. He gave the trucker a sob story about hitching in from Kenora. Said he was going to help his grandmother sandbag her little house.

Where is she? Over in St. Boniface? I thought you looked kinda Frenchy. Fantastic, the guy said. I can put you down right on the corner of Fermor and St. Mary's Road. We'll be there in twenty minutes. You'll be almost on her doorstep. Say, does your grandma make an apple pie?

She might. How'd I know? I never even met her, thought Paul. She might.

Man, you are one lucky son of a gun.

You betcha.

I guess I am, thought Paul.

He dropped out of the cab at a red light on a busy corner. A bus marked #16 Osborne came along to that corner within five minutes of the trucker pulling away. He hopped it because the girl (she told him her name was Georgie, but he wanted to think of her as the girl) said, she said something about living near that coffee shop in the Osborne Village and he didn't know fuck all about Winnipeg. He took the seat behind the driver so he could read the street numbers. They were way to hell out. He felt easier when they passed by a pub on a corner he remembered seeing from their drive out to the old monastery. He leaned over and asked the driver how much farther to the Osborne Village. Comin' up in ten minutes or so was the answer. The bus rolled on past miles of three-storey apartment blocks, the usual fast-food places, past donut shops, gas bars, 7-Elevens, through an underpass, and up into the heart of the city.

Paul stepped off the bus and into the same fancy coffee shop where he picked up the girl. No donuts here, so this time he took a blueberry muffin with his coffee and went over to sit on a stool at the counter in front of the window. This was good. He could watch the door and look out the window at the intersection easily. It was a pretty busy corner for the middle of the day. He watched people going in and out of the drug store, the bank, and the liquor store. No one noticed him. The daily newspapers were on the counter so he looked through them. The news that the coming storm was set to hammer the Red River Valley shared the front page headlines along with the report of a Native kid who got swarmed and curb-stomped in gang-related violence. Singer Joni Mitchell found her long-lost daughter, born in Toronto in 1965. No mention of a girl's body buried in the snow under a railway bridge.

He picked up a bottle of rum at the liquor store across the street and asked the smiling security guard he saw outside for directions to Roslyn Road. Incredible fucking luck. It was one block away. He headed for suite 14B, 21 Roslyn Road. It was a huge red-brick pile with turrets like a fortress and a green tiled roof. He slipped in the front door. It was so easy he was laughing to himself. A young couple, both thin, both dressed completely in black, passed by without looking at him. Fucking amazing! He found her apartment on the wing to the north of the central courtyard and, like she said, looking over the river.

Once inside, he set his tools on the doormat, locked the door from inside, put on the chain, then eased his wet boots off, and put them down on the mat. Fuckers were leaking bad. He was gonna hafta spring for new ones. Shucked his coat off and hung it on the inside doorknob. Jesus fucking Christ, he was cold, hungry and tired. Lucky to be in where it was warm and dry. He took his bottle out into the kitchen. The girl had some Diet Cokes in her fridge. Lucky for her because he was going to be in a bad mood if she didn't. He poured himself a big drink and looked through the fridge. There was some leftover rice and other Chinese-type vegetable shit in a takeout container. Yoghurt, apples, wilted lettuce, carrots, brown bread, wrinkled potatoes with sprouts growing out of them, five eggs, skim milk, orange juice, tofu and cheddar cheese. She must be a goddam freakin' vegetarian.

He found a pepperoni and cheese pizza in the freezer. Bingo! Not a vegetarian! He hucked that into the oven and went to sit in the living room. He had a second and a third drink. He was hungry waiting for the pizza so he rummaged through the fridge. He was really blasted on the rum and that felt fuckin'right, eh? He bit off a big chunk of her cheese. It was good. Cheddar. He chomped up about half the piece while the pizza cooked.

The ceilings in her apartment were very high and the wooden floors creaked with every step as he explored. If she had some cash hidden around the place he was going to find it. There wasn't much furniture in her living room. A smallish red velvet couch with carved dark wood feet, a 1950s brass floor lamp, an old TV sitting on the floor, and travel posters of some sunny beach stuck up on the wall. There were cold ashes in the old-fashioned green-tiled fireplace. In the bay window overlooking the river, he saw a birdcage draped with a piece of blue cloth embroidered in gold with some kind of foreign letters. Maybe like Russian or something. He lifted the corner of the cloth and saw a little blue-feathered bird cowering on the floor of the cage.

"Hey, birdie," he said, "Polly want a cracker?" He made bright chirping sounds and the parakeet took its bill out from under its wing. He spotted a package of birdseed on the window ledge and filled up the empty plastic dish that was fixed to the wire side of the cage.

"So she's got you in solitary, in the hole. You poor little guy, you need water too, don't you." He carried the tiny plastic water basin to the kitchen, filled it, and carefully replaced it in the metal cage.

"Here you go. Let's see how you make out with that. Eat up, fill your belly, damn you, I want to hear you sing for your supper."

Her bedroom was a real mess with clothes piled so high up on a chair he couldn't tell what colour it was. He found this disgusting. He could never live like that. He remembered how he learned young that he had to keep his bunk neat. A miniature dragon with a red bead in its mouth was sitting right in the middle of her dresser. He picked it up and thought about snatching it, but the little sucker was heavy. It was metal not china. He put it down. She had made her bed; it was a futon, covered with a dark blue comforter and some frilly pillows and stuffed animals. One of those Indian dream catcher things of yarns and feathers was hanging on the wall over the bed. Looked like an old spider web. Lots of Native guys he knew in the joint had them. They grew their hair long and got into that sweet grass mumble bullshit.

There was a dark wooden desk and bookcase on the opposite wall. Most of the books looked like they were for school: *Introductory Psychology, Bury My Heart at Wounded Knee, Anne of Green Gables, An Actor Prepares,* and *Introduction to Cultural Anthropology.* Nothing he'd ever heard of. He picked the last one up from the top of the pile and flipped through the pages. That was enough to give him a headache. Mostly writing, but with pictures of freaky people and stuff around the world. He reached over, turned on her computer, and watched it boot up. A picture of Tom Cruise dressed in a vampire cape came on the screen and a dialogue box requesting her password appeared. He didn't know fuck all about getting past that so he went to check on his pizza. The little blue bird was cracking open the seeds now and Paul thought he looked a lot happier.

Some of the melted cheese had dripped on the oven racks because he couldn't find a pan. The pizza smelled great and he managed to get the thing on a plate and hack it into four pieces. He carried the plate and another drink into the living room and put them on the floor in front of the couch. He put on the set and surfed through the channels until he found *The Simpsons.* Paul watched that dumb asshole Homer fuck up again and scarfed down the pie. The dirty plate got dumped in the sink with the crushed Coke cans and he was so blasted he pissed over all of it. His bottle was almost empty and he was close to crashing. He felt great.

He pulled down his zipper of his jeans and loosened his belt buckle, being careful not to unfasten the silver earring with its pink stone that he'd pulled out of her pierced navel. He fell asleep on her bed, rolled up in her comforter. It was early but he was used to early nights.

He almost shit himself when he woke up and saw where he had crashed. He thought he heard a knock at her door. Was it morning or night? The bedside clock read 10:55. A brown velvet stuffed toy monkey with a red plaid vest and a black bow tie was sitting beside it. The monkey seemed to be grinning at him. He reached over and cuffed it, knocking it to the floor.

There was another knock at the door. The second knock was louder, more insistent. His heartbeat sounded so loud in his ears it seemed like it was about to jump out through his chest. Sharp prickles heated up his armpits.

A woman's voice called out, "Hey, Georgie, are you home? It's me. Chick. I saw your light on when I walked home last night. You sick or something? Why didn't you come to work? I froze myself coming over here lookin' to find you. Listen to your answering machine. I called you three times. Bruce is scorched. He's pissed about the storm 'cause he couldn't leave for Hawaii. And millions of people didn't return their freakin' tapes on time. It's hell out here. You might get fired. Call me. Later. At the store. After three. I'm working late tonight, covering for you. I said you asked me to. Don't forget. Call Chick."

Paul felt in his pocket for his blade. Still there. The clock on the bedside table said 10:59. A.m or p.m? He heard her footsteps go trip-trapping down the hallway. He hunkered down and stayed like a stone until the hot prickling in his armpits stopped. No more sounds came from the hall. Fucking head was aching now. And he needed to piss.

He skated softly in his stocking feet down the hall to the can and took a long piss in the bowl. A steady dark-yellow stream. He blinked at his reflection in the white-framed mirror fronting the medicine cabinet over the sink. Same old badass there. He sniffed his armpits. He was rank. There was a showerhead on a rubber hose coiled around the taps of the old relic of a tub. He stripped off his shirt and turned the water on. A weak spray gurgled out. Not worth getting wet for. He walked over to look out the window. It was all white. He could see the back end of the Legislature building across the open river. The snow was falling thick and fast. The wind swirled it into drifts that covered the streets. A lone taxi rolled over the bridge in the tracks made by a larger vehicle. He was relieved to see that taxis were running. He could call one from the pay phone back at the corner.

He put on the TV and flipped through to find the weather channel. He kept the sound down low. Severe storm warning continues, said the printing at the bottom of the screen. Travel not advised, said the announcer on the CBC. Chaos in city streets as drifting snow blocks traffic. Thirty-seven inches of snow has fallen so far. The airport remains closed until further notice. Anyone with a four-wheel-drive vehicle is requested to call the nearest police station to volunteer for emergency services driving. He turned the volume down low and walked away. The one smart thing he'd did was to move her. The snow would bury her and keep her hidden there for a while. It would cover up the mess she made out on the ground at the old monastery when he'd moved her out of the car. Her blood spread out around her head like a fiery crown on the snow. It was snowing. Fucking A. Give him time to figure out his next move.

He decided not to take a shower. It would take for fucking ever and now he was thinking if he should get a room somewhere or head for a shelter. There must be a Sally Ann in this town. There were homeless and rubbies everywhere. He really didn't want to bed down with the Lysol and hairspray crowd but he had to watch his cash now or find some kind of work. Not what he had in mind. He was supposed to be on the way to Mexico. Wished he'd headed there a week ago. He had no driver's licence, and no ID that wouldn't bring him a hassle at the border. He'd hidden his parole papers in the bottom of his toolbox and carried the social insurance card and birth certificate he bought from that biker dude in the bar in Nanaimo. He needed a name he could get over the border with, be on his way to sunny Mexico and Pedro's farm. No *problemo*. Julian Russell. That's what he had to answer to. Buddy guaranteed him this Julian fuck died as a baby. Who's the dickhead calls a kid Julian? Assholes! It was a hassle driving around without a licence.

He should have headed south right away. Not east. Fuck what Pedro told him. He'd heard the bikers say that there were lots of back roads in BC that you could slip over the border on. And keep on driving, straight on through to Mexico. This was a total fuck-up. He liked boosting stuff. That was ace. Gave him a buzz that pumped him up. That little bitch made him off her and he hated her for it. The whole game was changed. He didn't want this. He never meant to kill her, for fuck's sake. He'd just wanted to get laid.

Paul stared into his own not so true blue eyes in the mirror and asked himself what the hell he was doing here in the fucking middle of the whole fucking country. He felt it, the hate rising in his gut like a river in flood. He pounded a good hard right shot straight at his reflection and hit the mirror dead on. His hand was on fire and blood was running back from his bitching fingers. He smiled at himself. He mouthed the word asshole at himself. Said softly out loud, "You are one stupid asshole." He cradled his whole forearm in the tiny sink, and ran the cold water over it until it numbed.

He eyed his hair. It was shaggy shoulder-length at the back and short at the front. Hockey player hair. It would look better cut short. In the joint guys grew it long for many reasons. Like the 'skins, they get into having it in one long braid, but for him, it was pure laziness. Outside, long hair was more noticeable. He looked in the medicine cabinet for scissors. He found a pair of manicure scissors and started to cut his hair off at his ear lobes. He dropped the wavy dark-brown hanks into the toilet bowl and flushed each time the surface of the water became covered. It took a while because he had to cut it in small sections. The result didn't look great. He couldn't see the back. He wanted to shave his whole head. Better wait 'til it warms up. The tiny triangle of beard he left directly under his mouth looked really stupid now. The girl didn't have any shaving gear in her cupboard. Stupid bitch. Didn't she know he was gonna need it?

A large colour photo of the girl standing with a man and woman on either side of her was hanging on the wall opposite the mirror. In it, she looked about twelve years old; she had on a Native Indian costume and feathers in her braided hair. He thought maybe it was from Halloween, but they were standing outside somewhere on grass that made it look like summer. He'd never a guessed that she was a breed. Too pale. He thought maybe she was French. She did look like the mother, but the guy seemed too old to be her dad. All of them were smiling. But the girl was the only one who looked happy.

Paul went into the kitchen and looked through the fridge again. He took out the eggs, milk, orange juice, and brown bread. He dug around in the cupboards for a pan and fixed himself a plate of breakfast. She didn't have no coffee in the place. He thought about washing the stack of dishes piled up in the sink and then thought better of it. That'd be too much like work and it wasn't like she'd ever notice anyway.

He sacked out on the couch again with his legs hanging over the end, thinking about what to do until it got dark enough for him to leave. He had to be pretty fucking quiet but he was used to that. Used to minding his own goddam beeswax. That was one of Charlie Hardwick's favourite sayings. Shame he had to miss the old man's funeral. Next time he saw a Legion Hall he promised himself he would go in and hoist a few beers in memory. Charlie would like that.

He fell asleep on the couch until he heard the phone ringing. The room was in shadows. He listened as the answering machine picked up the call.

"Hi, Georgie," said a soft male voice. "It's Uncle Markie. I thought I would find you snowed in like me and the rest of the city. Wanted to know if you would pick up a couple of movies, come over, and keep me company. I have some of that great takeout butter chicken that you like from the Taj. Haven't seen you in a while. Wonder where you are now. Call me when you pick up this message. Okay. Bye, bye."

Paul went into the bedroom to check the time. It was 4:57. Late afternoon, like he thought. He picked up the little stuffed monkey and grinned back at it. He carried it down the hall to the front door and set it on his toolbox. Time to check out of this crib.

The place was a lot messier than when he arrived, but the only clean up he thought about doing was to go around and wipe his prints off everything he remembered touching. When he was on a job, he always wore gloves but this was different. He didn't plan on ripping her off for any of her junk. He gave more seeds and water to the little blue bird and covered him up again. That might not last the little guy very long, he thought. He dumped the rest of the box of seed out along the window ledge, turned back the cage's cloth cover and opened the small wire door to the tiny cell. He never heard the little bird sing or even chirp. He decided to leave the girl's ID and keys on the table beside the bed. He tucked the little toy monkey inside his jacket, then closed her front door quietly and headed down the stairs and along the street to the 24-hour drugstore to find a pay phone. *Chihuahua, chihuahua, chihuahua,* he chanted, digging the way it sounded. *Choo, choo.* Like he was a train gathering speed.

Jane Eaton Hamilton

THE NIGHT
SS SLOAN
UNDID HIS SHIRT

SS Sloan oared behind Dame Judy Westwood while she read, stroking the millpond under pointillist willows in his paint-peeling pink skiff, a straw boater tilted precariously atop an electrical socket's worth of white wild hair. Blue shirt, dandy-ized trousers, one bare foot that I had oft-tongued draped across the gunwale.

The audience looked from the Dame to Sloan like fish leaping to hooks. It was his stone millhouse, his backyard, his river, his eponymous literary festival.

Spindle-shanked Sloan, scraggy and skinny and nearly seven feet tall. My SS Sloan, mentor and I suppose muse and, yes, lover. I had been on him about this year's festival after six Sloan Festivals to which I had not been invited, and he had, while nude and boozed, capitulated because of my novel, *Perch*, finally out from a small press. Sloan recognized the edge of first-book hysteria in my voice, and he knew that like any writer I was only ever ten fingers from a tell-all, so he added me to the schedule with Dame Judy Westwood and eight other CanLiteratis, our own diminutive murder. Never mind I was noted on all the posters as Annum, not Annette, Mockford – that was assumably a typo.

It was because of Sloan my work had been noticed to begin with; because of Sloan I had been netted up into anthologies, because of Sloan I wormily worked my way up the hook to my paltry book deal. SS Sloan, saw-toothed scalawag, scamp, rapscallion, scholar and teacher. He recently turned 50, with 50 or so mid-list books, and if no one exactly praised his literary prowess, they did praise his literary output-put-put.

On the millpond, Sloan unfolded like Gumby. Though I rather imagined him pitching into the drink, he had his footing; he poled laconically behind the Dame, thunder behind her dull cloud. (Even in bed, Sloan was a scene-stealer: I unfolded my orgasm like origami while he came in a cataclysm.) The scene was pretty; romantic in the September sunshine – the Dame's cultured voice, the boat, the trees in full leaf, the mist coddling the skiff. I sat up tall on my knees so that Sloan might see me. I'd been expecting him at my hotel the night before. While other writers I should have met congregated in the bar, I waited in my room, fish-lipped with Restylane, dressed and coiffed and laid out corpse-stiff on the shiny, slippery bedspread, the TV muted lest I miss my cell or Sloan's big-knuckled knock. I still had a fresh, fishy need for him. I was a walleye zooting across our pond, sending up humiliating thought balloons – *notice me notice me notice me.*

When SS Sloan first found my work in his wife's slush pile, he telephoned, scratchy with passion for my work. He was putting together an anthology! These, these, but more! More poems! Stories! Did I write novels too? "I've sent your work off to Martin Todd, my co-editor, and he agrees. We want to devote a significant portion of the upcoming *Toronto Island Anthology* just to you," he said. "You write like the fins of a flying fish."

(It was months before I paused to wonder.)

"I'll take the story, of course, and your poems *Schooled: The Mackerel Verses*. Maybe *The Electric Yellow Bass*. I could publish *Salmon,* but it's not your strongest. Will you write something else for me?"

"Yes, yes of course," I said.

Finally he said, "I have to come and meet you. Are you home Wednesday?"

I had to go to the library to discover just who, exactly, SS Sloan was, since I had heard his name but knew scarcely more. They had 14 of his books on the shelves, poetry and collections of short fiction and novels which I checked out. I haunted anthologies. I read biographical articles and discovered that he had been married 25 years to Gertrude Lennox, head of the determinedly feminist *Ms Morphic* magazine, that they had three grown children and two grandchildren, and that he had received several awards for mentoring young writers, but never an award for his writing, that the inaugural Sloan Literary Festival was the following fall. I checked the first two editions of the *Toronto Island Anthology* and found luminaries from New York's *86th Street* litmag. I munched through Sloan's works like a beaver. There were only a couple of pieces that brought down trees – a story of a boy and his milting father, a poem about guppy reproduction. But I was still gaga at the sheer numbers of his books, his longevity. I could build a whole lodge with just those, praying the water, Sloan, stopped where I wanted it dammed up, at me. I was new and naïve and had sharp teeth.

On Wednesday, SS Sloan slid from his cramped Porsche in my driveway and unfolded like a hickory tussock larva. His eyebrows caterpillared up his forehead on wiry white legs.

"Annette?" he boomed, waving, tilting forward. "Annette Mockford! Is it you? Is it really you? Why, you're as lovely as your poems."

He picked me off the ground and spun me around, cocooning me in silken arms. He was so tall that when he pulled me in for a hug my chin skimmed scarcely higher than his belly button. It was like hugging a branch. He took my chin, smiled down at me. "You are such a talent, Annette. Have you the faintest notion?"

I looked up, way up.

"You don't, do you? How utterly, adorably charming."

Not two hours later, as night fell, I clambered across his bony lap into bed. Not two hours after that, I insisted to myself that it must be love.

"Salmon-chanted evening," I said and smiling, I sighed. "Should I call you SS? What does it stand for?"

"Simon Scott. Or nautically speaking, Single Screw."

"'Naughtily' speaking?" I asked. I reached for a cigarette. "Please don't single screw me, you know, just for the halibut."

He laughed and tickled my nose.

After that, I wrote as I had never written before, stories and poems and then, in an ejaculatory spurt, the no-see-ums, deer flies, tiger moths, that would eventually form the backwoods milieu that was my novel, *Perch*.

Sloan was my eager guidance counsellor, my guru, my cod-father, and I submitted to the dangling lure of the thick blue pencil that rose between his thighs. His was the first eye on every of my manuscripts. ("Annette, you've dangled some participles here. Annette, you're using passive verbs. Annette, have you earned that metaphor?") In bed, we would catch up with what he called litsip – who was getting published where, even though they didn't deserve it, who was known to have chosen her best friend for first-prize winner in what contest, who was suspected to have made up the blurb that appeared on his back book cover, whose editor had actually written the entire of her book, who wanted to sue whom and for what. Indeed, it turned out that CanLit was a catfish-eat-excrement business.

The affair with Sloan was as good as a lottery win. I came out in the anthology and then, like dominos falling, in several others edited not only by Sloan but also by others. I sent work off to Martin Todd at *86th Street* itself, and though he had co-edited anthologies with Sloan which I'd been in, it still came back with just a friendly "Sorry" handwritten at the bottom of the rejection slip (and these rejections I framed and hung above my desk).

I couldn't write a sentence without passing it by Sloan. We spent countless afternoons tucked into my lumpy bed with my manuscripts finned out around us. We smoked, we dribbled red wine onto the ripply waves of the bedsheets. I expected he would leave his wife.

He didn't leave his wife.

And finally this year, he said, "I don't know if I can do this anymore, Annette."

"Well," I said, "do let minnow."

He began to publish other younger writers, while I stormed with jealousy.

"Sloan," I said the next time I had him in bed, his attention wavering, "Sloan! Sloan! For heaven's sake, do you need a herring aid? I need you."

"Annette, darling," Sloan said at last, wearily, "don't you see? They will suspect us if I don't cast my net a little further."

I did get that I could only have Sloan sometimes. I sent him love letters through his publisher. On weekends, I drove five hours to mass at his millpond, to watch through the window as Gertrude marked papers. Of course I attended Sloan Festivals – every year – but seemed far from getting the prized invitation to the yearly wrap-up extravaganza. I was forced to stand outside as Sloan and his wife entertained in yellow light.

I sucked up praise like a carp sucks up silt, every slim sentence of kudos generating a need a thousand times its length.

Feed me, said the greedy voice inside my gut.

Say it again.

Say it harder. Say it a little to the left.

Would you like me to sign that anthology for you?

For Julia. Just because. Love, Annette Mockford.

Say I'm the best. The best you've ever read.

Tell me you cried.

(Annette Mockford hearts Annette Mockford.)

The less SS Sloan wanted to do with me, the more I dreamed of his hands flying over the keyboard spelling out: Clitoris "A." Clitoris "n." Clitoris "n."

I was years away from publishing my first book before I was tired, tired not of writing but of the evidence of my own ego, that swelled leech that throbbed and bled internally. I was fatigued from self-googling, something I did furtively at my desk every night. I was middleaged, a mid-list writer, a proven mediocrity, a has-been before I had made it to an is. Perhaps worse, given I'd given my all to Sloan, I was a fish without a bicycle.

The reviewers were not particularly kind:

Annette Mallard tries hard to write like Dame Judy Westwood, but trying hard is obviously not enough.

Annette Mallard's story Viperfish *is a creek running through a hazmat site.*

I hung about under the surface of CanLit, lapping at the surface, always on the lookout for the bug, the lure, the fishing fly.

What's that? You like the writer standing next to me? Why, thank you very much. Thank you indeed.

Excuse me? You admire a writer who has my initials? Another Canadian writer? A writer from my time zone? I'll take it, thanks. Wonderfully good, thank you. Thank you, thank you, thank you.

And then, this spring, my novel appeared. A reviewer said, *Reading Mockford's* Perch *is like trying to dive into a wading pool.*

A line of poplars waved tiny green parasols. The river coursed by. I had just finished my own reading, having chosen a chapter from *Perch* where my protagonist, a fisherman, is diagnosed with colorectal cancer. By the end of my allotted time, people were leaving. As Don McIntyre took my place, I knelt behind a girl taking notes. I was able to read over her shoulder that I'd been boring. The 'i' of boring was dotted with a heart. *Colorectal cancer? Mockford's mediocre.* But she had asterisked me. I followed a fat arrow down her page. *"Buy her book!"*

There was a polite smattering of applause for Don McIntyre. I waited for Sloan to find me. It had been, if I told the cod's honest truth, almost two months since we'd slept together. I wasn't seeing anyone else. Over the years, I had sent Martin Todd three anthologies I'd been in, but hadn't heard a word in reply. I caught a bus back to my hotel to change for Sloan's after-party. I fussed with my nails, my hair, my make-up. I was still ready an hour too early. I lurked for a while in the lobby, hopeful, but after the 30th time I'd checked my cell and the fifth time I'd asked at the desk whether there were any messages for me – any phone calls? Faxes? But could you check, maybe, for a FedEx? I stopped by the bar for a fortifying shot of gin.

A girl sidled up to me, a slip of a thing not five feet tall or 20 years old. A book – *my* book, my over-fried *Perch* – pressed tightly between her palms.

I had not known the sides of my lips could touch my ears.

"I just wanted to tell you how much—" Here she leaned forward and I could see fully half of her stunning breasts. "—I admired your book."

"Thank you so much for taking the time to say so." *May I throw myself at your feet? May I nibble your feet with my mouth? May I give you next month's rent money?*

"Wou – would you sign it for me?" She thrust it towards me.

I took the wretched disappointment into my hands. There were, within it, at least two typographical errors and a single error of fact. The cover had been a complete rout – the colours muddy, the image (of a coiled rope and anchor, but it resembled nothing so much as an intestine) blurry, the font, Abadi MT Condensed Light, prissy and unclear. SS Sloan had blurbed the back: "Mockford's novel is a great fish story." I took the girl's proffered pen, moved my drink, lay the book open on the tiny bar table, smoothed its pages open

– they shone like scales. I did so admire pristine books…even this one.

"To whom shall I address it?"

"I'm Pauline Dark. You might have heard of me? I'm about to come out in *86th. Street*?"

I looked up at her. *86th. Street?* Was she kidding? But no, I realized she wasn't, and that actually, I had heard of her, Sloan himself had mentioned Martin Todd's new Canadian find.

"And in SS Sloan's new anthology?"

No! No no no no no! I had submitted two stories and had them shipped promptly back by some underfin underling.

I slashed the pen through my printed name and with a flourish dedicated and autographed.

Pauline Dark did not move after I had returned the book. I gazed desperately around the bar for help.

"Don't you just love that guy? Isn't he, like, *such* a Canadian idol?"

Sloan? Didn't I just love him? I had loved him in most of the positions of the Kama Sutra. The man definitely had groupers.

"And Martin Todd, too. He's gay, but he's something, isn't he? Didn't you love *The Magnet*?"

She paused. "He asked me down to NY and took me to dinner after he accepted my piece." She called for a crantini and sipped it through her young lips. "But he's not as nice as SS Sloan. Did you know SS stands for Single Screw?" She giggled. "Sloan is wonderful. Sloan is fantastic. Sloan is—" She smiled shyly and ducked her head. "I guess you can kinda tell we're sleeping together."

I almost choked on a pretzel.

"Oh yes!" she bubbled. She wore a whale pendant; the fluke fell into her cleavage.

Keep your anemones close, I thought. I rolled my eyes as if I knew something about him that she did not, as if to give her the idea that I was an insider. Much more of an insider than she, since, after all, on numerous occasions I had stuck my finger up his ass. "Tell me more."

"Not— You?" Her hair was razored to the side of a very small head, and her nose ring caught the light.

"No," I said quite firmly. "Not me. Never me. But there have been, I understand – others. A great many others. Schools of women."

"No. He swears this is his first affair. He is going to leave his wife." She looked at me. "He is!" She said she was a BA student, and just about to declare her major, which she now understood must be – must be because of *Sloan*! – creative writing! She now understood she, like Sloan, had a novel in her. More than one novel. Two novels. Five novels. The world was *actually* a novel, didn't I see? Well, of course I did see, didn't I? She held up my book as if she'd won a contest.

I was a tiny bit drunk. "Stop being so shellfish," I said. "He's married." It sounded cold and moralistic; I attempted modulation. "It's sexual harassment. He shouldn't have seduced a student." I added, "Another student."

"Not hardly," she said and snorted. "It was all me. Well, okay, *and* him, but, like, I wanted him to."

I wanted him to, I repeated to myself. *I wanted him to, I wanted him to.*

She put her hand on my wrist. "Ms. Mockford, Annette, that's the thing. I, that is – I hadn't figured out who I could tell. And then, well, I heard you read at the festival, and I realized that you were bound to know him, SS Sloan, since he blurbed your book, so you might be, uh, friends—"

"After you, it will be some other vulnerable fishlet, and after her, some other." I stirred my drink with my finger, then sucked gin from it. "We women must swim together. We women *writers* must swim together."

"No, no, that isn't it. It's just—" Her cheeks were the colour of a red snapper. Pauline brightened. "He says I'm very talented. I mean, Martin Todd said the same thing, and, well, between the two of them? Sloan says he hasn't seen a writer quite as – *original* – in many years." She pulled her shoulders up around her neck and beamed.

"But you can't want to make it as a writer, Pauline, by sleeping your way to the top? What self-respect would you have?"

"Oh no, Annette. You don't get it. I mean, yeah, Sloan and I are having sex, but my work is *separate*. He hasn't *hurt* me, Ms. Mockford. I mean, sometimes he ties me—"

I waved my hand, dug in my purse for a twenty. There were literary types passing through the lobby. "I'm sorry, but I have to get to the party. I'm already late."

"Say hi to him for me, okay? Get him alone and tell him I love him. I do. I really think I'm in love with him."

"You're not in love with him. You just want him as your mentor, and I urge you to go to your faculty advisor at once. I can't say this strongly enough." I left her in my wake.

I was in a most foul mood when I returned to SS Sloan's. I came upon Dame Judy Westwood nursing a sore ankle in Sloan's den, and cast my name at her.

"Well, young lady," she said, looking up at me above her glasses, "if you have anything you feel compelled to say to me, do it now. There is bound to be a lineup later."

The thing had just started and I'd already haddocked enough. I found a washroom, sat on the toilet and fanned myself with the new issue of *86th Street*. I flipped through to see which fiction writer had won the issue's lottery, whose story was included, and was nonplussed to see it was the much-dead bard who once had written of the invasive New Zealand mud snail. One of his *undiscovered stories*. I had written about fisherwomen – what, really, was the difference?

As I slipped from the safety of my refuge to begin hunting down Sloan, a girl stopped me. "Annette Mockford?" she said. "You're Annette Mockford, aren't you?"

I nodded.

"I'm Sole Duvet. Know how I know you?"

She was eager, bright, I would give her that. I shook her proffered hand.

"You were part of that anthology launch at Tide Gallery where I launched my novel *Morphing*. The same day, afternoon to my evening. People who meant to be at my launch ended up at yours by mistake."

I'd like to clean the scales off of Annette Mockford's Perch, said *Toronto Today*.

Mid-summer, and except for Sloan himself in his nautical whites and blues, all the writers, me included, wore black. My need for Sloan shivered raw in the thick, firefly-lit night air, wiggling like a dew worm, gyrating like bait on a hook.

An older woman came to stand beside me. "I'm Gertrude Sloan. I don't believe we've had the pleasure."

I've had many, many pleasures with your husband, though, I thought. She was as short and fat as her husband was tall and lean. I shook her hand with the fingers that had masturbated her husband.

"I was interested in what you read today. My husband was right about your talent."

"Well, thank you," I said greedily.

"Did you know I'm the editor for *Ms Morphic*?"

"Of course, yes. I'm pleased to meet you. It's lovely of you to have hosted this party."

"Sloan found you in my slush."

"Not on porpoise," I said. "You have a really lovely home. I'm sure I'll never read anywhere as beautiful again. Your husband has been very kind to me."

She said, "He *is* a character."

"They broke the mold etctera," I said.

She met my gaze, touched my arm. Her eyes were soft, green, watery. "Well," she said, "at least we can be thankful for one miracle."

Gertrude and I turned for a second to look at SS Sloan. We turned back to each other to speak of other matters – the heat, West Nile virus, the mayor, the utter impossibility of heating their old stone house if the price of gas rose.

There was a sussuration, a stir, ripples on a still pond.

In the arched doorway, a white silk scarf thrown around a wattling neck, was the *86th Street* editor and writer, Martin Todd. I recognized him at once.

"Martin Todd, in person," I breathed.

"In person," Gertrude repeated. She squeezed my elbow. "No, wait. *Is* he a person?"

"Is that his wife?" I said.

"Leslie," Gertrude said. She put a smile on her face, raised her hand and bustled towards them.

I drank glass after glass of Sloan's plonk until I had screwed up courage to wiggle through the school of Martin Todd's devotees to give him a tug; I had the book published, now, after all; I had earned my spot. But the ambience shifted. Todd had actually left, it was whispered. Todd had excused himself. He had a private matter to take care of before he and his wife drove back. Yes, tonight, to Saratoga Springs. Yes, near Yaddo.

I ran to Sloan's staircase. Where had Martin Todd gone? I looked around but did not see him. I slipped outside. I don't know what I was thinking – that I could waylay Todd and convince him to read my novel, to excerpt it in *86th Street*? There was no one around. The night had grown cloudy, but it was still humid and hot. I went along the road. The streets were deserted. The volunteers had finished with cleanup – the only sign there had been, just hours before, a literary festival was a stack of brochures tucked beside a heap of green trash bags at one street corner. The road veered sharply to the right. I crossed a one-lane bridge that arced over the little river, stopped at its apex to listen to the sounds of merriment from Sloan's place. I kept going under Victorian streetlamps.

I came to the banks of the millpond. It was now very dark, the moon snagged behind clouds. Reeds and bulrushes dotted the shore. A bat looped, scalloped wings briefly outlined against the white sky. I heard something, some odd noise like catfish gulping, and slipped behind a tree trunk. The water was murky and still. I could just make out a ladder leaned up against a barn to my right. I saw them before I identified who they were – two figures, the first bent over and clutching a rung, the other behind, rutting.

It was SS Sloan's hair, wild white hair that cinched it.

SS Sloan was pronging Martin Todd. SS Sloan's shirttails jumped like dolphins. His pants were a puddle around his ankles.

I got green shivers.

It was intolerable to be inside my own body. There were exclamations of arousal, grunts. I had an urge to dash forward and slap Sloan's buttocks. I suppose I must have loudly moaned, because just as I stepped out from my hiding place planning to turn away, both men swivelled to look at me. I met Sloan's panicked gaze first, and then, for the first time ever, I locked eyes with the distinguished, illustrious, powerful, married, closeted Martin Todd. As he was being fucked up his ass.

They were very near climax.

"Annette!" Sloan yelled and pulled out, put-put-putting all around the paddock.

Todd approached me with a plate of strawberry shortcake heaped high with whipping cream.

I accepted it.

"I'm Martin Todd."

"How lucky for you," I offered coldly. I resisted the urge to praise his work, to tell him what a fan I was.

"I'm a heel, Annette."

"Pond scum," I agreed. I tined a strawberry and pretending it was Sloan's heart, consumed it.

He put a hand on my shoulder. "Your story 'Octopus Rex'?"

He had my attention, though I pretended nonchalance.

"We'd like to make an offer."

"We?" I said.

"*86th Street.*"

"*86th Street* wants to publish me? You've rejected everything I've ever sent you. You rejected 'Octopus Rex,' in fact, just a week ago."

"Rejected it? I'm sure not."

"I received a rejection slip. A blanket rejection slip."

"In error, my dear girl, I assure you. We have any number of college students working for the magazine, and so naturally, sometimes…" He paused. "We will want some minor changes to the text, of course."

"Naturally."

"I do value my marriage," Martin Todd said, his lips glubbing around each word.

"I'm certain that you do."

"I will call you next week, Annette."

I nodded.

He stuck out a hand. "We have a firm deal, then, the two of us?"

We shook on it.

Sloan approached me, steering me by an elbow away from the party to the damp grass by the prow of his pink skiff. "I'm sheepish, Annette."

"You're a little late to be saying this now, Sloan. I should tell Gertrude."

His nose tip quivered.

"I ran into Pauline Dark today. Is there anyone you haven't fucked?"

"Who on earth is Pauline Dark?" He seemed genuinely not to know.

"I mean, anyone you haven't fucked *over*? I should tell the Dean." I had a sudden crick in my neck, from staring up.

"Space has become available in *Ontario Anglers*, Annette. I was planning on coming round the hotel tonight to let you know."

"Stuff your bloody anthology up Todd's behind, Sloan."

"Don't, Annette," he said, touching my arm, electrifying me. "Don't do this, I beg you. I need you onboard. Let me come see you later."

"Not tonight, Sloan. Really. I've got a haddock." I flounced away.

I should've gone back to the hotel to gloat, but stayed, God forgive me, I stayed and watched Sloan get drunker and drunker, which was like hearing a very tall tree bough crack off a tree in the wind. Mucid, fly-blown, contaminated SS Sloan. Feral; glottal-stopped; frenzied. His voice was a gong, his arms Big Bens of oversized motion. Plethoric exhibitionist who would have been laughed out of any other arena but literature's.

He stood on his porch bellowing. My hair was zinging in the current. A story about a no-talent writer who tries to sleep her way up the ladder rungs. Her name was Seine Fockman. Everybody was watching me, even Gertrude, with her eyes darting back and forth between us, her hand over her heart. As Sloan read, he ripped open his shirt button by button, top to bottom. Irascible, choleric, stumbling with drink, he several times lost his place and picked up from somewhere altogether new, but linearity scarcely mattered since Seine Fockman not only had my career, and my looks, but my bad literary luck and my exact skills – or non-skills – in bed. A fireball cackled out along a live wire; I might as well have been standing in water.

"Sloan, don't, don't." Gertrude tried gingerly to interrupt, to lead him away, but he swatted at her. She pulled at his shirt, but only succeeded in pulling it down one white-skinned, flaccid arm, so I could see how old he actually had gotten. He swayed on his size 14 feet like a bottom-weighted frigate.

"Don't you like my story?" he slurred to everyone. "Don't you like my festival?"

He caught my eye.

"You!" he cried. "You're a bloody *mediocre* writer, Mockford. You never were any good. You never will amount to *shit*."

"When did you write that?" I demanded, stepping forward. It had to have preceded today. Now I was yelling, arms in air. "When did you write that?" On his chest was a whale pendant identical to Pauline's, which I tried to rip off of him.

He tugged his shirt free. Then his pants fell so that his boxers, awash in fishing rods, puffed out over his grey-haired stick-insect legs.

Martin Todd came out on top. So in a sense did I, though I was embarrassed a good long while.

Of us all, only SS Sloan was devastated, when the video of his strip appeared, getting hundreds, then thousands upon thousands of hits. Pauline Dark brought the man up on charges; Gertrude left him.

I should know more, of course, I should have some better, longer denouement to offer, but lately I have not returned SS Sloan's phone calls.

And nobody else has, either.

I don't know what comes next. It probably involves a flounder. On a dock. Beyond that, I don't want to know. I just don't want to.

Lisa Pike

STELLAS

There's not much to think about once she's dead. Just that it's two more weeks till the end of the month and that the cheque should come on the 18th. There's still unpaid bills from last month but it should be okay, they're both on the account. Her Canada Pension is 800 and the Old Age Pension 500. Plus the 400 dollars widow's pension that Henry never thought well enough to sign her up for – Stella and Judith talked about it so much it sometimes seemed they actually had it. "Even though I looked after him all those years, cooking and taking him to the doctor's every week to have his blood checked, making sure his blood thinners were alright so's he wouldn't have another stroke. If I'd a known I wasn't even on there as his wife, I wouldn't a done it, believe me! He coulda found somebody else to do all that for him," Stella would always say.

The VISA bill would have to be foregone, its minimum payment far beyond what Judith could ever pay. Months of not making any payments at all, not being able to spare any money until the weight of the phone calls became too great – calls at dinnertime just when the two women were trying to relax, put food in their mouths, the moment when they wanted still, in some small way, to nourish themselves. Golabki, sauerkraut and kielbasa, bigos – or hunter's stew, if it were winter. The apartment faced the Detroit River and even though Stella always did want to live on Riverside Drive, it was too noisy and it was always 8 or 9 degrees below the temperature anywheres inside the city so they always suffered the cold. And the dampness. But neither one wanted to move or could afford to. It was enough to complain about it.

Judith had finally started putting $25 a month on the VISA and the line of credit; it would never address the thousands of dollars now and the more than 85 years the statements kept saying it would take to pay it off at the current rate of 21.8% a month and at the minimum payment now up at near 1700 dollars. "But I didn't use it to go on a vacation! I used up that amount to pay for my other bills! Heat, water, electricity!" Judith would shout when she was still getting tangled up in the conversations the creditors wanted to have to make her feel like a bad person, a failure, a loser in life. "I had kids to think of, you know! And now, I've got my grandmother to take care of. What do you want me to do? Shoot her?"

"Oh, you don't have the money?" said the last snide young man in his 20s, living off his parents' money or still in their basement, Judith thought, though she didn't bother getting into it with him. And then, there were the others. People in their mid-30s or early 40s incredulous at her situation because it did say "Dr." on her file. How did they get that information, Judith some time ago wondered – she certainly didn't go announcing herself as "Doctor" everywhere she went. What would be the use? Doctor of Philosophy? Who the hell understands that? It must be because of the student loan she finally (and correctly) decided. She had to provide proof every year of her enrollment and when she finally graduated and had no more proof to qualify for the 8% interest rate, they must have looked at her status and decided that she must now be a

Doctor. The client now had a PhD – time to flip that up to the regular interest rate of 21.8%.

Judith remembers Noam Chomsky, the famous linguist and cultural critic, coming one year to the university to talk about student debt and how people were enslaved for the next 10, 15 or even 20 years of their life, unable to ever be free enough to participate fully in society. The Marxist idea of the wearing down of the worker, he'd said, only this was the wearing down of the intellectual, of those people who saw the bigger picture of things, of how things might be changed, how the world might be improved in ways that had nothing to do with money. How PhDs were now living on food stamps and that pretty soon the universities themselves would become creditors, joining the banks in a variety of partnerships. Donations, sponsorships which finally led to ownership. The University of Toronto, for example, with the Scotiabank Information Commons Computer Banks put in the library during the late 1990s easily imaginable as the beginnings of Scotiabank University of Toronto. Or perhaps Toronto TD University, the more logical pairing since the logo was already so similar – that kind of austere formality hearkening back to pride in British imperialism and all that.

But that was so long ago and so far removed from Judith's present life. At least the theoretical aspect of it anyway – the call for change, resistance, the kernel of Chomsky's lecture. The pragmatics of his prophecy, she was indeed living. Sometimes when she and Stella were sitting outside on the second-floor balcony of their apartment having their morning or afternoon cigarette, the old woman would sum it up nicely by saying on the exhale of a long, thoughtful drag: "Well, I'm really disappointed with this whole school thing."

The only thing Judith could do, really, was to warn her own kids when it came time to go to university. Help them choose programs that could potentially lead to a job and show them how not to get bogged down and caught in the machinations of the corporate university. The idea of higher learning, enlightenment, of the phrase which still called out from behind the ivy – The Truth Shall Set You Free – carved in stone, a mere marketing tool now with no hope for anything more.

~~~

The sour-cream dough has risen in the old woman's bowl. Judith takes it out to knead before working it into a long coil to lay on the floured surface of a baking sheet. Then she begins to form it into balls. At intervals of six, she flattens them down slightly, flours them again, and piles them one on top of the other so that they all fit in the palm of her hand. Folding fingers down and pressing as the dough circles move clockwise round, they are flattened out enough to start to make the sweet pierogi. Sometimes Judith makes them with *powidla sliwkowe* – plum butter jam – inside, but the old woman likes these better. Sugary and sweet, the plum still whole but soft inside the boiled sour-cream dough.

Judith puts the dough circles aside and washes and dries the last of the plums. She will make the usual two dozen, slicing each plum lengthwise to remove the pit and then filling each empty cavity with a quarter teaspoonful sugar before returning the two halves together. Each of these will find a home in the centre of one of the small circles, the dough folded over carefully and the ends pinched secure with thumb, forefinger, and flour. One dozen for the freezer, one dozen split fresh between them; Judith likes hers fried in a bit of butter, the old woman likes hers boiled. A bit of granulated and white confectioner's sugar sprinkled over all.

Leon. That was the thing that split the two Stellas apart for good. Judith had dug up some of the old photos just the other day when they were reminiscing over coffee after cigarettes smoked standing just inside the screen of the sliding glass door to the balcony. Sitting in front of the old wooden chest where the old woman liked to keep all her pictures. Since Judith had moved in, Stella had spent a number of hours putting batches of them into the extra large Ziploc freezer bags they got on sale one day at the Price Chopper up on Tecumseh Road near Fontainebleu. At first, she was doing it all secretly, grouping pictures together without telling Judith why. But once she started writing family members' names in her scrawl of blue ballpoint ink, Judith understood that this was part of the unspoken project of the bits of masking tape torn from the roll kept in the kitchen drawer under the dark brown aging microwave beside which her grandmother faithfully kept, for some unknown reason, two flyswatters of orange and bright green plastic. Judith moved the flyswatters to a spot under the sink daily, a spot beside all the cleansers which was, of course, more hygienic, but each day at some unspecified, hidden time, Stella always moved them back. The two women never spoke of this, just as they never spoke of the bits of masking tape stuck to all manner of objects in the small two-bedroom, fourth-floor apartment in Harbour Tower facing the Detroit River. Bits of torn tape with the same blue ballpoint ink and scrawl of family members' names: Wanda (daughter), Bob, Louise and John, Larry, Walter (nephew), Stella (great-grand-

daughter), Judith, Lucy, Maudie and others. Everything par-
celled out so there wouldn't be any doubt as to who gets what.

Even if they used the platter with the blue roses, faded now
into a teal green after decades and decades of use, Judith would
find a new bit of masking tape with the name Wanda (daughter) written on the back if the old one had fallen off in the
process of washing, drying, and putting it away. In all truthful-
ness, Judith thought the platter should go to her. And not
because of the plain fact that it was she who actually cared
about the old woman and took care of her in her old age, but
because Judith was the only person who knew the stories.
Bothered to hear them and remember them, fix them in her
mind in the same way the old woman had them fixed in hers.
"Partners in crime!" Judith often said to people in the elevator
when she first moved in with her grandmother after her two
kids finally left for university and Judith had, in earnest, begun
to accept that she'd probably be living the rest of her life on disability. Wanda (daughter), of all people, did not deserve the
worn, discoloured, beautiful rose-patterned platter with the
two deep chips on the right-hand side. She didn't even bother
to know or remember her great-grandmother's name, the original owner of that platter. Madeleine. Madeleine Mokriski.
(Judith always felt bad that she didn't know Madeleine's
maiden name, but then again, neither did the old woman, or
she couldn't remember that far back.)

Leon had come up in a few of the pictures. One at a Legion
Hall table with Judith sitting squarely on Stella's lap, smiling
for the camera. "It'd be okay if we cut that part out," said Stella,
without mentioning anybody's name or why "we" should get
up to go get the scissors to actually do it. Then, in another,
when Judith finally got up the nerve to say: "Who's that man

hugging me? He sure looks happy," Stella said: "Oh. That's Leon."

For years Judith had called that smiling face the mystery man, not wanting to probe around in that period of everyone's life when Stella finally divorced. Judith had been content to simply think of the mystery man as one of her grandmother's boyfriends before what everybody called at the time her "new" grandpa – Henry. Henry seemed okay to the eight-year-old Judith – he was tall and dressed well and liked to do things like wash his burgundy car and build whole barbecues out of brick around which people would drink and eat. Henry seemed okay, but Judith always hated how the new replaced the old and how talk of the real grandpa and who he was, and what he'd done, and how he, finally, after the divorce, wound up dead, all, quite abruptly, went underground. The only signs of the past were brief eruptions from Stella, often incomprehensible because of the non-sequential ways in which they were told, or because of the ways they were immediately shoved back down from where they came by still years-angry listeners – her children.

Judith's mother had sometimes held the others at bay and this is how Judith got any details she had, and living with the old woman, struggling along after her own divorce and the bad luck she'd encountered with the whole school business, not finding a job with so much debt after her nervous collapse and months of hospitalisation, Stella warmed up a bit to speak things, at least sometimes, in their coherence. That, and the fact that she felt time was running out anyways, so why not?

"That is going to go by my tree," she'd say, holding a ceramic angel that sat on the cabinet beside the door to the apartment where she and Judith always left the keys. There was a piece of masking tape underneath the base of the angel announcing this as so. "I already had it planted, and paid for the plaque that says: '*for my dear children.*' They don't let you plant it by the headstone per se, but off to the side down the path. It's not far. The casket's paid for. I already went down there last summer to meet with the girl, I don't remember her name, the old one was Janet, I know that. She's the one that arranged for the tree, where it would get planted. I got the kinda casket you can burn 'cause I'm gonna be cremated too, just like your mother." And this was the real problem, the real dilemma that faced her now, Judith thought, picturing the old woman there on the bed where she'd gone for her usual after-noon nap. How could she deny the woman the fruits of all she'd worked so hard to plan?

The water boils and Judith adds a bit of vegetable oil to the pot so the pierogi with the plums filled with sugar won't stick to each other. She follows the old woman's ways now without questioning. The little things are there as they've always been – the small ceramic pig that sits atop the edge of the control panel of the old stove, its dials of metal and plastic, the wish-bone of a roasted chicken bought already-made from the gro-cery store drying in the crook of its little brown and pink perked-up ceramic ear. This has always been so, Judith remem-bers without thinking. The plaque nailed to the wall just above that, a bit grimed-up from the steam of food cooking – World's Greatest Grandmother, the ribbon attaching to the nail faded. When they boil to the top, floating, that means they're done, the old woman had said thousands of times. Judith puts in only three at a time because the pot is small. The slotted spoon is the one made of plastic, chipped and cracked, that the old woman refuses to throw away. Judith has been meaning to buy a plain metal one from Home Hardware and simply replace the broken one with that, the latest act in their string of unspoken exchanges.

~~~

The road to the two Stellas went back before Leon or Henry or the first grandpa. Back to the open fields of Morris Place and wooden walkways in front of weather-worn houses (their screen doors with holes), streams and the road that was lined so well with chokecherries, bending down together to collect them in the gathered-up parts of your skirt. The road to the two Stellas went back to Sundays with heavy glass Coke bottles and store-bought ice creams, pictures taken standing amid fields of chest-high poppies, dresses bought to match and a pair of shared shoes between.

The road went back to the mothers' (sisters') wombs, putting forth the two Stellas (cousins) just three months apart. "We were more than cousins, we were friends!" Stella would say to Judith as they looked out onto the Detroit River, the old woman getting up now to straighten out the plants in the white plastic swan planter at the edge of the balcony after she'd finished her cigarette. "Would you just look at that!" Stella would continue, her arthritic hands fingering the dark purple petunias with that mild look of disgust Judith knew so well, *"The wind just whips the life right outta them!"*

"We'd go see Jean when we wanted to know something, though. She was already married so she'd tell us the things we wanted to know. A course, you wouldn't dream a asking Mother anything like that! Finally my cousin Stella went to Dr.

Stewart down on Rupert Street. He'd do anything you asked. It was pregnancy, a course, that you had to worry about in those days – you didn't dare do anything that would risk you gettin' pregnant! So Stella thought that would be a good idea, going to see Dr. Stewart. A course, later when she married, Larry was wondering why they weren't having any kids. But she never told him what she done. *Why should she anyways!"*

Judith had, in fact, been hearing a lot more about cousin Stella since she was dead. Her grandmother would go on about the funeral, who was there, what was said, what everybody ate and wore. "Stella looked real pretty. She had on a blue dress and inside the casket was that pale pink rose-coloured satin. I wasn't sure if I should go. Even up until I was drivin' there in the car. I thought everyone might see me and think: *Oh well, what's she doin' here now?* But they didn't. They were all real nice to me. There was a lunch too after the service, but most everyone's gone now. Even Chuckie. Died last year and I didn't even know about it. I really liked Chuckie!"

And if Stella wasn't going over the details of her cousin Stella's service, she was contemplating the events leading up to it: "Well, she was in a nursing home but the family didn't want her there. She wasn't doing good there at all. So it was Chuckie that said maybe Marian could take her since she didn't have any kids. So Marian did take her. And that was good of her to do that, a niece and all. She even took her to Florida one year on vacation. Stella had started with the Alzheimer's then too. When she'd get real bad, Marian said it was like a devil was inside her and she'd have to get real firm with her so she would stop and that devil would get cast out."

Leon treated the two Stellas equally well. Leon in his dark blue polyester pants, white short-sleeve pressed cotton shirt and his genuinely kind smile. If ever there were a second chance in life, it was to be found in Leon. And this is what each of the Stellas knew because each of them had married and divorced badly, as Judith's grandmother liked to phrase it. "Marrying Larry was the biggest mistake of Stella's life! One time he beat her up so bad she nearly died. Tossed her when he was done on Auntie's lawn. Marian was telling me too that at the end, just before the Alzheimer's set in, she was living with some guy who didn't treat her well at all. Now, why would she do that at her age?"

Stella had asked it as a favour, the other Stella meeting up with her date Leon. "Stella, do me a favour. Go down and meet Leon 'cause I have to work an extra half-shift and I'm worried he'll be sittin' there all by himself, not knowing where I am. I tried callin' but he's already left. Could you would you do that for me?"

"Of course I can, *Stella*."

Leon's mouth down there on her so soft.

No one had ever touched her like that. Not rough and scratchy and greedy and hard. He did it soft, careful and gentle. And it wasn't like he was just somehow slowing things down, some sort of variation for variety's sake. No, no. It was like that's just how he did it no matter what. Soft and careful and gentle. Tender.

"Come here Stella," Leon said when he was done. Sitting there on the edge of the bed now, feet on the floor, holding his arm out to her, inviting her to climb on top of him. He was sitting facing the large antique dresser with the round mirror. Stella looked at him there, waiting, his words and tone not saying at all, "Come here because I want to fuck you in front of this mirror," but rather, inviting her in, telling her, "Please come, fall on me and I'll hold you while we watch ourselves…" And the feeling that he could do that, hold them both safely. The tattoos on the insides of both forearms he'd gotten before leaving for the Army, shipped out of St. John's, somehow adding to this feeling of security.

How they'd moved together on the bed next to the night-stand with the small black and silver alarm clock and the lamp with the light-green coloured glass ball just above the switch, he on his back, uncontrolling, giving into whatever she might do, want. Then when he'd somehow moved everything so that he was on his knees pushing hard into her as she lay on her back with legs, calves resting on each of his shoulders, and she'd started to cry, he just stopped. Pulled himself out of her, brushing her hair gently back to say: "Hey, it's okay," look-ing on quietly now as her cries turned into heavy sobs. Who would want to give up that! That was worth having, fighting for even, wasn't it?

"Where are your towels?" Leon had said when they were done.

"In the cupboard in the hall."

He'd gotten up to go to the old wood door that always stuck and took one out. "There, we'll get you all cleaned up," he'd said as he wiped the cum off her stomach, hip. And then: "I should go. Wait. *You want me to stay?* You'll feel too alone? Okay, I'll stay, but I snore so that might keep you up. I don't know if that's what you'll want, to be kept up all night."

"Of course I can meet him, and will, Stella," Stella remem-bers saying, the smell of sex on her fingers and the aftertouch of Leon's mouth still there between her legs.

~

Judith stares at the pot of boiling water, waiting patiently for a few of the pierogi to begin their ascent to the top. The fan with the filter that still needs to be changed whirs along the best it can and from the corner of her eye Judith sees that light in the corner curio cabinet, filled with a Christmas tree somehow made out of multicoloured plastic beads and safety pins, is still on. The funeral itself, Judith didn't attend. She didn't have it in her to accompany the old woman, and this was something that Stella, for some reason, understood. It was that period when Judith was becoming so obsessed with small things, like change. Pennies, to be specific. She had set aside a special zippered compartment in her wallet just for them. Pennies from the good years. The ones she wanted to keep, hold on to. Judith was aware that this would be seen as odd so she never bothered tell anyone but her grandmother about it. She'd stand at the counter of somewhere, a store, out to buy cigarettes or escape the apartment for a while, to go have coffee at the Tim Hortons on the corner of Chandler and Tecumseh, looking across the street at the field of the Catholic school, where she was baptised *Most Precious Blood,* while sipping her coffee and reading one of her books. While she liked mostly to reread the books she already had, she had taken to letting a few new things in, mainly fiction. Like that crime writer she'd recently discovered, originally from the Ozarks. The Ozarks with their rocky paths, streams and hidden caves, seems like you could bury anything out there and get away with it.

In the time it took for Judith to scan her pennies for their dates, she would make offhand small talk with the cashier and pretend that she was searching for the precise amount, like she was taking all that time to do somebody a favour. "There you go," she'd say, "a dollar sixty-five exactly," giving all the bad years away to the cashier. "I hope you like pennies!" Sometimes the cashier would engage in the small talk, smiling, taking the change and saying, "Thanks for that, I really was getting low on coin," but mostly they'd just take it, polite but indifferent. Judith knew too that when things were kind of bustling or busy, the time it took to sort out her change started to annoy those people in line behind her. But ever since she had started to live in the world again after her nervous collapse, this sort of thing didn't bother her. In fact, it was like it didn't even exist, other people and their preoccupations, worries about being late for some thing or other they deemed important but wasn't.

The odd time she came across a few good nickels, but she didn't spend a lot of time going through them like she did the pennies. Only if they really caught her eye. Pretty much any-thing from the '70s could be considered good and when she got one of these or a few at once, it would be a matter of reflecting on the individual years themselves for particular memories of her life. 1974. The first memory of consciously writing her name beside the date, focusing and concentrating hard with pencil in hand over the open ruled notebook her grade one teacher Mrs. Copage had given everyone in the class in September. 1977. A good year just because of the way it sounds (that and the fact that double 7s are always lucky). 1975, nice because it was situated right in the middle of an overall solidly good decade, and anything from the early '70s was worthwhile because of the free warm summers of being a kid, running around, the feel of bare feet on the cement of a sidewalk, grass and then sidewalk again. Chasing, being chased, long hair hanging down loose, soft baby curls growing into straggly little-kid hair knotted in places, and falling out of lopsided plastic baby-blue and white butterfly barrettes.

Late '70s, riding your bike alone or with friends. Falling down and scraping your palms and knees. Getting back on. The sting of being alive on your skin. Judith had mixed feelings about the '80s, though for the most part she kept holding onto them – the '90s and anything in the 2000s was unloaded onto the cashiers. Sometimes there were special coins that came her way. Pennies from the 1950s. 1953, the year her mother was born. And anything from the 1960s was worth having. Sometimes Judith's little zipped pocket in her wallet bulged too full of the good years in all their varying degrees, and she was obliged to take some of them out, putting them in a small pile on the left-hand corner of her antique wood dresser, right next to the picture of the real grandpa the year before he wound up dead.

"Even when Auntie was dyin'. Well, she wasn't dying per se, she was in a coma for eight years before she finally died. I'd go up to the hospital to see her, sit with her a bit, and if Stella came in I'd just leave. So we avoided each other like that. There was the times we'd see each other in the grocery store but we just pretended not to know one another. I didn't have nothin' to say to her and she, well, she'd never bother offering up an apology for what she done. I really liked Leon and she knew that. But it was really all those lies she told about me to him that I couldn't ever forgive. Then when Marian called me up to say: 'Aunt Stella, Aunt Stella's been asking for you. She keeps saying, 'Marian, I'd really like to have a cup a tea with Stella, please call her will you?' But she lost consciousness and I kept delaying. It was on the Tuesday that I finally bought the red rose to bring over to her. But I was too late. When I called Marian to say I was comin', she said: 'Auntie, you're too late, Auntie Stella just passed away not an hour ago.' So we missed each other. Even if she did come to visit me. I heard a knock on the door and when I opened it, no one was there. *So I guess she came to say goodbye since I didn't go to her."*

Judith lifts the two pierogi out of the pot with the broken slotted spoon and adds two more while waiting now for the third one to rise. She puts them in the large clear wide-rimmed bowl that has served up countless salads for family gatherings back in the day when people still gathered. Oil and vinegar to coat the torn leaves of green, bits of raw broccoli, chopped tomato, cucumber, radish, red or green onion, and then small cubes of cheddar cheese. Coated and salt-and-peppered and set on the table alongside the dressings that everyone likes: Thousand Island, Ranch, Italian, Blue Cheese, Raspberry and Poppy-seed. When all the pierogi have been cooked and put in the large clear bowl that can still hold so many more, Judith shuts off the stove and empties the small pot of water into the sink. She grabs her cigarettes and white plastic lighter with the dice on it off the top of the brown microwave with the flyswatters tucked along the side to go out on the balcony, alone. She watches the cars go along Riverside Drive as they always have, day and night. In her lifetime, anyway. She looks at the river as she and the old woman have done so many times over the years, the two of them together. The sliding glass door to the apartment has been left open. Judith scans the apartment: the corner curio with the light inside that the old woman liked to leave on at night, the cabinet with all the items that nobody wants after she dies – the little Asian girl dressed in pink on her knees with flowers in her hair; the little red and blue Dutch girl with the glued-on head; the Christmas tree made out of safety pins; a set of ceramic containers with an orange and brown mushroom for a top handle sitting on an angle; a fake golden clock with a little crystal heart in it that dangles above the words *I Love You*, all things bought at the dollar store or five-and-dime if they were old – the sofa and matching loveseat facing each other over a small table, whose base is made out of ceramic birds and a clear glass top; Henry's painting above the couch that was really an oil landscape done by his first wife who had died so young from asthma, leaving behind a small child that Henry had no idea what to do with; and the embroidered picture of *The Last Supper* that one of the daughters-in-law had made to try and quit smoking sometime in the '70s, under which Judith always puts the new bills in the order they need to be paid. The purple petunias ruffle in the wind behind her as she steps over the threshold of the balcony door.

Judith goes to the closet in the bedroom that was extra before she had to move in. She takes out the flannel sheet with the small dark-pink roses on it. It is ripped on one end but like so many things the two women continued to hold onto it because it reminded them of better times. Judith, of her childhood when her grandmother would take care of her, tuck her into bed on those nights when her mother was in some undefined place and she would have to sleep over. Stella, of when she was a middle-aged woman, young strong and competent, the start of a new life after her divorce. The sheet smells of her grandmother: fresh laundry soap and Downy softener, the musty smell from her knitting and crochet books that have been stuffed in a box in the back of the closet along with her canister of needles, and the soft smell of smoke that has drifted from the spot overlooking the balcony to find its way here. Noam Chomsky smiles out at her from the cover of his seminal 1989 work *Necessary Illusions* that Judith always keeps placed right beside the framed photo of the children on her small bedside table.

As she walks on the cream-coloured plush carpet toward the old woman's open bedroom door, Judith begins to feel it coming on, that unreality feeling she'd had all those years before. The disconnect that left her always tallying up how many steps it might be, say, to the kitchen, bathroom, one of the kids' bedrooms when she was married and contemplating the possibility of her legs, feet actually taking her there. Objects taking on personalities – the pair of her daughter's tap dance shoes that would continuously mock her, their ribbons spread wide in a smile lying across the floor. By the time the tap shoes began openly mocking her and she felt like there was a real possibility that she might become a thin sheet of loose-leaf paper that could easily be slipped beneath any door, Judith had been confined to the suburban house outside Toronto where her husband was working. The danger of things like buses and downtown subways removed. Just the one-car garage calling, luring her in from just beyond the kitchen window shutters. She'd not been allowed to go anywhere after she told the doctor how it seemed that there was something stronger than she was, some kind of presence, heavy and inevitable, that eliminated the distance between her and the edge of the platform every time the train approached, flurries of people and coats and things, the smells of their workplaces, apartments, families, lovers, pets, the business of some sort of life that did not seem in any way part of hers all mixed in. How could it be my fault if there was this thing there, always pushing me, Judith had asked the doctor in earnest.

~~~

So tiny she's become, and thin in death. Not even her at all really, Judith thinks. Just a collection of bones now under thin layers of skin. Skin became thin through the prednisone she took to help her with the arthritis she had since her forties when she became a grandmother for the first time. A corpse is not a person. It's just a remnant, a shell of something Judith thinks that was once her, a woman who used to hug and kiss and love and dance. How much you've danced is a good measure of life, the old woman would sometimes say, smoking her cigarette at the half-opened sliding glass door of their balcony.

In fact, it is so small and tiny that anyone could lift it without much trouble at all. And it wouldn't be a desecration to think of those bones wrapped up in her own flannel sheet, the one she'd slept in winter after winter – her very own sheet-cum-shroud. The bones halfway to their disintegration already after a full 87 years on earth. Hair on her head missing, patches at the top and the back which Judith helped her cover up by combing and arranging the other hair on her head just so before spraying it all with the large can of aerosol hairspray Stella bought on Seniors' Day (10% discount on selected items) at the Shoppers Drug Mart up on Wyandotte Street and Pillette Road. Her teeth had been removed long ago when people of her class found it more practical to have everything pulled and replaced with dentures than to keep returning and paying a dentist monies they really didn't have to spare. The veins in her legs collapsed finally after so many years with the stent helping the blood be pushed along up and down around the various paths of its circulation and the half a bottle of nitroglycerin she'd been carrying around since the heart attack she'd had in her mid-50s still in her purse. Judith looks at the label. The old woman always kept it in the pocket with the bit of broken rosary that was her mother's. A string of black beads from a longer, broken string of prayers. That too kept in there since her mid-50s when her mother, Tekla, finally died.

Judith wraps Stella up in the flannel sheet with the small pink flowers, a set that was bought sometime in the 1960s – the top sheet with the raggedy edges that Stella refused to throw away. The bottom, its match, sacrificed long ago to a tear that couldn't be repaired. Judith starts to feel the weight of her grandmother lift, flannel sheet warm against skin. Her mind wandering now down to what once was the edge of town, along that craggy path by the water and the once-towering Riverside Brewing Co. with the crumbling red brick and faded paint signs. To those lots, long since abandoned, golden-rod in full bloom.

Bruce Meyer

TILTING

They ought to make a movie about Terry. I could retire and go live someplace on the earnings if I wrote the script. For the time being, I raise chickens. I've always raised chickens. My father and my grandfather before him were, to put it politely, in the poultry and exotic fertilizer business. Eggs, legs, and fertilizer. I've learned a lot over the years from those birds. Chickens don't care about anything. People say they are stupid, but they are focused. They chime in with their own opinions if you understand that opinions are just clucking. They do what they do. They lay their eggs. They know when you are going to push the cage through the rows of pullets and pick out the ones that seem fatter than the others. They are brave but they suffereth long and are kind. Terry's family never got around to raising chickens. Chickens might have saved him from the windmills. Terry hated wind turbines.

Sometimes, parts of Terry's nemeses would fall off and go flying through the sky as if they were launched. Apparently, when the windmills rose out of the landscape, the company that made them hadn't laminated the blades properly. Terry and I stood for several hours one day watching a workman rappel from the top down to the edge of the huge knives in the air so they could be glued back together again. We took turns saying, "He's gunna fall, that fucker's gunna fall right about NOW!… nope. In five minutes? Betcha five minutes."

Anyone who met Terry knew those forty-foot blades sliced the air inside his head as much as they cut through a good midwinter wind. The whirr of the turbine hummed a constant B flat like a song stuck in the brain. Terry told us about the music one winter day down at the gas station where we used to gather to gab about stuff.

"That's the way Schumann went mad," I told him, because I read that somewhere and wanted him to think I am musical. "And A flat kept playing over and over in his brain. The song had nowhere to go. It just kept turning."

I'd look out my kitchen window across the way and see Terry. He'd stand out where his yard met the field, lean on his fence, and by the hour look up at the flickering between himself and the sky. After a storm, big chunks of ice would go flying through the air and he'd wait to see where they'd land and write it down in a little notebook he carried in his workshirt pocket. In spring and again in the fall, birds would drop into his hands as he stood beneath the spinning blades. Their blood rained from the sky. Heaven was crying, he told us. Heaven was bleeding. He caught their broken bodies and you'd see him disappear behind his dilapidated smoke shed and bury them with dogs and barn cats he'd loved.

Within weeks after the windmills went up, Terry's cows stopped giving milk. The incessantly spinning arms caught the sun and strobed and flashed into his bedroom as each day began. His cows ambled to the far end of his outer field one afternoon and pressed their bodies against the barbed-wire fence until their skin split open as the razors gave way beneath the weight of their black and white Holstein bodies. They headed down the Eighth Concession and disappeared over the hill. The police asked him if they were his as he stood beside an overturned transport on the main highway and stared at the bodies down the road and in the fields to either side where they had been knocked dead. "Yes," he said, "these were my milkers."

"No, no, no, a thousand times no, a million times no," Terry had insisted for years at meetings and deputations, but the local corporation was not interested in his protests. We should have had the courage to speak up more, maybe do a protest or something, but we had enough problems of our own without taking on the government. Yet the more he said the word "no," the more it blended with the rhythms of the hammering metal workers and the engine of the crane as the white tower rose in the middle of the next farm on our line, a place that had been in the Jessup family for generations.

Jessup needed the money. Terry met Til Jessup one day at the gas station and the neighbour said that his wife's headaches had driven her to try and hang herself in the cellar, so they were moving away, walking away, leaving everything behind them, and going to live with their daughter in the nearest town fifteen miles away. He blamed the wind turbine that had been set up too close to his house. The whirr was something a person didn't hear if they listened to it long enough, but his wife kept trying to hear it because she played the piano for local weddings and when we got together for parties. The music in her drove her over the edge.

The neighbour had an old horse named Mary. "Come by and pick her up. I don't have the heart to have her butchered and I don't have the bullet to do it myself."

Terry and that horse got on well. Sometimes old horses are assholes. They arrive at your farm and when you put them out to pasture they go home even if they no longer have a home to go to. But Mary knew that Terry was her best shot at a longer life. He brushed her, and tied ribbons in her mane. One day he rode her bareback past our farm and my wife and I just stood where our old front porch used to be with our hands across our foreheads to shade out the sun, and watched him saunter by. He probably thought we were saluting. We couldn't hear what he was saying, but he seemed to be talking to her and she was nodding her head.

My wife had remarked several weeks before that Terry didn't have enough to do now he was out of the dairy business, so I went to the shed and hauled out a box of books left over from the church rummage sale and left them on Terry's kitchen stoop. Old crap. Long stuff. The kind of stuff no one wants to read even if they have the time. The day he rode by our farm he had a book in his hand, so he must have been reading to the horse. I liked that. My wife thought it was daft, but she knows I talk to my chickens, so what's the difference with a horse?

Winter came too early to Terry Thurm's farm. Snow danced like a runaway bride as it crossed the open fields, some of it piling up against the side of his barn where it could not run any farther. Every time he looked out his front window Terr, like the rest of us, saw lovely straight ribbons of snow cross the open road. They blew in lines as if they were off to tie someone down to the place they'd always been.

Down at the gas station, Terr would read aloud copies of the letters he had sent to the corporation. "My cows wouldn't milk and ran away. My neighbours ran away. I have an old horse. It is sick and I can't afford the vet because my cows are dead and even before they died they wouldn't milk. No, no, no, I say to the wind turbine. Have mercy on me. God have mercy on me. Stop the goddamned arms now." We'd all nod because we understood what he was going through. The corporation had stopped answering once the machine had turned on and the arms spun. "I am still paying in pain and suffering for my hydro," he wrote. "Fucking well paying for the electricity that has ruined my life."

The corporation loved to tell us that the turbines generated enough power to light the entire town even though the town was nowhere near any of us. Our rates would go down, they said. No such luck. We paid and paid. Some of the fellas down the road couldn't pay any more so they just upped and left. They left their great-grandfathers buried in the corner lot at the crossroads of the Ninth Line and the Fifth Concession where someone had meant to build a church a hundred years ago and couldn't find enough faith hereabouts to gather a flock.

As far as the eye could see on the horizon south of my farm and Terry's, the turbines rose out of the landscape. Their arms waved in the sky as if they were beckoning us to come closer and embrace them. Come! Follow us! We know the way. But up close they were more enigmatic. Each tower had a set of steps and a small steel porch as if they were homes to thin Methodist needle creatures. An oval-shaped door ten feet off the ground led to a circular staircase that corkscrewed through the hollow interior. I know because I pried one open the day I was out chasing a deer across my property.

The deer thought she would run for the thicket that lay a hundred yards away from the base, but the corporation had cleared all the scrub so there was no place to hide, and someone who had probably come the week before to do maintenance had failed to lock the gate around the barbed-wire frost fence that kept the tower enclosed. I had the doe trapped. She ran back and forth looking for a way out but I stood at the entrance to the pen. Her front hooves beat against the fence as she frantically tried to get away. I raised my rifle.

And what did she do? She turned and stared at me. She stared like one of those female heroes standing before a firing squad in a war movie. "No blindfold for me. No, sir. I want to look into the eyes of the men who are going to shoot me." I slowly lowered my weapon. The buzz of the arms through the winter air and the groan of the turbines, lower now because we were directly beneath it, ate into my soul.

"Get outta here," I said to her. Rather than hightail it out with her white flag flashing behind her, she sauntered through the gate, her head held high as she walked so close to me I could have thrown my arms around her. As I left the enclosure, I shot the lock off the open gate, and fired two more shots into the hinges so that trap would never close again, at least not until the next time a repairman came around.

The weather remained January even when it must have been February. Goddamned awful winter. Sometimes I couldn't see across the fields, but one day a circle of sun appeared above our farm and even through the clouds of snow I could see someone down by the turbine. It was Terry. He was mounted on his horse and had a long piece of what looked like a length of round dowling under his arm. Something that looked like a rusty screwdriver was tied to the end of it. The rod drooped and pointed down. The horse was shifting from leg to leg. I got on my jacket and walked out through the stubbled heads and almost snow-bare fields to the base of the tower I had left open. Terry was shouting now, not at the horse, but at the turbine. Mary was rearing up and snarling because she was as into what he was doing as he was.

"Hey, Terr, what's up?"

"I am about to remove a monster from the world."

"Okay. Say, Terr, how?"

"How what?" he shouted to me as he started to back Mary up, and then gradually turned her in a tight arc until they were facing the tower again.

"How you gunna remove it?"

"Rosamunde and I shall do battle."

"Shit, Terr, you're not Don Quixote."

"No, I am Sir Terrance, knight of the sorrowful concession, and I yield no more to these beasts."

"You're shitting me, right?"

With that he dug his heels into Mary's side, or should I say Rosamunde's sides, and the horse and rider charged the tower. I tried to stop them at the entrance to the gate but they galloped past me, the snow flying in the wake of every hoof print. Together, horse, lance, and rider, they slammed into the tower. Terry went face first over the horse's head. The horse tried to veer off at the last second but the rod hit the metal wall and snapped. The screwdriver end flew up in the air as Terry bounced off the steel porch. The rod and Robertson came down squarely into the centre of the horse's head and the animal toddled sideways, struggled for its footing, before kneeling before the victor. The creature shook its head in disbelief and fell over on its side.

"Holy fuck, Terry!"

He lay there stunned. He had broken some of his teeth. His shoulder was still part of his body but in a different way, and a meander of blood tried to find its way from his forehead to his feet. I dragged him home to my house. My wife was out. She would have shit herself if she'd seen him. She would have been all over me for not stopping him if she'd come home early.

But what was I supposed to do? The guy went idiot. Right there. Full idiot. Can't say I blame him, though, but full idiot though.

I sat Terry down at the kitchen table and gave him a glass of Johnnie Walker, but he said it hurt his teeth so I drank it even though some of his blood had dropped into it. I grabbed my rifle and went back to do the right thing for the old horse, but by the time I got there the Lord had done his work, so I just put a bullet into the door of the tower and went home. By the time I returned, Terry had wandered back to his place. I knew he'd gone home because he'd left a dribbling trail of his blood in the thin dusting of snow from the bottom of my stoop all the way down to the end of my lane.

That night I borrowed Jeff Tyne's four-wheeler and I dragged the dead horse into the bush beyond the corporation's clearing. I felt sad for the horse. I'd never seen something die in a pointless cavalry charge like that. Granted, it was a sick horse. It probably would have keeled over in Terry's barn before spring arrived, but my heart ached nonetheless. A person gets used to the life and death of animals on a farm. That's the way it is. But not like that.

I didn't see Terry for a week until I heard the sound of an axe early one morning. It wasn't the *pock, pock* of someone having a go at a tree. It was a *ding, ding* of someone striking an empty oil drum or breaking apart an old tractor. My wife sat up in bed. I got up and looked out the window. It was Terry. He was having a go at the tower again. This time he had an axe. *Ding, ding.* He'd cuss and continue the work.

"Aren't you going to go out and stop him?" my wife asked as she bent down and peered out the window with me. "He's gone bonkers."

"I can tell you more, but not right now," I hollered. She stood up puzzled, and pulled her flannel nightgown tighter around her throat.

I hated going out before I had my coffee, but I also hated to see a friend in trouble.

"Hey, Terr, whatcha up to?"

"I'm going to chop down this huge tree and haul it off with an ox."

"Where'ya gunna get an ox?"

"I found one. It was just standing out in a field five farms the other side of your place."

I glanced to the side of the tower. There stood an ox, chewing on some scrub that was poking up through the snow. "You mean Frank Jatther's ox?"

"It isn't his any more."

"I dunno. Didja ask Frank?"

"He wasn't home."

Terry had put some good dents in the side of the tower. The blows had taken the white paint off the surface so that the scars were silver. He hacked and hacked, huffing, his face turning redder and redder with each blow as he shouted, "Fall, you bastard," through his broken teeth that were turning brown already along their fractures. Then the axe snapped. Terry fell to his knees and wept.

"C'mon, Terr, let's go to my place and get some coffee." He was weeping and shaking as I put my arm around him and led him off. I wished I knew what to do with the ox because I didn't have anything to tie it up with to the fence. I looked at the ox and it looked back and me. "Stay!" I shouted.

I wished I hadn't ruined the gate. It was an open invitation for Terry to take out his frustrations on the corporation. After an hour or two, Terry seemed to be okay. My wife's bacon and eggs settled him, and he warmed up. But he had gotten a faraway look on his face. It was the look of a man who was seeing into the future and did not know what he saw there.

Thank God the winter wasn't a long one. The groundhog was right, and spring came just around the corner. The ribbons of snow turned into ribbons of dust because we hadn't had enough snowfall to wet the soil and keep it down. As I passed by Terry's farm one day to check on him and kept going along the concession, I saw signs of life at the abandoned Jessup place. A young guy and his wife were moving in, so I turned up the lane and went to say hello because I figured it was the neighbourly thing to do.

The new guy was about twenty-five or thereabouts, his wife was pregnant. She was wearing a black parka with a big hood that hid her face, and he was in an open plaid shirt that had quilted lining. A green toque sat perched on his head like a tea cosy. He'd grown what we call a "grandfather" all over his lower face because even though most of us don't shave every day around here, we do manage to shave on Sundays when we don't go to church just because we gotta respect the Lord in some little way. The new guy had a canvas mailman's bag slung over his shoulder and heavy suspenders holding up his jeans, like the kind my pappy used to wear when he got old. The guy came up as I got outta my pick-up and extended his hand.

"McCuddy, Buddy McCuddy, and this is my wife Tiffany. We've come to help redevelop the local economy. We're going to grow lavender and make beeswax candles."

A bit of a wind was picking up as I said my name, and I knew he didn't catch it because it got blown away, and he probably didn't care. The pregnant woman turned her face from me because the dirt had devilled up and was getting in her eyes. I chatted this and that with Buddy. I told him who lived where and what they tried to farm. He told me he was going to grow lavender to dry and sell in the city, and that he didn't mind the windmill turning on his land just near the edge of his back forty because it was "eco-friendly, man, and everyone has to, like, get into the earth." I just nodded, called "Welcome" over my shoulder and drove away. Then, I thought to myself, "Who the hell eats lavender?" I mean, I guess you could, but everyone around always thought of themselves as useful in a humble sort of way. We raised things a person could eat. People always need to be fed.

I had to go into the gas station because the package people had dropped off a part I needed for one of my ventilation fans. When I got to the crossroads the provincial police were there and the guys were standing around a broken window at the back and shaking their heads. Jeff Tyne was shaking his head as we all stared silently at the glass on the floor and the table of tools strewn haphazardly more than they usually were on the workbench.

"Someone broke in last night."

"Kids?"

"Dunno. They stole the acetylene torch, some gloves, the goggles, the torch cart, a couple of crowbars... cuttin' stuff."

My first thought was that someone was going to plan a bank heist and cut their way into a vault if they drove all the way to town. There wasn't much worth stealing in our local bank though. Then the wildest though hit me.

"Holy shit!" I ran out of the gas station and jumped in my truck. I broke some land speed records to get to Terry's farm. I opened the door and shouted hello, then shouted his name. He wasn't in the barn. He wasn't in the shed. His truck was still there, but that was nothing new because most people knew he didn't have the money for gas anymore. I went out and stood in the wind at the edge of his yard, and that's when I saw him. He was over at the turbines on the McCuddy's land, so I drove over lickety-split to the hydro access lane.

"Hey, Terr, how's it going? Whatcha up to?"

"Won't be long," he hollered back as he stopped, and pushed his black goggles up on his forehead so he looked like an aviator.

"Just working on this one. Then I'll get to the next and clear the land just like my great-grandfather, and then, as they say, after a long time the cows will come home." He laughed and repeated "the cows will come home."

He pushed the goggles down and snapped the sparker, and the nozzle came to light again with its pinpoint blue flame. Terry had been making good headway. The acetylene hissed and snapped as a snake-shaped black line traced its way from one side of the tower and was almost ready to meet the far side.

"Tough job, eh, Terr?" I shouted.

It was hard to talk and Terry just nodded.

"Wind is coming up. There's going to be one helluva storm." I tried to converse, but the sound of the torch and the whirr of the blades drowned me out. I went up to him and he shut the torch off again.

"What the fuck do you want now?" he said, annoyed at being interrupted.

"Hey, Terr, why don't you finish that later," I said, hoping to use some psychology on him and persuade him to come back to my place for a drink. He just smiled at me as if he thought I was daft. His front teeth were now black, and his shoulder drooped as if it didn't want any part of him. "You know, you don't want to be beneath one of these things in a spring storm."

Lightning was flashing to the north and the storm was headed our way. "See that bolt? That could hit us right here, right where we're standing. C'mon back to our place and we'll have a Johnnie and wait for it to pass, and then you can get back to work." I was hoping the provincials would follow me to my place or at least to Terry's and put two and two together. They hadn't.

Terry made the final cut in the windmill's skin. "I also cut the spiral staircase inside," he said with a proud smile on his face. "Take you up on that dram now!"

We sat at my kitchen table. I sat Terry with his back to the window so I could face looking out at the tower. My wife muttered something about us drinking during the day and went upstairs. "Call the police," I whispered to her. I sat there waiting. No police. Where the fuck were they? Terry was into his fifth tall Johnnie.

The storm came faster than I had anticipated. The sky grew dark over our little no place in the middle of the world, and the wind became so fierce and the clouds began to turn a yellow grey. I wondered if a tornado was going to touch down. The rain fell and fell so I could barely see the tower.

Then I heard a sound as if a monster was having its body ripped apart. It was a sound of metal groaning and shrieking, a loud "EEECH!" but in a high note, and as a curtain of rain passed away to the south I could see the tower leaning and leaning as if it was dying in tremendous pain. The blades were spinning, faster and faster as the storm caught it at its odd angle, and then a tremendous crack broke over fields in an explosion. The turbine hit the ground, and its head came off the neck. But as the blades hit the ground they continued to spin. They walked on three legs across the open space the corporation had cleared. They stepped over the fence between the lots the way a giant or a monster in a Japanese B-movie strides over buildings. I stood at the window, and dropped my glass in disbelief and Terry turned, raising his glass and shouting in victory as if he had just won a championship.

One of the blades smashed through the McCuddy's house, right dead centre, and jammed in the foundations, before the other two, their arms up, dropped their hands like a pair of scissors, and cut the dwelling in two. I ran out of my house as fast as I could, leaving Terry laughing and stomping his foot on the kitchen floor, and my wife almost falling down the stairs screaming, "Christ-ee, Christ-ee, Jes-Us, holy Jesus!" in panic.

I arrived at the McCuddy place. The husband and wife staggered from the remains of their house, and I stopped in shock to look at them, splinters and plaster covering their heads, and bits of plaster and lathing stuck in his beard. They fell to their knees and tried to hug each other, and all I could smell in the soft rain was the scent of lavender, and for a moment I thought it was beautiful – the perfume, the newly rearranged beams and walls, and the white blades reaching up to the sky. Then a bolt of lightning came out of nowhere, raced down the blade to the foundations of the Buddy McCuddy house, and struck the furnace's oil tank. The explosion knocked me to my knees, and it was the explosion that finally brought the police around, bless'em.

The ambulance was a long time coming because it is a long way from somewhere to nowhere. The McCuddys were fine. They were homeless but fine. The quantities of lavender seeds they had stored inside their home in lieu of furniture went up like incense, and I thought of the holiness of what I had seen, the power of God who speaks in odd ways and appears in angry clouds and threads of lightning just when you think the storm has passed. And back at my place, with my wife hiding in our basement, Terry was dancing with the almost empty bottle of Johnnie Walker, his legs kicking high in the air and his arms raised like some Judith who celebrated the drowning of an army. The police took the bottle from his hands, wrestled him to the ground, and cuffed him. One of the officers read him his rights as they lowered his head into the back of the cruiser.

About five months passed before the corporation and the hydro folks figured out what to do with the remains of the tower. It did not fall down completely. It tilted to the east but in such a way that through the long summer months when the sun was slow to set, its shadow, like a tower of Pisa, passed over the fields of the abandoned McCuddy farm and my back forty. The shadow crept over the hydro right-of-way lane and counted the hours over Terry's empty place just before the sun went down.

The guys at the gas station would sit around as we waited for someone to find they were short on fuel, and we'd fill the hours between my morning egg collection and cleaning of the white shells, and my evening return to the cluck of my brood, and they would ask me to tell the same story I told my hens. My wife had heard it a million times, and the more I told it the less she believed it had actually happened right before her eyes. I'd end my version of the story for her with, "You know, it was probably those books you made me leave him to pass the time – that's where he got his ideas. You're culpable, sweetheart, culpable."

The local people believed in Terry the more I told the story, for they too had shouted "No" and no one had listened. Now, they had something to believe in. They had a hero and they had his legend. There was even talk down at the gas station of building an enormous, twenty-foot-high statue of Terry with an acetylene torch in his hand and a pair of black goggles over his eyes, just like the Paul Bunyan statue tourists flock to see somewhere in Minnesota. Nothing came of it, though. But when the next election rolled round, we all voted out the bastards on our local council and wrote letters to the government to say we weren't going to pay our taxes until we were compensated for the damage the windmills had done to our way of life. No one answered us, of course, though to have a voice felt good. Gotta shout at something. But the windmills kept on turning, either right before our eyes or in our dreams, as if they were hands of a clock trying to time the length of our remaining days, and the power they made flowed through us and beyond us and became someone else's light.

When I told Terry's story, I always ended with the bit about how my days with Terry ended. I could hear the police radio on the dashboard, the voice asking and asking for a reply from the officers on the scene.

"Come in, 942. Someone cut down a what? A house was chopped in half with scissors? The baby was full term but delivered on the way by the husband? Repeat, 942. Repeat, 942. Come in."

Before the officer pushed me away, I was able to get close to the cruiser. Terry was shouting out the thin opening between the no-draft and the glass as he swivelled round in the back seat so he could see me.

"Hey, Terr, what are you saying? What in God's name did you do?"

"I'm a goddamned legend now! And forever and forever, whenever people in these parts stand in the middle of nowhere and wonder where they are, you can tell them Terry Thurm made this place. You can tell them this is where I killed a monster. You gotta admit the world is a better place now. Yes, sirree, a goddamned, fucking good place."

Linda Rogers

RAGING BREATH AND FURIOUS MOTHERS

Usually, especially on warm afternoons, she falls asleep counting sheep, the drowsy clouds, *nuages*, such beautiful words for drops of water suspended in air, *nubo* in Esperanto, baby shoes about to drop, precipitation, lovely consonants, lovely diction, the beat.

Grace herself has now given in to woolly speech. "Are you deaf or stupid," is the louche question people keep asking, and she answers, moving her lips but not making a sound, making the louche questioners read, as she must, "I am deaf and you are thick as fog, thicker than cardboard, deeply, deeply stupid." Unkind stupid is the worst kind.

Her sleepy tongue embraces the new inconsonance.

Wool-gathering. Her mother encouraged it, gave her every opportunity to consort with fluff. Grace grew up on a sheep farm. She was the gatherer, the child who went to the hen house thrumming with *berk, berk, berk* before breakfast and thrust her hand under cosy hen-breasts to collect the eggs, the one who picked watercress from the stream that ran through the orchard, the wild asparagus that grew beside the river and tasted of tides, and the tufts left behind on thistles and barbed-wire fences, wool she used to felt hats for her dolls and for the bush-tit sock hotels she felted for avian tenants.

This was dreamtime with sound: hens, roosters, sheep, wind in the grass, hummingbird wings and rain. She gathered light, framed her dreams the way photographers choose their shots, with her fingers, two thumbs and two pointers, a rectangle. Her mother called it Grace TV. "Say Grace," Mum said at the table, and her hippy siblings, Summer and Forrest, made frames, hummed in funky keys and rolled their eyes while Grace got ready to lick her plate and make it laugh, then tell.

"Enjoy. Children are starving in Bangladesh," her mother said, approving of Grace's hunger, spooning out more as she waited for Grace TV.

"What's on today?"

Grace swallowed her mouthfuls and spun her stories, describing a world always moving like clouds across the sky. Sometimes she spun herself and the colours ran together: rainbow spit, Technicolor smiles.

Sometimes life was a bucket of blood.

And sometimes tears held in suspension. "Fog is clouds on the ground," her mother said, while she sewed muslin bags for the spice she put in her stews and their sheep grew back the wool her father had sheared. "Cotton in German is *baumwolle*." Grace closed her eyes and saw rows of sad-trees shawled in wool. "*Gift* means poison."

She's telling me everything means everything, or maybe nothing, Grace thought while she watched birds play hide and seek on the infinite screen upstairs, fluffy clouds shaped like her mother's hair, now a lamb, now cantering horses.

She watched mother eagles circle the fields, teaching their young to hunt, to gouge out the eyes of newborn lambs and eat them, what her father called "contemptible snacks."

"Kids need dreamtime," her mother insisted when teachers complained about Grace. Grace TV didn't work on blackboards or lined exercise books, but classroom windows were her silver screens. Grace stared for hours and hours, watched flowers open up in movie time, watched snow make beds where angels lie down and frozen branches blossom.

"Grace is an anomaly, a witness, the essential nonessential invisible in mutable sutras," her fluffy-headed hippy mother explained. The teachers thought Grace's mother should go back to the city she came from and seek help, but Grace thought her mother was special; she understood the beholding.

"You are an uber ewe," Grace said, trying out a new concept, best of the best, snuggling into the soft sweater her mother had spun and knit from clouds of carded wool, combing her mother's tangled wild-woman hair with her fingers, the reason, she said, little girls should not put their fingers in electrical outlets. Grace has not done that. Her hair is straight and auburn like her dad's.

"She's a wool-gatherer," her mother apologized to her father when he was annoyed after an eagle stole a newborn lamb from the pasture where Grace had been sent to watch over the flock.

Why did her father call her mother "My Old Lady"?

"He doesn't get us," she told Grace.

That was a bucket of blood moment, although Grace didn't realize it until later, when her mother hopped aboard a different cloud.

One day, her mother turned into air loaded with wet regret and the Internet stole her, took her to join the bloggers in Middle Earth. Uber Ewe mother had transformed into pixels and her confused husband buried her purse and her shoes under a willow tree.

> *Oh, bury me beneath the willow*
> *Under the weeping willow tree*
> *So she will know where I am sleeping*
> *And perhaps she'll weep for me.*

He is a confused coffee-house back to the land hippy, handier with a song than with women and girls and ewes.

Then and now Grace visits her mother under the willow that weeps like men who can't understand why on earth their wives would leave them, especially for another woman, a valkyrie clearing the battlefield.

Ombre, she thinks today, years later, AD, for storm clouds, the black sheep, growers of dark wool and typeface, black on white, ominous script. Now the air smells different. She shifts and closes her eyes. Patterns of light flicker on her lids, herding floaters off the main stage to her mother's things buried under the sorrow tree.

Zap. Zap. Zap. She feels the current, mother to daughter, husband to wife, wife to wife. She understands about electricity, AC/DC, alternating currents. Power shocks. Power failures. Her world is divided in similar ways, everything by halves. Up where her mother wandered into a binary cloud and fell down to Earth, and Down, to After Deaf, nothing to do with religion, miracles, nothing to do with Jesus the time marker, just her way of being, before he turned off the sound.

What happens first, she wonders, do married people stop listening or does one of them simply turn down the volume?

After her mother drifted away, she grew up, left the farm and found a room in the city, in Chinatown, where she scavenged for images and materials for the small (*amuse bouche?*) paintings and collages she sold in street markets and the co-op gallery.

Before Silence, she framed Him with her fingers. She was sketching on the patio at The Ocean Garden, dreaming her way through a pot of *Moonlight on the Grove* and a plate of fortune cookies when he found her, "Do you mind if I sit here?" Click, her hands went up, made the frame, and her aperture stalled – Northern Chinese, long nose, slender fingers, and soft voice. Photogenic.

Magic will transform your life, she read as he pulled up a chair. He talked. She listened. He said he was a magician, and she blinked and read her fortune again.

"The human body is an electrical grid," he said, taking her hand, squeezing the little pad between thumb and first finger. She felt a jolt from her groin to her brain and she couldn't let go because he was pulling her way past the *let go threshold.* Later he observed that he was action, she was reaction, yin and yang. Perfect. Just like electricity, one electrode jumping to or on another.

He massaged and relaxed her fingers, especially the web parts from the time before, when she was a fish that swam right up to him, sudden love.

"Are you hungry?" he asked. He whispered in her ear and he knew what to say, the menu: *shrimp balls, wor wonton, pork buns, green peas with garlic prawns, ginger beef, eight jewel duck with crispy skin, cod with black bean sauce* in Mandarin and English.

"What do you do?"

"Wool-gathering," she said without thinking, when she should have said, "I am an artist." He might have noticed the paint under her fingernails.

"Wool-gathering?"

"I dream and then I translate my dreams into little pictures."

She ate with him. Even before her left-brain went along with the decision to stay, she was already there. One mother-generated Grace factoid is that Grace is like a stray cat; once you have fed her, she's yours forever. That was a great family joke.

"Now you've got me," she said, after the magician dipped in the wonton bowl with his soupspoon and slipped a quivery noodle on her tongue.

"The cod's eye is a delicacy," he said when the fishplate arrived. He plucked it out for her and she saw eagles circling lambs, going for the eyes.

"Then *you* eat it," she said, shivering.

They opened more fortune cookies and he read his first, *Your dreams will become reality,* and she added words her mother taught her, "in bed."

Later, in his manbed, only a few doors from her studio couch as it happened, he whispered dessert: *lychee nuts, almond cookies, quivering coconut jelly,* and a night blooming lotus opened between her legs as her private lake trembled then shuddered like fragrant petals reaching for the moon.

So they continued. He practiced his magic tricks and she moved in, gathered wool and assembled her dreams, cityscapes with clouds, children who looked at clouds that became animals. Sometimes he surprised her by pulling things from his sleeves, a beautiful scarf or jade earrings. Sometimes he lit flash paper in the dark and startled her out of her sleep.

Every morning rain or shine, she crawled out the bedroom window and sat on the fire escape to watch the sky and he passed out cups of jasmine tea. Every evening, he whispered in her ear while she held her phone to her other ear, ordering between moans: *ants climbing trees, ma po tofu, moo goo gai pan, bang bang Ji, dragon's beard candy, ginger ice cream.*

By the time the delivery boy came with their cartons, they would be dressed and waiting at the kitchen table – chopsticks, bowls, tea in order, and every hair in place. She moaned when she ate, always licking her plate, making it laugh.

It is the adorable things that first become irritating when the bloom is off the rose.

"Do you have to do that?" he asked, after a while. "You'll lick the pattern off." The pattern was bamboo leaves, very pretty, his mother's china. His mother's flesh was dissolving in a jar filled with wine at the Chinese cemetery. His father's too.

"Earth calling Grace," he complained, when he caught her gathering, her brush suspended in mid-air, the paint drying on it. "Earth calling Grace." Sometimes he said it more than once.

"Let's have a child," she said, and he asked if she would pay attention, if her child might drink turpentine or put its fingers in an electrical socket while she was wool-gathering.

"You can't just pull babies out of your sleeves," he told her. "You can't put them back when you're having dreamtime."

"You could drop a bomb beside Grace when she's wool-gathering," her father advised her lover when he was visiting, meaning, leave her be; *if it ain't broke don't fix it.* But her lover was not used to this sort of proverb. He came from a Confucian family with homilies about social order.

Disorder is not sent down by heaven. It is produced by women.

And fixed by men, of course. It was Chinese New Year, their third together, a time of whispering and feasting. They went to Quon Lee's and bought tins of special New Year's cookies and fireworks wrapped in colourful papers, and, even though the bloom was off the rose, they ordered take-out to celebrate in the usual way.

She put on her red silk *cheongsam* and felt how beautifully it fit over the secret child in her slightly swollen belly – so soft, like stroking an animal's flanks. It was the Year of the Horse. She looked out the window and watched white mares canter across the sky. Then she sat down and imagined them galloping through cloud tunnels to the sun. *What is the sound of hooves cantering on air,* she wondered. Her secret child, running in circles around her belly, was still as invisible as air; and she was hungrier than ever.

"Earth calling Grace," he insisted. The delivery boy rang and rang the doorbell.

Her eyes stayed shut. White horses circled the sun, one continuous solar cloud. She heard her lover go downstairs, then up, with paper bags full of sticky rice and singing chicken carolling in his arms.

"Earth calling Grace," he shouted one more time, a warning.

She heard him strike a match, and then she smelled sulphur.

"Bang!" The room rocked and filled with smoke.

She remembers saying, "Your people invented fireworks." What a silly thing to say when her ears were bleeding, when he might as well have stuck a chopstick in her ear and driven it right through her brain.

They both lost their hearing.

She considered the verb "lost" as if hearing loss was love gone missing, something they might find if they looked hard enough. They looked under the bed, in the phone book, at the clinic. They tried magic, but there were no new ears up his sleeves or inside his top hat, and no enduring love. He was sorry. She was sorry. They took care of one another even though the bloom was off the rose. But it would never be the same.

There would be no more whispering, no more ordering dinner, no more feather dusting the glorious tchotchkes they'd collected in Chinatown and beyond. She found it hard to remember the sound of his voice. Worse, she began to imagine herself ramming chopsticks in his orifices, in his ears, his nose, his anus, driving them right up and into the source of his magic.

He never noticed the child, or, if he did, he pretended not to know.

"So long," she said some weeks later, after she'd packed her paints, her brushes, her sketchbooks, her toothbrush and not much else, and left the red silk *cheongsam* on the bed with Proverbs 21: 9 pinned to the sleeve.

It is better to live in a corner of the housetop
than in a house shared with a quarrelsome wife.

She moved back to her studio and, shortly after, to the farm. It was too difficult in the city, where crossing the street was dangerous and people asked her if she was deaf or stupid when she read their lips incorrectly, especially the ones attached to their devices. They were the least kind. Who would protect her child from traffic? Who would protect her child from fireworks and people with iPods?

What was the sound of hooves cantering on air? It was still the Year of the Horse. Time to ride home.

The big silver screen still hangs over the field where she's back to her usual and her father still sings to the rose on her mother's grave; but now it's a silent movie, no murmuration of swallows, no rain on leaves, no bees buzzing or hawks squawking, and most of all no sheep mother and child radar, familial bleating.

Her father, bereft of his wife and his other grown up children, is learning sign language. Grace has been learning to cook lamb short ribs and pineapple upside-down cake, and the rest of her mother's repertoire, root beer chilled in the well and wild flowers in jars. Every afternoon, she lies on her back and watches the sky while the child sleeps inside her.

Once, before he cut the hay, her father almost ran over Grace and her unborn child. Then he jumped right off his tractor, held her and wept under the weeping willow, next to the rose where her mother's purse and her shoes lie buried.

It's past solstice time, time for the sheep to mate and for her baby to arrive. She feels the pull and so does her lover, who has sent her a box of divinity with a note. It came in today's mail. *I'm learning to cook and I've started with divinity candy. Beat egg whites and pour in sugar and the secret ingredient. Nuts are not optional.* She can guess what the secret ingredient might be. She sniffs the candy. It smells familiar. She takes it to the willow tree and eats it, greedily, guiltily because she will not be responding to this overture. It does occur to her to send an egg by return mail. Would it survive? She could wrap it in wool, like an infant. Not.

Solstice or no solstice, it's a firmament-troubled day. She's near her mother, marvelling at how everything changes in a moment: sun to rain, girl to woman, woman to mother. The sky flock is restless. She feels but doesn't hear the thunder and is so intrigued by dark sheep chasing white sheep across the heavens that she fails to run and hide from the lightning that strikes the sorrow tree and invites her child to come suddenly, painfully, jolts of electricity bursting her water right there, no time to get to the house.

Grace is surprised, but calm, alone with her dreaming as usual. Magical thinking will get this life out of her just as it got in. She thinks of her velvet crease as a sleeve full of tricks, a silk sleeve filled with fingers and toes stretching and pulling, petals convulsing, opening, flesh-coloured skirts. More lightning. Flash paper. Fireworks, all of it silent. Not a peep from the sky or from her or the willow splitting open, not even the sound of flesh tearing.

The head has crowned. She's crossing the *let go threshold* again, clutched by contrary motion. She pushes, reciting the ingredients for a post-partum menu: savory dumplings, *sik foo,* bitter soup. What was it they ate the day the child was conceived?

More thunder, lightning and rain.

The storm passes. She lies exhausted on her mother's grave with her baby dangling between her legs, its cord still attached, waiting for the next moment to find them. She and her magic trick are soaked with rain and blood and she shivers, expelling the afterbirth.

Grace and the child doze and wake as the sun slowly warms them. Her *petite jouissance* stretches, brushing her thigh with her fingers. Now she's a mother, her third eye opening. She watches an eagle emerge from its storm shelter at the top of a tall cedar and she covers the tiny face, remembering the fish eye quivering between her lover's chopsticks.

Wherever she goes, it seems, she is tracked by the mute traffic of predatory birds.

Fear stalks freedom and the sky distorts once again. A giant sky mouth opens, her mother's mouth releasing crows and seagulls, angry birds bereaved of their young. She can see right to the bottom of the silent scream, to the light at the end, where a rainbow shatters, spitting shards of glass in every direction, disassembling her mother, no longer a billboard face, just pixels again.

Isn't that what Grace the child said at the end of every story? Again. Start at the beginning and read to the end. Don't skip a page. Don't change a word. *Put the story back together.*

This is how it goes. She doesn't hear the birds. She doesn't hear the ewe approach and paw the ground with her hoof. She doesn't hear the bereft mother rage at the sky that took her lamb. But she does see the eagle vanish, chased away by crows and gulls, raging breath and furious mothers. She undoes the top buttons on her shirt, gathers her slippery child and lifts her to her breast. The baby kneads and gropes with hungry lips and fists, then latches on. Grace is surprised by love. More powerful than lightning or fireworks or lust, the current moves from her nipple to her groin and she knows it will never let go.

Lisa Foad

HOW TO FEEL GOOD

It's Monday and my bottle of vodka is almost empty and my old friend is meddling in my life. "You won't meet for brunch. You won't meet for drinks. You never leave your house. I bet you wear pyjama pants all day long. I don't even know if you're showering."

I say "old friend" because she is no longer my friend. She is from last year. She belongs to old me. I used to hang up on her. But she kept calling. She likes to yak.

"I'm worried about you," she says.

I think about Kay, with her boring Japan-based modelling gigs and her boring tiny dog and her boring self-help books and her boring cocaine problem.

"I think you are bored," I say. "Besides, how would you know anything? We haven't seen each other in months."

"Maybe you're right," she says. And then she begins yakking about the new shoes she bought and the mediocre date she had, and the latest self-help book she read and how her mind is a trick because it's always wandering and wanting and that if she wants a better life she needs to trick her mind by meditating more and wanting less.

This is why I still take Kay's calls. How else will I know what I'm missing or not missing now that I've stopped leaving my house?

I stopped leaving my house because I was tired of going home with men who disgust me. Men with ponytails. Men with shit cologne. Men with mother issues.

One of these men became my boyfriend once. It went on longer than I would've liked. I kept pretending he was someone else. But he was only ever himself. Ketchup smears on my remote control. Shit smears in my toilet bowl. And every morning, him jerking off in my bed while I drank coffee and watched the birds fly by my window. He'd use my discarded T-shirts to wipe the splunk from his stomach. "Why don't you use your socks!" I screamed one day. He raised a lazy arm in the direction of the socks that were balled up on the floor. "I can't reach," he said.

He was an angry musician who played guitar poorly and wrote sentimental lyrics. He had no phone and he hated his mother. He was always complaining: "It's too hot," and, "You don't spend enough time with me."

How could I?

We fucked like dogs. We were hungry and desperate. It was the only thing that felt right. Afterwards, I'd feel dirty, like I was made of the street.

He read my text messages, my emails, and my journals. He was jealous of those I'd known, and those I knew. He threatened to cut off all my hair. We fought often.

Once, I complained about him to Kay. I said, "He is a monster. Everything about him is wrong. He has taken me away from myself. He has taught me not to trust. Look at what he's done to me. I feel so violated."

She shrugged. "You let him."

In my head, I slammed hers into the table. It didn't make me feel good. But it made me feel better. On my way home, I was seething. *You let him*, I mimicked. *You let him.*

But she was right.

When I think about my old life, it makes me want to stick my fingers down my throat.

Me with my slingshot eyes, my tight jeans that screamed *ass*. Really struttin' my stuff.

"You're hot," some idiot would say.

Oh, wow, I'm hot, I'd think. *How fantastic!*

I wanted to be wanted. And I liked the idea of feeling fantastic.

Sometimes, this was easier than other times.

I had no standards. I was ugly with need. Always smiling and getting my hair styled and pushing around the food on my plate so I wouldn't look too hungry. Looking for someone. Looking for anyone. It's like I was leaking.

Right before I stopped leaving my house, I met Kay for drinks at the bar I'd made a fool of myself at the weekend before. Remembering the details made my head hurt so I didn't bother. Besides, slurring my words and vomiting on the sidewalk was how I knew I'd had a good time.

We were two drinks in when some idiot approached us with a round. He was wearing snakeskin boots and silver chains and a silk shirt, and his hair was tied in a bun. He looked like he was pretending to own a nightclub. He was repulsive. He leaned close. He said something about the blow-job I'd given him in the bar bathroom last weekend, and how about a repeat?

"How could this have happened?" I said to Kay.

She shrugged. "You have no self-esteem. Or you're unlucky in love."

What do you know about self-esteem or love, I thought. *You're bulimic.*

And then, flashing her whiter than white teeth, she tried to say it all boiled down to unresolved childhood trauma.

My mother was a young woman who didn't want to be a mother so she gave me to her mother. My father was a bum who left before I was born. So what?

"These are core issues," she said. "Core."

"What a bummer," I said, and rolled my eyes. Still, I let her yammer on about abandonment and insecurity and bodywork and yoga. Why burst her bubble? *Oh, this babbling brook.* Let her think all her self-help books are good for something. She already spends enough time jogging and crying.

And then the stupid dog she carries in her purse started whining and we had to take him outside so he could pop from the purse and do his business.

I looked around. Everywhere, people with greasy eyes and greasy hands, wanting someone else to make them feel good. It made me sick to my stomach. I looked at Kay, with her "I'm jet-lagged from Japan" attitude, her starving clothes-hanger body, her self-help and her self-destruction. I thought about the rouge on my cheeks, the alcohol that helps me say yes when I want to say no, and the way I lick these lips of mine like they're bones. All of us, lonely and pathetic. Trying to be worth wanting. Trying to look good, be good, so someone will make us feel good.

"Anyhow," Kay said. "Do you want a bump? It'll help."

But I was tired of looking for help. *Let these idiots help each other,* I thought.

And so I locked the door, with me on the inside. And it didn't make me feel good. But it made me feel better.

I used to want to be a writer. But all that imagination made me tired. *Oh, this babbling brook and this bull in a china shop.* Who cares? It's just leak on the page. And then what? The end.

What have I done? Nothing. Unless you count the arts degree I never finished. When I enrolled, my grandmother said, "Who goes to school for 'arts' except lazy people who don't want a real job? I won't be footing this bill." I went just to spite her. I took classes in English and philosophy and film and psychology. I told myself I was finding my way. But after the first year I was $10,000 in the hole, so I quit while I was ahead. Afterwards, what? I bartended at this dive and that dive. I met Kay. I developed a cocaine habit. I quit bartending. I quit my cocaine habit. I got a job teaching night classes because I lied and said I had my degree, and those pencil-pushers with their bureaucratic shit for brains never asked for proof. I thought I'd like the job but I didn't. My students were hopeless. "Gum couch" (read: "gym coach"). "Drug attic" (read: "drug addict"). "Past tents" (read: "past tense"). "Sorry this is late, Miss. But I was sick with the fly." I grew tired of explaining how Spellcheck works and how Wikipedia is not a valid source of research. It was a college prep class, and it was graded on a pass/fail continuum. Most of my students failed. Maybe I was too hard on them. Maybe I expected too much. At any rate, I quit. I couldn't take all that failure. Anyway, knowing the shit-for-brains way things are, I knew my students were, despite me, bound to succeed. And so these days I sit on my ass in my pyjamas and eat the potato chips I've had delivered and watch the birds fly by my window while I write user manuals for a living: *How To Use Your G– Brand Vacuum Cleaner*; *How To Use Your L– Brothers Adding Machine*; *How To Care For Your New Goldfish*. I like this work because there's always a right answer.

I like right answers.

Grey areas are for old me. *Who am I? What do I want?* Useless questions. All they do is lead to existential thoughts and self-absorption and second-guessing. I'm going to die one day. I'm pretty sure I have one of the cancers anyway. So what?

Sometimes I get drunk and call my grandmother, talk about my problems. She's hard of hearing and has dementia so it doesn't matter that I'm drunk and senseless, repeating things over and over, caring deeply about things I don't actually care about when I wake the next morning, having passed out on the couch, my stereo still on, surrounded by slices of toast I kept making because I kept forgetting I'd already made toast.

I say things like, "Who is my father? Where is my mother? How could she leave and never look back? What kind of wretched mother must you have been. She left you too, you know."

She says, "What is this weather you're talking about?"

I say things like, "I'm a horrible person. I blame you. You were never supportive of my dreams. You told me to be an x-ray technician. You were horrible. I used to be smart. I used to be hopeful. I could've really gone places. But I wasted my potential. Now my life is meaningless. How could you have let this happen? You ruined me."

She says, "Who is Ruby?"

When I burst out laughing at the sheer absurdity of our back and forth, she asks me why I'm singing so loud.

She calls me by the names of dead friends, and tells me about the visits she's been having with her dead husband. She says the nursing home looks nice from far away but that up close it's poor quality and she needs more electricity. She says, "Where are you living? Not the big city, I hope. It's dangerous."

In the morning, I want to call everyone I know and apologize for living. But I don't.

Instead I wait till noon and pour myself a glass of vodka and watch the birds fly by my window. *Oh, this babbling brook,* I think. And I don't feel good. But I feel better.

Bart Campbell sets his stories and essays it his home city of Vancouver. His book, *The Door is Open: Memoir of a Soup Kitchen Volunteer,* was a finalist for the City of Vancouver Book Prize, and the BC Book Prize for non-fiction.

Maggie Dwyer was born in Stratford, Ontario. She began writing mid-life, and prefers the short story to the novel. She spent 20 years in Winnipeg, 16 on Vancouver Island, and now lives and writes near Commanda, Ontario.

Lisa Foad of Toronto debuted with the collection *The Night Is A Mouth* (Exile Editions) which won the 2009 ReLit Award for Short Fiction, was a *Globe and Mail* First-Fiction Top Five of 2009, and received an Honour of Distinction from the Writers' Trust of Canada Dayne Ogilvie Prize for Emerging LGBT Writers.

Veronica Gaylie of Vancouver is a poet, writer, teacher and environmentalist. Her work has been published in literary journals around the globe, including *Poetry Review* (UK), *Crannog* (Ireland), and the Canadian journals *Geist, Grain, Geez, Lake, Ditch, Room, Carte Blanche* and *Filling Station.*

Hugh Graham of Toronto has written for the *Toronto Star* and the *Walrus,* and his fiction has appeared in Canadian journals. He has twice been shortlisted for, and once won, the Carter V. Cooper $15,000 Short Fiction Award, those stories then appearing in the *CVC1, CVC4* and

CVC5 anthologies. He has published two books, with Exile Editions: *Ploughing the Seas* – a first-person account of CIA operations in northern Costa Rica during the war in Nicaragua – and *Where the Sun Don't Shine*, a gothic black comedy in dramatic form. The author lives in Toronto.

Jane Eaton Hamilton of Vancouver has pub-
lished eight books of short stories and poetry.
Her memoir was a *Sunday Times* best-seller and
included on the *Guardian*'s Best Books of the
Year list. She is the two-time winner of Canada's
prestigious CBC Literary Award for fiction
(2003/2015). Her work has appeared in *Salon, NY Times, Seventeen, MS blog, Full Grown People* and many others.

Bruce Meyer of Barrie, Ontario, is author of 44
books of poetry, fiction, non-fiction, literary
journalism, and pedagogy. His recent books of
poetry include *A Book of Bread, Testing the
Elements* (Exile Editions) and *The Seasons*, which
won a medal from the Independent Publishers'
Association of America. The collection of stories, *A Chronicle of Magpies*, will appear in July. He was the inaugural Poet Laureate of the City of Barrie and teaches at Georgian College and at Victoria College in the University of Toronto.

Christine Miscione of Hamilton, Ontario, has
appeared in various Canadian publications,
including *Exile: The Literary Quarterly, This
Magazine*, and *The Puritan*. In 2011 she was
the recipient of the Hamilton Arts Award for
Best Emerging Writer. In 2012 her story
"Skin Just" won the Carter V. Cooper Award. Her debut story collection, *Auxiliary Skins* (Exile Editions), won the 2014

ReLit Award, and her debut novel, *Carafola*, came out in in 2014.

 **Lisa Pike** of Windsor, Ontario, has published fiction and poetry in *Re: Generations: Canadian Women Poets in Conversation*, and the journals *ditch, the poetry that matters, CV2, The New Quarterly, Riddlefence, SubTerrain* and *Whisky Sour City*. She is the author of a poetry chapbook, *Policeman's Alley*, and most recently, the novel *My Grandmother's Pill*.

Josip Novakovich emigrated to Canada from Croatia at the age of 20. He has published a novel, *April Fool's Day* (in ten languages), the story collections *Infidelities: Stories of War and Lust, Yolk* and *Salvation and Other Disasters*. He has received the Whiting Writer's Award, a  Guggenheim Fellowship, the Ingram Merrill Fellowship, an American Book Award, and in 2013 was a Man Booker International Award finalist. He has been a writing fellow of the New York Public Library and has taught at the Hebrew University of Jerusalem, Die Freie Universitaet in Berlin, Penn State and now Concordia University in Montreal.

 **Linda Rogers** of Vancouver is a broadcaster, teacher, journalist, poet, novelist and songwriter. She has received the Stephen Leacock Poetry Prize, the Reuben Rose Poetry Prize (Israel), the Dorothy Livesay Award for poetry, the Hawthorne Poetry Prize, the Saltwater Festival Prize, the People's Poetry Prize, and most recently was co-winner of *ELQ/Exile Quarterly's* $2,500 Gwendolyn MacEwen Poetry Competition.

Leon Rooke of Toronto is one of Canada's most prolific writers, and the author of over 20 books, among them *Shakespeare's Dog, The Fall of Gravity, A Good Baby, The Magician of Love, The Beautiful Wife, The Last Shot,* and *Wide World in Celebration and Sorrow: Acts of Kami-*  *kaze Fiction.* He has been widely anthologized, has won the Governor General's Award, and with John Metcalf annually runs the Metcalf-Rooke Award for short fiction.

Nicholas Ruddock is a physician and writer. He has won awards in Canada, Ireland and the U.K. for his poetry and short stories. His novel, *The Parabolist* was shortlisted for the Toronto Book Award in 2010. *How Loveta Got Her Baby* (stories) was published in 2014 – one of the stories was filmed by the Canadian Film Centre. A novel, *Night Ambulance,* is due in the Spring of 2016.

Priscila Uppal is a Toronto poet, fiction writer, memoirist, essayist, playwright, professor of English at York University and a Fellow of the Royal Canadian Society. Among her critically acclaimed publications are ten collections of poetry, most recently, *Sabotage, Traumatology,*  and *Ontological Necessities* (Exile Editions, Griffin Poetry Prize finalist); the novels *The Divine Economy of Salvation* and *To Whom It May Concern*; the memoir *Projection: Encounters with My Runaway Mother* (Writers' Trust Hilary Weston Prize and Governor General's Award finalists); and the collection of short stories *Cover Before Striking* (the title story won the 2013 Carter V. Cooper Award). Her work has been published internationally and translated into Croatian, Dutch, French, Greek, Hungarian, Italian, Korean and Latvian.

Carter V. Cooper
Short Fiction Antholgy Series
~ BOOKS ONE THROUGH FOUR ~
Prepresenting the best
of today's Canadian writing!